VAMPIRE

HERETIC

The Immortal Knight Chronicles
Book 5

Richard of Ashbury
and the mass murderer Gilles de Rais
1429 - 1440

DAN DAVIS

ISBN: 9781791708740
First Edition: December 2018

1

The Bishop of Nantes
April 1440

THERE WAS NEVER in all my life a story more depraved and hideous than that of Gilles de Rais. For all the horrific, evil deeds that I have both witnessed and myself committed over eight centuries, it causes even me to shudder to relate the crimes of that great Marshal of France.

It was a dark time for England.

Our King was Henry VI, a young man who had been gifted the crown of France by the military successes of his father and who seemed determined to piss it all away. He was timid, soft in the heart and in the head, weak-willed and cowardly as a man and a king and sought only peace instead of victory.

And so we lost.

Before his majority, England had been ruled by a gaggle of

lords who were the fading echoes of their mighty fathers. Administrators in their hearts, the only fighting that they excelled at was the squabbling of the court and in battle they were hesitant and had the alarming tendency to flee when defeat reared her head.

The series of wars that we had waged against France for over a hundred years was limping toward a miserable end. After the soaring, magnificent glories of Crecy, Poitiers, Agincourt, and Verneuil we were brought crashing to earth by the ignominious defeats at Orléans, and Patay.

We were undone by many things but principle among them was the divinely inspired leadership of Joan the Maiden of Orléans.

Those military defeats weighed heavily on me and the knowledge that the figurehead of our destruction had ultimately been burned at the stake for heresy brought me little comfort. I was heartsick and disillusioned at the collapse of our fortunes and had spent years in London, miserable and unable to summon the will required to return to France before it was lost forever.

It was nine years after Joan's execution, in early April 1440, that I received a hastily-written letter from Stephen Gosset begging me to join him in Brittany.

Richard, I pray this letter finds you in better spirits than when we last spoke. There are rumours here of a familiar nature and it is imperative that you join me in Nantes immediately. The subject of said rumours is a man known to you and is one of remarkable power and thus I implore that you come attended by our strongest comrades. As always, our business in London can continue to be maintained by the Lady of the house. I beg you, Richard. Hurry.

The scrawl was barely recognisable as Stephen's, though it most assuredly was, and his usual care to encode the business of our Order had been abandoned for open clumsy innuendo. It was not even signed.

"What do you make of this?" I asked Eva, who was the Lady that Stephen had referred to.

"That you shall shortly have some bloody business to attend to," she replied. "And I will be able to run our affairs here in peace without your glumness seeping from the walls."

I had found little to fulfil me in the running of our estates and managing trade. I had no aptitude for it. Nor did I enjoy the gathering of political and commercial information by the management of our agents and preferred to travel to see events for myself, whether it was to Scotland or Ireland or further afield. Even so, the concerns and passions of the people engaged in the local and regional events seemed so petty and transient, no matter how deeply felt they were for those involved.

So Eva's accusation of glumness was true, and I had been out of sorts for some time. My men liked to joke that all I needed was a battle to wage and a war to win but I had been fighting those for so long and all for nought. What did it matter whether this king or that sat on the French throne? They would all be dead soon enough, and the lords that supported them and the men who died fighting for them, and so what was the use in fighting?

But on reading Stephen's letter, I felt an ember deep within me begin to burn once more. Could it be true, I wondered, that Stephen had uncovered an immortal in Brittany? And a powerful immortal at that. Scanning the words again and again, I felt the stirring of my true purpose once more.

I quickly summoned back to London Walter and Rob, engaged three trusted young valets, and arranged for our journey across the Channel to Nantes in Brittany, where Stephen was currently employed.

On his most recent period away from England, Stephen had fulfilled an old ambition by attending the College of Sorbonne in Paris to study theology and law and thence had become a lawyer for the Church. His intellectual excellence, enhanced through his unnatural long life, had enabled his swift progression through the institution. Despite his repeated insistence to his masters that he lacked any professional ambition, he soon found himself so well regarded that he was able to apply for and was granted a position in the episcopal see of Nantes.

Why would such a brilliant young man, they asked him, seek to bury himself so far from Paris, which was the centre of learning for all the Earth? Of all the great lords of the Church that you could serve, why request the service of the Bishop of Nantes?

Stephen had made his typically smooth excuses and they in turn had waived him off as another fool who would rather never reach his potential than to fail in the attempt.

But it was not the Bishop himself that attracted Stephen, nor the lowly position as episcopal notary, but instead was whispered rumours that had travelled all the way from the distant wastelands of Brittany to the grand halls of Paris. Rumours that hinted at a great and bloody evil. Some months after his curious relocation to Nantes, Stephen sent his scrawled letter.

One line in that letter was ever on my mind during the journey and I wondered what it might mean and who it might refer to.

The subject of said rumours is a man known to you and is one of remarkable power.

"Damn you, Stephen," I muttered on the dockside in London. "Why must he speak in unanswerable riddles?"

At my side, Walt shrugged. "Likes being clever, don't he."

We crossed from London to Nantes by ship, travelling along the southern coast of England across to the northern coast of Normandy and then following that dangerous, craggy coast around headland after headland in choppy dark seas until finally we reached Saint Nazaire in the mouth of the Loire. From there we travelled upriver to the great city of Nantes.

"Strange," Walter said as we passed through that country. "Strange to be back here again."

We stood at the rail of the boat as it sailed up river on the flood tide, pushed by a stiff westerly wind. It was cold and spring seemed delayed, as if the land lacked the strength to throw off the remains of winter.

"Is it strange?" Rob asked, wistfully. "Seems fitting, to me. We brought much evil to these parts."

"Wonder if they remember us," Walt said. "If they remember the White Dagger Company and that bloody banner we fought under."

Rob nodded. "A field of red with yellow flames beneath rising up to touch the white dagger in the centre. Who could forget it."

"It was not evil we brought but justice," I said. "And all who lived then are long dead, as are their grandchildren. Whatever strangeness you feel comes not from the land but from your own imaginations. Pull yourselves together."

They said nothing in response which spoke volumes about their true thoughts. And the truth was I felt disquieted myself. Not so much by memories of the distant past when I had hunted Brittany and Poitou for the black knight Geoffrey de Charny but by more recent ones.

Our disastrous losses to the French a few years before had shaken me to such an extent that I was not the same man as I had been. It seemed so unnatural that our veteran army had been defeated by a mad young woman still in her maidenhood. An unholy reversal of the true order of things and it was simply the final insult for our nation, which seemed to me to be in sharp decline.

The Loire, up which we sailed was the great river of France, stretching more than six hundred miles from the central highlands in the south, up and across the land to the west coast and its waters fed the richest valley in Christendom. The very same river had formed the limit of the English dominion in the war, making a great front line upon which our armies had pressed for years.

It was the great bastion on that river, the city of Orléans, that we had needed to crush for us to become masters of all France. On the Loire was it that the French armies led by that mad young woman Joan of Lorraine had instead defeated us time and again, earning herself the name the Maiden of Orléans.

And it was where my own weakness and indecision had led to the slaughter of thousands of magnificent English bowmen.

But Orléans was halfway across France to the east and there was nothing to be done about the war any more. Through treaties wrangled and petty sieges conducted, King Charles VII was carefully and inevitably winning back his entire kingdom from the English and Henry VI was gladly giving it to him. Order had finally been imposed on the countryside and the bandits and thieves, the bands of routiers, and rampaging free companies driven out by forces loyal to the king.

Nantes was the picture of peace as we moored in the city on the 15th May 1440. The grandest buildings were of the typical Loire sandstone; either grey-white or yellowed-cream depending on the way the sun fell on the walls or beautifully carved columns and reliefs of the towers and facades. Still being built and covered in scaffolding, the cathedral was already grand and well-proportioned and perfection itself without being ostentatious. At first glance, the same could have been said for the city as a whole, although there was much in dire need of repair when we got into it. A large portion of Nantes had been reduced by a terrible fire and the acres of blackened timber, jutting up at all angles like the limbs of burned corpses, were yet being cleared.

Thinking of the urgency expressed in his letter, we did not pause even to secure lodgings in the city but went straight to the cathedral and asked after the Bishop's notary Stephen le Viel, which was the pseudonym he was using. It seemed as though we were expected and while Walter, Rob and our servants waited below, I was shown up almost directly to an antechamber and bidden to wait before the porter left by a different door to the one in which we had entered.

I sat waiting in the antechamber, listening to the hustle in the hall beyond and the shouts of the builders working on the cathedral outside. The decoration all around me was quite beautiful and even the tiles on the floor were bright and shining reds and greens, glistening in their rich glaze.

"Richard!" Stephen cried, flinging the door open and striding toward me. "How quickly you have come."

His clothes were rich and his hair cut into a fashionable length beneath his cap and he seemed rather fat and happy.

We embraced and I held him at arm's length. "You insisted upon urgency and so here I am. What is it that you believe you have uncovered in this damned duchy?"

He glanced over his shoulder into the hall from where he had emerged and, taking me by the elbow, pulled me away and lowered his voice.

"Rumours of children going missing from lands to the south of this city, about twenty miles away, right across a great swathe of countryside."

I sighed, feeling the ember of excitement fading fast. "Is that it? Missing children again, Stephen? How many times over the years have we followed rumours such as this, only to find the most mundane of causes? They are almost always found drowned in some overgrown pond or wash up miles downriver. It has never once been an immortal."

All while I spoke, he flapped his hands at me to lower my voice and he hissed at me. "It is dozens, Richard."

That gave me pause. "Dozens? Are you certain?"

He looked me in the eye. "Scores, sir. Perhaps even more. Scores of children gone missing, never to return."

I pursed my lips. "And you think an immortal is the cause? Why so? Why not slavers, taking them off the coast and from raids inland? Probably the damned Moors again."

He opened his mouth to answer but a powerful voice rang out from the hall beyond where we stood.

"Stephen? Is it your man or not? Where have you gone, Stephen? Why are you always vanishing when I need you, Stephen?"

My friend straightened up and whipped around and raised his voice. "Yes indeed, Milord Bishop. We are coming now, Your Grace." He rolled his eyes at me and lowered his voice. "Quickly, Richard. I have told the Bishop that you are a faithful man who has conducted many investigations of a secular nature for various lords over the years, especially in Normandy. Only by telling the Bishop this has he allowed me to bring you here to be engaged in a secret but official capacity to investigate these rumours."

I nodded slowly. "I am a faithful man, am I? Faithful to whom?"

Stephen swallowed, his face growing pale. "Why, to me, Richard. It was the only way to get them to trust you enough to bring you in."

"I see."

The voice from the chamber rose again. "Stephen! I hear you hissing out there like a pair of old maids. My patience grows thin, sir."

Stephen, as outwardly subservient to authority as ever, turned on his heel and strode into the chamber with his head bowed and I followed.

The Bishop's audience hall was sumptuously decorated with wood panelling and fine carvings covered in gold leaf and painted in rich vermilion and indigo. Elegantly proportioned windows filled one wall, overlooking a portion of the cathedral that was covered by scaffolding swarming with builders.

At the top of the chamber the Bishop sat on his throne, which was quite tasteful, as far as thrones go, and it was positioned behind a long table where clerks and priests examined papers filled with tabulated texts and calculations, and architectural drawings. None of the other men paid us any attention at all as we approached the great lord who was Bishop of Nantes.

"My apologies, Milord Bishop," Stephen said as we drew near. "It is indeed my man who has come, finally, from his recent work in Normandy. Please allow me to introduce—"

"Fine, fine," the Bishop said. He was a tall, fat man with a rather kindly face. Some Bishops, grasping and ambitious as they often were, aroused in me nothing but immediate and lasting contempt. But I must say that the Bishop of Nantes did not. His manner was rushed but his tone was not overly rude. "So, you have experience with this sort of thing, do you?"

I glanced at Stephen. "I have some experience with the investigation of certain dark crimes, Your Grace. Only, if you will permit me to say, I am afraid I do not yet know what you mean by this sort of thing."

The Bishop pursed his full lips. "No, indeed. Well said, sir. We must reserve our judgement until the facts are established. But this business with le Ferron is cause for concern enough."

"Le Ferron?" I said, addressing Stephen.

The Bishop nodded to Stephen, who turned to me. "Two days ago, at Pentecost, a priest named le Ferron was seized. Dragged from his church before the parishioners and thrown into a black dungeon. Le Ferron and his brother are noblemen and vassals of Duke Jean, the Lord of Brittany, and so this is a grave crime against the Duke that must be answered for."

"Bah," the Bishop said. "The Duke will order the release of le Ferron and if he has any sense, the Marshal will give him up."

"The Marshal?" I asked. "What Marshal?"

The Bishop raised his eyebrows at Stephen. "You did not inform your man of the subject of his investigations?"

Stephen made a little bow. "I thought it best not to put such a thing in writing and was a moment ago about to explain it to Richard before you requested that we attend to you, my lord." Stephen fixed me with a warning look before explaining. "The man who has broken the Duke's peace is also the subject of our investigation in the missing children. He is Gilles, Comte de Brienne, Lord of Tiffauges, Laval, Pouzages, and Machecoul, the Baron de Rais, Marshal of France and Lieutenant-General of Brittany."

I believe that my mouth gaped open like an imbecile's for a moment but swiftly I found my jaw clenched in quivering rage.

The name was known to me. It was one I had not heard for almost a decade but a name that had often been spoken in the past along with that of another. For Gilles de Rais had been the closest companion to and steadfast captain of the Maiden of Orléans. And I had always suspected that it was he who had been the architect of her victories. It was he, surely, whispering in her ear, who had directed the French to victory and not the divine voice of God's angels in her head, as she had claimed. For why should God send angels to aid the French and not the English?

It was not only I that held these same suspicions about Gilles de Rais, for he had been rewarded with high honours. Indeed, Gilles was one of only four lords granted the honour of bringing the Holy Ampoule from the Abbey of Saint-Remy to Notre-Dame de Reims for the consecration of Charles VII as King of France. It was at the coronation that Gilles was also made Marshal of France in recognition of his superb generalship in the campaigns. His appointment as Lieutenant-General of Brittany also meant that he was the King's representative in the region, similar in some ways perhaps to the sheriffs of English counties. These were the highest possible appointments that could have been made for a young military leader.

In contrast, Charles had soon tired of and discarded the poor mad girl before she was captured, tried and burned to death. And the newly feted Gilles de Rais had callously abandoned his former companion to her fate.

"Gilles de Rais?" I asked Stephen. "Did you say that this killer of children is Gilles de Rais?"

"Yes," Stephen said, watching me closely. "Almost certainly."

"Now, now," the Bishop said, chiding Stephen. "We have nought but unsubstantiated rumour about murders and witchcraft. I must stress that currently all of these horrid claims are nothing more than hearsay. Come now, you men, we all know how village folk like to gossip about their betters and there is not a single body nor bloody blade to add credence to this talk. They say that children have disappeared but have they truly? And if they have gone then who has taken them? And what then was their true fate? Do you know, Stephen?"

"No, Milord Bishop."

He nodded his big head sagely. "This is why we must have evidence before anything can be done. Evidence, do you see? Stephen here has my written authority to travel from place to place and take depositions from anyone who is willing to provide them. But this investigation must be conducted in full secrecy, do you hear me? None of this shall get back to my cousin the Duke until we are certain that crimes have been committed. And of course, we certainly do not wish to alarm the Baron de Rais himself, do we." He broke off, looking me up and down. "You have the bearing of a capable man but I warn you. Do not alarm the Marshal or any of his men. He maintains a personal army of two hundred superbly equipped veteran soldiers, mounted on the finest horses and if you go blundering about then you will end up thrown in one of his dungeons just as le Ferron has. We do not have a force capable of resisting them in Nantes, and even my cousin's personal guard is not so large as that. Do you understand?"

"The Marshal maintains a personal army of two hundred mounted veterans?" I asked. "Men who fought against the English?"

Stephen shot me a look.

"Why certainly, Master Richard. And you are quite right to be fearful as these are men who are not to be trifled with and neither is the Marshal. If we go making unsubstantiated rumours then the King himself may intervene and take steps to protect his man from proper justice." The Bishop cleared his throat. "Assuming he is guilty, of course. Bring me evidence, sirs, evidence. We must have blood and bones, God forgive me for speaking it, the blood and bones of these innocent children and also sworn statements from witnesses to murders and witchcraft or else we have nothing at all. Now, God be with you."

2

A C u r s e d L a n d

M a y 1 4 4 0

STEPHEN KNEW THE WAY south from Nantes to the lands
around Tiffauges Castle and we rode out together, we four
immortals and our servants, across the Loire and out into the
wilderness beyond.

Most of the Loire Valley, hundreds of miles of it, provided
fertile soil and a delightful climate for producing abundant crops,
healthy people, and wealthy lords. But south of Nantes, it was
rather different.

It was an area where met three regions of France; Brittany,
Poitou, and Anjou and it was a broken country. The land itself
looked like it had long ago been smashed, shattered, and wrecked,
perhaps at the dawn of time or during some great catastrophe. All

hard earth, thin rivers, or dank marsh, with scattered fragmented jumbles of grey rock and the people were sullen, scrawny, and bitter and the lords were few and far between. There was not enough wealth in the land itself to sustain many knights or gentlemen but there were prosperous commoners who carried on trade up and down the Loire.

Those people that we saw as we trotted through their villages either hid from us or cast unfriendly glances in our direction. I made sure to wave, smile, and call out greetings but not one gesture was returned in kind.

We were dressed in ordinary clothes, as a reasonably wealthy townsman might wear. All of us but Stephen wore a sturdy, padded doublet beneath those clothes but these were thinner than the gambesons we would wear beneath plate and mail armour during warfare. Thick enough to protect from a slashing cut and would perhaps serve to resist the thrust of a dagger but little more and I knew we would have to avoid full combat at all costs, especially if the Marshal's small army was properly equipped for war. We did not even have steel helms to put on, should a battle threaten.

Likewise, our horses were well bred and rode wonderfully but they were not trained for battle and so we could not hope to fight from them. Wherever we went and whatever we did, we would have to avoid combat wherever possible.

In spite of the poor weather, bleak landscape, and unfriendly welcome, I felt reinvigorated by the ride. Once more, I felt wrapped in the comforting cloak of purpose.

By the end of the day, we drew near to our destination and we slowed to a stop as the battlements appeared on the horizon. Our horses were tired, and I was wary of alerting even a fraction of the Marshal's personal army to our presence.

The castle itself was a substantial fortress. Standing on a massive outcrop overlooking two ravines through which ran the rivers Crume and Sevre. Towers of differing heights jutted up over thick walls, silhouetted against the sky.

"Have we not been here before?" I asked Walt. "I look upon those walls and it feels somewhat familiar."

He nodded, pursing his lips as he recalled it, but Rob answered in his stead. "Came through this way a few times when we was looking for the black knight and when we was trying to bring Jean de Clermont out from hiding. Our lads needed somewhere to spend the winter, probably, what was it, ninety years ago now? By God, that's a long time. We talked about taking this place with our company of fifty men."

"Well," Walt said, "you talked about it, Richard."

Looking at the imposing fortress, I scoffed at the notion. "I must have been mad."

Walt laughed, as did Stephen.

"It has been much added to in the years since," Rob said, appraising the place. "More towers, new walls. Higher than before. We would need an army to take it now. Five hundred, perhaps."

"Five thousand, more like," Walt said. "And a score of cannon."

But we were not going to take the castle. Not with an army or in any other way. Gilles de Rais was said to not be in residence and instead he was at another of his many castles, in Machecoul, thirty miles west toward the sea. When a lord was not present, with his court and household, a castle would be almost entirely empty. Perhaps a caretaker or two to guard against burglars and squatters, and to fix a leaking roof to stop the place falling into ruin before the lord returned. But we could not be certain that Tiffauges was not also guarded by members of the Marshal's army. It seemed unlikely to me but Stephen claimed the villagers believed those soldiers and the Marshal's men resided in the empty castles. I had not believed it but smoke drifted from within and from one of the towers and so it was not worth the risk.

Instead, we wanted to speak to the people in the villages subject to Gilles de Rais. And we had one specific man in mind.

"Come," I said to Stephen, "let us find this village of Tilleuls and get a statement from this physician of yours."

All about the landscape was bleak and wind-blasted. Underfoot, the ground was stony and the soil so thin that the trees grew stunted and were bent over by the endless winds. Water pooled here and there in hollows, their surface choked by weeds and green slime. Above us the sky was low and dark, like a roof of broken slate.

"Best wrap up your bow," I said to Rob. "You look like an Englishman."

"Plenty of bows like this in France," Rob objected. "In Brittany, too. Not just hunters but soldiers, too. Some of them. Levies, mainly, when raised from the country."

"I'd rather you did not look like an Englishman or a poacher or do anything that might make the commoners mistrust us. You will unstring and sheath your bow and hide the arrows. From the first moment we make ourselves known to the people of these lands we must be beyond reproach. We will pay for everything we use, and we shall pay handsomely. We will be courteous even when treated rudely. Do you hear me, Walt?"

He affected outrage. "Why do you single me out?"

"Do you hear me, Walt?"

"Yes, Richard."

"And we are all from Normandy. Even Walt."

"That's right," Rob said. "And if anyone asks, we just say his mother was ravished by an Englishman."

"Don't you mean a Welshman?" Stephen said.

"Oh, charming," Walt said. "Even my dear old friend Stephen Gossett is having a dig at poor old Walt, who never did his friends no harm in his life and then this is how they treat him in his turn."

"That is enough, now," I said, seeing the roofs of houses up ahead for just a moment as we went over a rise in the road. "We must present ourselves as trustworthy men who can be relied upon to get the evidence needed to arrest their lord and to put him on trial."

"Why can we not just kill him?" Walt asked as our party picked our way along the narrow tracks toward the village. "Just ambush him, cut off his head and be done with it."

Stephen sighed elaborately. "He may be both mortal and innocent, Walter. We cannot murder an innocent man."

"Innocent?" Walt said. "Of course he done it. People don't talk about things like that if it ain't true. And if he has done things that that, like what they say he done, then he has to be immortal. Don't he?"

"Not necessarily," Stephen said, sniffing and lifting his nose up. "Immortals do not have a monopoly on violence."

"But if he is guilty of murdering children," Rob said, speaking slowly and frowning. "Why do we not just kill him anyway? Whether he's been drinking their blood or not? Mortal or immortal, he will deserve death."

Stephen lifted a finger up and took the kind of breath he often took before launching into a pompous lecture.

I hurriedly spoke before he could get started. "Because our Order exists to kill William's immortals. Not to assassinate common murderers for the sake of it. If he has committed crimes, then the Bishop and the Duke must be the ones to pass judgement. Only if he is an immortal is it our duty to put an end to him."

Stephen and Rob nodded in agreement.

"You're saying we first have to find out if he is a killer and then also find out if he is an immortal before we can do anything?" Walt said. "Be easier if we just take him, that's all I'm saying. It's what we done before. Take him, cut his flesh and have him confess that is guilty and a spawn of William de Ferrers before we slay him. Like we done before."

"That was different," I said. "That was war. There is no war here. And the easier route is not often the right one to follow. We must act rightly for we are knights, we three, and Stephen is a moral man, are you not, Stephen? Despite once being a monk and now being a lawyer."

My words drew laughter from all three but they quickly fell silent and I hoped they would think on what I had said. Even so, I was not feeling so confident about doing the right thing myself.

Gilles de Rais had been one of the architects in the downfall of the English armies and the revelation that he may have been an immortal the entire time brought the whole conflict since Orléans back into relief. He was at Joan of Lorraine's side during every battle and thus it was he who had been whispering stratagems into her ear.

Our defeat suddenly made sense to me. And I had an opportunity to put it right, to take revenge for the losses we had suffered.

But perhaps Gilles was not an immortal. Perhaps it was my desire for him to be so that coloured my thinking and twisted my thoughts.

And if he was not an immortal then was he a man capable of murdering children? Dozens of them at that, so Stephen had suggested. Dozens or even scores.

Whether Gilles was good or evil seemed to rest on whether the Maiden of Orléans had herself been divinely inspired or heretical. Had she been practising witchcraft all those years ago when she led armies while dressed as a knight? Had she drawn from the power of evil? If so, then it seemed likely that Gilles was also evil.

Or had she truly been divinely inspired, following the directions of angels and God above? For if that was true, as the French yet claimed, then how could Gilles be either evil or immortal?

I had no answers but I hoped to find some amongst the commoners of the region and first of all from the people of Tilleuls.

"Here we are," Stephen said as we rode into the centre of the village.

There was a stone church, quite plain but in good repair, and a group of good houses around the large central square, built tall and with tiled roofs. The gardens were well-kept, and the stink of the middens and cesspits was not as foul as in many such places. In fact, it was as fine a village as I had seen in the area.

When we approached there were children playing a game of some sort in the middle of the village before the church but before we came close they scattered beyond the building and into the houses. In the silence after the children's voices stopped, all I could hear was the sounds of our horses breathing and their hooves echoing from the walls of the church and the houses all around.

A movement caught my eye and I turned to see a pair of shutters slam closed in the upper window of the house there. Almost at the same time I heard a door bang shut on the other side of the church and there was the scraping of a bar being pushed into place behind it.

The wind blew up a swirl of dust beneath us.

"We mean no harm!" Stephen bellowed suddenly, right behind me.

I almost jumped out of my skin and my horse sprang forward in surprise.

"For God's sake, Stephen," I said as I reigned my horse in.

"Do you think that will bring them running with jugs of wine and a platter of almond tarts?" He began to answer but I did not let him do so. "Get off your bloody horse and lead us to the house of your potential witness."

Sheepishly, he pointed to the grandest house in the village. A two-storey place with an attractive tiled roof and windows with sound panes of glass in them. "The physician's house."

"Watch the approaches at both ends of the village," I said to Walt and Rob. "Do not let the servants wander. Be respectful to all the folk here but remember also that any of them may be in league with the Marshal."

Both men nodded and moved to instruct the valets. I noted that Rob checked his bow in its sheath and loosened the cover on his quiver.

Stephen was speaking through the closed front door of the physician's house as I approached. He turned and his face was one of despair.

"The physician is away," Stephen said. "And they will not admit us."

I sighed, for it suddenly seemed obvious that he would not be there, for physicians who do not reside in large towns travel all over visiting the sick. "Where is he? Do not tell me he has returned to Nantes? We could have stayed and met him there."

Stephen jerked his head at the door. "The woman there will not say."

"Is there no other within who will help us?"

Stephen shrugged and stroked his chin. "To speak plainly, Richard, I was doubtful whether even a man as learned and decent as the Master Mousillon here would speak to me in an official capacity. His servants would certainly lack the courage to do so."

"You are the one who lacks courage," I said and stepped up to the door before banging on it with my palm. "We are on official business, madame. Is the lady of the house within?"

There was a pause before a soft voice answered. "This is she."

"Please would you open the door but a little, madame, so I may state my business? We have come as previously agreed with Master Pierre Mousillon, some weeks ago now. Perhaps you already know of why we come but I must say that we come from Nantes on peaceful, legitimate business, and not from Tiffauges or Machecoul or any other such place."

After a moment, the lock turned and the door opened a little.

"Thank you, Madame," I said, "I appreciate the—"

My tongue stuck to the roof of my mouth as I laid eyes on a beautiful young woman who was not more than twenty years old. Perhaps she was a servant or perhaps Master Mousillon had got himself an especially lovely young wife, but I suspected she was a daughter.

"Ah," I said, softening my tone and lowering my voice, "my apologies, mademoiselle, I believed I was speaking to the lady of the house. Is your mother present?"

"My father is Pierre Mousillon," she said, in the most delightfully high, clear and yet warm and steady voice. "I am the mistress here. Now, my father is away and will not return for some time. Please, sir, I beg that you leave me be."

"A moment, if you please," I said, placing my hand gently on

24

the door frame and leaning forward. "I shall certainly do whatever you wish but perhaps you can help me before I go?" She paused, looking up at me. I snatched off my hat and clutched it in my fist. "You see, mademoiselle, we have come about the boy. His name is Jamet. Forgive me but he is your brother, is that correct?"

She breathed in and held up her chin, her eyes shining. "He was."

"I see. And as I understand it, young Jamet Mousillon disappeared last year and I am here to discover what occurred and also to see justice done."

"Justice?" She hesitated, peering at me through her fierce eyes. "And who are you?"

"My name is Richard. This is my friend Stephen. He is a lawyer but try not to judge him too harshly, for he is not so bad, as far as members of his profession are concerned. Stephen here is the one your father spoke to in Nantes, about your brother."

She peered at Stephen, fixing him with a fierce gaze. "What did my father say to you in Nantes?"

Stephen swallowed, bewitched by her beauty and disconcerted by her directness. "That he could no longer keep silent about what all in these parts know. He provided me with the particulars of his own tragic case and outlined many others. When we parted, we agreed that if I could get others to swear a witness statement, he would do also."

The young woman lifted her chin and unflinchingly fired her next question at him. "Where was it, precisely, that you met my father?"

"My lord the Bishop of Nantes had taken ill, and your father was the third physician called, as the other two only caused the Bishop's condition to worsen. After your father had administered his treatments, I asked him if he knew anything of the rumours in the area in which he lived. I admitted that I was keen to find a legal resolution to these concerns, no matter the social standing of the potential criminals involved. I believe I said I would prosecute the King himself, if he was the culprit. It was then that your father told about little Jamet. He was receptive to speaking further and so I said I would attend him here, as soon as I was able."

The young woman nodded once, confirming this was correct. "You are late. You said you would come by the end of last week, sir, but you did not and my father had to leave."

"I am at fault," I said. "As Stephen had to wait for me to arrive in Nantes."

"Neither of you are Breton," she said, prompting us.

"I am from Normandy and Stephen comes from Paris," I said. Small, necessary lies such as these came so easily to me by then that they were undetectable as such. Deceit is a skill and just like any other it may be improved through rigorous practice. "And this is why those in authority here have engaged us to make these enquiries. Because we are uncorrupted by any taint that might have crept into local men. May we come in to speak with you, please? It would be just for a few moments and then we will return at a time convenient for your good father."

She glanced over her shoulder, took a deep breath, nodded once and stepped back, opening the door wide.

Inside, the house was dark. An old man, a servant, stood in

the back of the room with his hand on the pommel of a short sword that he held, sheathed, but ready. He was withered and bony but his eyes were unwavering and I recognised in him a man willing to do violence. That was more important in a bodyguard than physical strength. I nodded to him in greeting but he gave no response.

The house was sparsely furnished but what furniture there was spoke of a certain wealth. The fireplace crackled with warmth and every surface appeared clean and the home was well cared for.

She invited us to sit at the dining table which dominated one side of the main room, which we did, though she herself remained standing with the old servant behind her.

"Now, to get started," Stephen said, opening his satchel and pulling out a sheaf of parchment, an inkpot, and a pen, setting them each in turn upon the table. "Might I have your name, mademoiselle?"

She scowled and glanced around at the old man before looking at Stephen again with irritation and considerable nervousness.

"For God's sake, Stephen," I said. "Put your lawyer's tackle away, man."

"I have no desire to have my words recorded, sir," the woman said.

"No, indeed," I said. "Is that not so, Stephen?"

He shoved his things back in his bag and lowered his head. "My apologies."

I leaned forward, planting my hands flat on her table. "Please understand that Stephen is entirely unused to the company of decent people, for he spends all of his waking hours amongst dusty law books and dustier old priests."

She smiled, not because my jest was amusing but because she appreciated my attempt at levity. "No apology is required, sirs. My name is Ameline Mousillon."

"Thank you, Ameline," I replied. "We do not wish to pry into your particular tragedy, unless you wish to tell us of it, but we would greatly like to hear about what it is that goes on in these parts. You see, we know of rumours but because we are outsiders and completely new to this land, we have very little in the way of facts."

"None at all," Stephen muttered, before wiping his mouth, for the woman's beauty had quite stoppered up his lips.

Ameline took a breath. "What is it that you wish to know, sir?" The servant behind her hissed a warning I did not catch but she turned on him. "Oh, enough, Paillart. Do you not think we have had our fill of keeping silent? I think you will find that it is the prolonged silence of too many souls in these parts that has allowed the evil to grow as it has." Her cheeks became flushed as she spoke and she ended with a tight clearing of her throat. She pulled out a stool and sat at the table opposite us and took a moment to compose herself before continuing.

"I do not know when it began. It was some years ago, perhaps four or five years. I do not know for certain and I am unsure if anyone does. Children going missing. It was only one or two, I suppose, from each village. One or two per year, perhaps. And each village knows mainly of itself, of course." She cleared her throat again. "Paillart, could you bring me some water, please?"

With a glare at me and Stephen, he left the room for the rear of the house.

"Speaking to us about these things shows remarkable decency and bravery, Ameline," I said, softly. "Please, do go on. Can you give us the names of the missing children?"

Ameline bit her lip and hesitated before shaking her head. "Their mothers and fathers would not wish me to. They would not speak with you."

"You are speaking with us," I pointed out.

She smiled. "I am not as they are."

"Oh? How so?"

"We are foreigners, you see. My family, we came here fourteen years ago from Poitiers. We are outsiders and always will be."

"You and your father," I said, "and your brother?"

"My mother also and my sister. They died. My sister before Jamet and my mother soon after. It was a fever but my father could do nothing for her. The villagers say she died from a broken heart but of course that is mere superstition."

The servant Paillart returned and placed a cup of water in front of Ameline. He did not bring any for us and Ameline did not offer us any either. She was yet unsure about us and remained nervous. She wanted us gone and I sensed she might throw us out at any moment.

I sat back and looked at her again. "Were you in receipt of an education, Ameline?"

"I can write in French and Latin," she said, surprised by my question but proud enough of her accomplishments to speak of them. "And I manage the household finances and my father's business."

"You have books here?" I asked by way of conversation.

She frowned. "Only my mother's book of hours. It brings me great comfort."

I nodded, smiling. "May I ask why your father remains in this place? Why not move to Nantes or back to Poitiers?"

She coloured and lowered her head. "We live here."

"Of course, of course. Tell me, does your father have much business at the castle? At Tiffauges?"

The name of the place was like a jolt through Ameline and Paillart both and I thought that we would be asked to leave immediately. But the moment passed.

"On occasion, my father has been called on to attend to a member of the Marshal's household," Ameline said. "But the Marshal has other physicians, thanks to God."

Sensing I was on dangerous ground, I spoke softly. "I wonder if I wanted to speak to a servant of that place, who might I speak to?"

From behind her came a gravelly, Breton's growl. "Say nothing, my lady." Paillart stepped forward behind Ameline. "These men must go."

I looked at him and spoke in a low but firm voice. "We are here for justice, Master Paillart. We are here for Jamet and for all the other boys and the girls who have had no justice. Mademoiselle, I know you are afraid and I am sure you are right to be. But look at me. Look closely at me. I say again that I am here for justice. And I am not afraid."

Ameline sat up and seemed about to speak but Paillart got

there first. "Then you are a fool. Mistress, these men must leave. They have been here too long. Your father would wish them to leave, Mistress."

I stood and dragged Stephen to his feet. "Of course, we shall take our leave. Thank you for speaking with us, Ameline. We shall, I think, be staying at the inn north of here, in Mortagne. When your father returns, we shall speak with him then. And I hope that I shall see you again, also."

She smiled. "My thanks, sir. I hope for that, also."

As we walked through the quiet village to our horses, the evening sunlight broke through the low layer of clouds and I slowed to savour the feeling of warmth on my face.

Stephen looked up at me, shaking his head. "Why must you seduce every pretty young woman you meet, Richard?"

"Seduce?" I said. "You mistake courtesy for seduction, sir."

"Hmm," he said. "Your courtesy is so forward it is enough to make a whore blush."

"Do stop acting the old maid, Stephen. Why are you in such a foul mood?"

Our pages brought our horses and held them ready. In the distance, I saw Rob at one end of the village and Walt at the other. They both reported, through gesture, that all was well. The daylight would soon be gone.

"I am in no foul mood," Stephen replied. "But if I were, it would be because we have wasted our time coming here."

I swung myself into the saddle and looked to the north. "Oh, I would not call it wasted."

"Yes, and we both know why. But we have nothing to do now

but wait for Pierre Mousillon to return, and who knows how long that will be."

"No, there is much to be done. Let us return to the inn at Mortagne. We may begin asking the locals for what information they are willing to give. And, if at all possible, I will go to Castle Tiffauges."

"What? You are mad. The Marshal is not there, so why would you go?"

"Someone may be there. A servant, at least, who might be willing to reveal his master's secrets."

"Richard, you agreed to conduct yourself in accordance with the law. If you go around torturing people for information, it risks invalidating all of our—"

"Keep your hose on, Stephen. I said nothing of torture." I patted the purse on my belt. "I mean to obtain information by way of bribery."

"We must be careful," he argued. "The poor commoners of this land have been much abused by their lord."

"So it seems, at least," I pointed out.

"Whatever the truth of it, you must admit that something terrible has been going on here. The people are mightily oppressed and have absolutely no legal recourse to do anything about it."

"Of course not," I said. "Why would they have?"

"But do you not see how powerless it makes them? How utterly at the mercy of their lord they are?"

"That is the proper way of things," I pointed out and not for the first time.

"Their collective will is close to being crushed and so we must tread carefully and not go barrelling about with random questions and so risk ruining our investigation before it begins."

"Do not concern yourself, Stephen. One way or another, we shall learn what we need to know. And then we shall have our revenge on Gilles de Rais."

"Revenge?" he said, aghast. "What do you mean revenge? This must be about justice, not revenge. Richard?"

I ignored him and rode north to find the inn at Mortagne.

That night, I lay awake, looking up at the gloomy beams and ceiling above my bed, thinking back with deep dread and clinging regret to eleven years earlier. It had started at the battle that ultimately brought me into conflict with the mad girl Joan of Lorraine and her captain Gilles de Rais.

34

3

The Battle of the Herrings
February 1429

THE ENGLISH AND BURGUNDIAN armies were besieging the great city of Orléans. It was a cold February in 1429 when I joined a supply column heading south from Paris to our forts ringing the walls of Orléans, bringing three hundred carts and wagons laden with arrows, cannons, cannonballs, and barrels of herring. The tons of preserved fish were because Lent was approaching and even on campaign the proper fast was attempted to the best of our ability.

There were a mere fifteen hundred men in our supply column. We were led by Sir John Fastolf and I was posing as a common man at arms, though a well-respected and well-equipped one. The only authority I commanded was that which was expressed naturally by my manner and bearing and I was contented to quietly follow Fastolf, who appeared to be a competent captain.

I had known some of his ancestors over the decades. The Fastolfs hailed from Norfolk and ruled over boggy coastal lands quite competently and every so often a son would rise to prominence as a bishop or a sheriff. A perfectly conventional English noble family. The kind of family that quietly and dutifully served its king and its people and thusly made England into the magnificent kingdom it was.

By 1429, Sir John was getting on a bit. Almost fifty, he had married a wealthy older widow, passing up the opportunity for sons in exchange for fortune and now held a series of rather splendid estates all over England.

I had seen him conduct himself well during the siege of Harfleur, fourteen years earlier but he had been wounded and sent home and so had missed the bloody glory that was the battle of Agincourt. All men who had been abed in England thought themselves accursed that they were not at Agincourt and no man thought it more keenly than Sir John Fastolf. Though I was a nobody, a poor man-at-arms with inexplicably fine armour, I had been there and Sir John, I am certain, held it against me.

The relief column that he led seemed to be protected well enough. Our eventual defeat at the hands of the French was yet many months away and it seemed to me, and to many of those fighting on both sides, that an ultimate English victory was almost inevitable.

Why was I fighting there at all? It was a question I asked myself even at the time and more so ever since, for my duty was to the Order of the White Dagger and not to the King of England.

And yet, we had come so close to taking the crown of France for the English king but after Henry V's untimely death, it was in danger of being snatched away.

And so I fought because I was an Englishman, first and foremost and also because we had uncovered no more immortals after the nest of them we had cleared out almost ninety years before.

That was why I found myself fighting once more with the English army against the French. Not as a lord, because I wished to keep out of the politics and the endless questions and plots of the nobility and because I believed it would be easier, simpler, to fight as a common man-at-arms.

I was wrong. Utterly and idiotically wrong to think such a thing but I did not know it yet.

In those days, there were spies everywhere. The front line of the war, that is the extent of English control from the north coast and Paris, was the Loire River but it was far from a solid barrier. Indeed, it could hardly have been more porous to enemy incursions and our coming was well noted. Indeed, it was essentially impossible to hide our coming across the featureless plain as we approached our siege works, far beyond the horizon to the south.

I was in the vanguard at the front of the long wagon train but had sent Rob and Walt further ahead to watch for ambushes. Vigilance was our only defence at being caught out in the open.

Both men came back, riding hard, to our convoy, their horses breathing heavy.

"Enemies, Sir Richard," Rob called to me from the saddle.

He had been knighted on the field of Poitiers, as had Walter, and all three of us were posing as mortal men-at-arms fighting for the pay and for the promise of spoils and ransoms. Yet, old habits die hard and especially when feelings are high and battle may be near.

"How far?" I replied. "How many?"

"Thousands."

Sir John Fastolf rode up with his retinue behind him. "What is this you say, man?" he cried. "Thousands of French? I doubt that."

He turned to the knight at his side. "Send someone credible to the south, Hugh, see what this is all about."

A few moments later and two riders trotted off.

"Sir John," I said from my horse. "Perhaps we should bring the men in to make a defensible line here?"

"Here?" Fastolf looked around at the flat plain. "There is nowhere to make a defence. Besides, our supplies are needed by the army. No, no, we shall continue onward, I think."

"But sir!" Walter called. "There are thousands of mounted men-at-arms not three miles southward. Coming this way, sir."

Fastolf hesitated. I knew he doubted my men's judgement but if they were right then an enemy force of such a size and strength would mean the death of us. Our three hundred wagons were spread out over a vast area and our mounted men and archers would be unable to protect them.

"Order a halt," Fastolf commanded. "We shall wait here until we can confirm this rumour."

"Most likely it is our own men, sir," Sir Hugh said to his friend and commander. "Our own men come out from the forts to meet us. Escort us in."

"No, my lord," Rob blurted. "Forgive me, sir, but the enemy had banners unfurled and the ones I recognised were French."

"And Scots," Walter added. "Bloody treacherous Scots, hundreds of the bastards. No doubts about that, sirs."

I kept silent, watching Fastolf's face crease into frustration. The wagons creaked to a stop behind us and the men drifted forward to see what was occurring.

In little time, the two men who had trotted off came charging back in full gallop. Before they even came close, Fastolf was calling out orders to prepare for battle.

"We shall make for that hillock," Fastolf said, pointing with outstretched finger. "And prepare stakes."

"What about the wagons, sir?" one of his men said.

"We must leave them," Fastolf said. "It is regrettable but we cannot defend so many and they would take too long to traverse to our defensive position upon the hill."

Walt and Rob glared at me, for the hillock was low and small and entirely unsuitable. And indeed I felt compelled to speak up.

"Sir John?" I said, drawing sharp looks from his men. "Might we not draw the wagons up here? If we make a wagon park where we stand, forming a great square or circle or any shape that creates a perimeter, then we may bring the men and horses safely within. Our brave archers may then shoot the enemy at will. We shall be unassailable."

"How dare you, sir!" Hugh cried. "Do not question your captain again. Sir John has spoken and it is our duty to follow his commands. When he says—"

Fastolf held up his hand. "Peace, Hugh, I beg you. Peace." Sir Hugh fell silent and glared at me while Fastolf, to his great credit, continued. "Richard's suggestion has merit. Command the drivers to bring the wagons up into a perimeter. And have the archers plant their stakes beyond."

His men gaped in astonishment for a long moment until one of them began shouting commands. Soon, they all followed and our great convoy of three hundred wagons and carts, was arranged into a rough and large fort, where the walls were wagons. It was conducted swiftly but only with much shouting and cursing and with such great clanking of wheels and chains and neighing of horses that any enemy within ten miles would have thought we were having a battle all by ourselves. The archers were commanded to plant their long wooden stakes on the outside of the wagons, most at the front and others on the flanks, so that the enemy horsemen could not charge close and push their way through by weight of horse.

"Thousands, was it?" I asked Walt and Rob, as we watched the madness behind us.

They exchanged a look. "We're in for a rare scrap, Richard," Rob said.

"Don't really think this will work, do you?" Walt asked, nodding at the chaotic mass of wood and wheels being shifted into position.

"It was a proven tactic employed in open country by the people of the grasslands against the Mongols," I said.

Rob scratched his head under the rim of his helm. "I thought no one ever defeated the Mongols in battle?"

"The French are not the Mongols," I pointed out.

Even as we drew the last of the wagons into position at the rear, our enemy came into sight through the woods and hedgerows up ahead. First, it was scattered groups of horsemen emerging from the shadows beneath the bare trees to watch us and our strange behaviour. But very quickly the main force followed, already deployed into a broad front and flying their banners and with lances held high. They had horsemen, infantry, and crossbowmen, and their colours were bright and their armour shining in the late winter sun.

"Should we perhaps retire to within our wagon fortress, Richard?" Rob suggested.

"I think perhaps we should."

Their forces were commanded by Jean, known as the Bastard of Orléans on account that he was the illegitimate son of the old Duke of Orléans. The Duke was long dead but he had been the second son of the old King of France and so Jean the Bastard had royal blood and was first cousin to the Dauphin.

And the French were indeed supported, as Walt had claimed, by a powerful contingent from our old enemy, the cunning Scots. They were led by a superb soldier named Sir John Stewart of Darnley. He was a wily old sod who had fought and won a dozen battles in France against the English over the previous decade.

"It would be pleasing to me," I said to Walter and Rob as we watched them approach from atop barrels of dried herring on the back of a wagon, "if we could put an end to Sir John Stewart."

Rob nodded and caressed the side of his bow stave. "I'll put an arrow in his eye if I can, Richard."

More and more companies emerged and took position a mile away. The mounted men alone outnumbered us and there were thousands of spear-armed infantry and crossbowmen in formations

"They're taking their sweet time," Walter grumbled, leaning on his poleaxe.

"They are right to be afraid of us," I said, looking over my shoulder at our archers. "We shall pick them apart and drive them away."

Rob grinned. "Another Agincourt."

Walt scoffed. "You're always calling everything another Agincourt, Rob. You said that after Verneuil, five years ago."

Rob's grin fell into a scowl. "Well, it's true, ain't it?"

Walter ignored him, squinting into the distance. He tensed.

"What is it?" I prompted.

"Those wagons," he pointed them out amongst the colourful pageantry of the men-at-arms. "See that. And there. Also there. They're carrying cannons, Richard. Are they preparing them to use against us?"

It was already cold and yet I felt a sudden shiver of fear. "Warn Fastolf," I said to Rob, who raised an eyebrow. "No, no. I shall do it myself."

"You see!" his man Sir Hugh cried when I relayed the warning. "We shall be blasted into pieces. We should have abandoned the wagons. Sir John? We must retire to a more favourable position. The hillock yonder, as you first ordered earlier this day. Shall I relay your order to the men?"

Fastolf glared at me while his man was speaking. "It is too late now, Hugh. If we leave the protection of the wagons, they shall run us down. We are vastly outnumbered, are we not? How many are there?"

"A thousand, my lord," one of his knights said, shrugging. "Perhaps a little more."

The others in his retinue nodded.

"They are four thousand," I said. "See for yourself. Count the banners, my lords. There are five hundred Scots alone, you can see it with your own eyes. My lord Sir John is right. There is no leaving this place now so we must weather the storm. Have no fear. These cannons are barely capable of hitting a castle wall, let alone striking us here. We must sit and listen to them blasting their filthy, stinking smoke at us for half a day until they run out of gunpowder and cannonballs and then we can be on our way to Orléans and reach the forts, God willing, by nightfall."

The first of their cannons fired and the ball flew just over the front row of our wagons, killed two horses and smashed a wagon at the rear that was still being eased into position. It exploded into a shower of splinters and its cargo of arrows was tossed into the air like sparks from a bonfire. Men ran screaming and pages fought to control the panicking horses.

"Get out of my sight," Fastolf said to me.

I returned through our soldiers and archers to Rob and Walt who were cowering against a wheel of the wagon we had been standing on.

"Did you warn him about the cannons, sir?" Walt asked.

I looked down and sighed. "I do not think that wheel will serve to protect you, men."

Another cannon fired and the ball ripped through the air over our heads with that sound that I would come to know so well over the coming centuries. It landed unseen beyond our wagon fortress but other than being a few feet too high was right on target.

"I think I may have understated their effectiveness a little," I admitted, crouching down beside Rob and Walt.

Another cannon sounded and a ball bounced in front of our position before crashing through a wagon at the right flank of our fortress. It took off a wheel and the whole thing collapsed, spilling its barrels of herring outward onto the archers' stakes beyond in a mound of dried fish.

Our men were shouting continuously now, yelling at each other in their fear. Many sat on the ground and hunched over with their hands over their heads. Some already lay stretched on their faces which was certainly the most sensible but also least dignified form of repose one can effect.

The bombardment continued for some time but after their first successes, their balls went too high or too wide just as many times as they hit us. In those early days, the practice of field artillery was hampered by the inconsistency of supplies, as it was by the lack of expertise. Gunpowder was variable in quality, as were cannonballs and the cannons themselves. Each one had its own unique issues that had to be adjusted for and with repeated firings the barrels grew hotter, expanded and were in danger of breaking or even exploding. I would not see the science of cannon artillery reach its peak until I fought against the armies of Napoleon almost four hundred years later.

We took casualties but not so many that our men dissolved in panic. Indeed, the more we took, the more the men-at-arms and archers grumbled about their inaction. They wanted to ride out and take the battle to the enemy. A natural reaction but to act upon it would have been foolhardy in the extreme.

"I believe their rate of firing has slowed," Rob said from where he sat, leaning back on the wheel of our wagon and sharpening his arrowheads one by one. His fingers were white from the cold.

"I believe you are right," I said, grasping the side of the wagon to pull myself up. I poked my head up over the top of the barrels. "Well, would you look at the mad bastards."

Walt and Rob scrambled up beside me as the cannons fell silent and we heard the familiar sound of kettle drums beating and war pipes droning.

"The Scots are attacking," Walt stated. "But not the French."

I laughed because it was true and because it might just mean we would not be pounded into dust after all.

Hundreds of Scots came forward on foot, clutching their weapons and cheering themselves on with the banners waving above them.

"Archers!" I shouted. "Archers, stand and come forward. String your bows, you blessed bastards. The Scots are crying to be filled with English arrows once more. Come on, up you lucky bunch of bastards. Now is your time for glory."

In my excitement I had forgotten my lack of formal position

and yet the men responded. They were professional enough to need little encouragement at such times and their captains organised them efficiently. As soon as the five hundred Scots were in range, our shooting began.

The poor Scots fell. Our arrows smashed into them and many of the mad sods were wearing inadequate armour which our arrows easily pierced. Still, they came on like the wrathful devils they were and when they came close to our stakes, our archers climbed on the wagons to shoot down into them.

Their success in reaching us must have encouraged the French for then their mounted men-at-arms came across the plain to crush us with their horses and steel.

We had thousands and thousands of arrows on our wagons and so our archers did not hold back but instead shot and shot at the Scots and the French as they charged us. Our arrows alone were enough to drive off the French who fled back to their lines.

The Scots, though, were filled with a murderous rage that the French did not feel and they pushed forward again and again. Their final assault reached the walls of our wagons and many of them clambered up the sides before they were struck down.

Thousands of French men-at-arms held in the rear and watched their allies being killed.

Was it a ruse to draw us out? It likely was but then the French were ever filled with terror of the English archers and so I suspected that they were genuinely frozen in inaction.

"Bring the horses," I commanded our pages, raising my voice so that other men would hear. "Bring the horses up and move aside that wagon on the flank there."

Other knights wondered aloud what we were up to and I answered, again speaking so that scores would hear my words.

"We shall ride out. Do you hear? We shall ride out and come at the Scots from the rear. If they do not flee, they will be killed to a man."

No order was given, as far as I know, and yet a hundred men and then a hundred more streamed out of our fort on the flank. We came at the Scots just as I said and ran them down. Those few captains of theirs who were mounted chose not to flee and to instead die with their men.

I aimed for the banner of Sir John Stewart of Darnley and charged him alone on my tired horse. It was a hard fight, but I brought him down and quickly dismounted. I strode forward and shouted that he was to surrender himself to me. Instead, he rolled onto his feet and rushed me with his poleaxe and I drove my sword point through his visor as I bore him to the ground.

"The French come!"

At the cries of warning, I leapt back atop my horse and prepared to meet the attack. Our lines formed as the French approached and I found Walt at my side once more, riding a horse that was not his. He opened his visor to lick an enemy's blood from his steel gauntlets before closing it again. His face had been contorted into a wide grin.

Our enemies were led by the Bastard of Orléans himself but as the great wall of steel that was the French came close to us, a massive volley was loosed upon them from hundreds of English archers standing on the backs of the wagons. Another volley smashed into them and the French approach was halted. Horses fell as another volley crashed in a great cacophony of clanging iron against steel and then a volley of English jeering went up as the French turned and fled.

"Did you see?" Walt shouted. "The Bastard of Orléans fell!"

We would later discover that the cousin of the Dauphin had been merely wounded but the sudden shock of it, on top of the total slaughter of the Scots, was enough to drive the French from the field.

As our convoy unwound itself and continued toward Orléans, the archers and the men were thrilled by our unlikely victory. All knew how it was my defensive strategy that had saved us from being caught in the open, and they knew it was my tactical decision to counter-attack. I was feted and I felt good about their praise, for I have always been vain.

But as we rode, Sir John Fastolf glared at me with hostility. He would claim the victory as his own, of course, but the men would know the truth. And he would know it himself in his heart. I had made an enemy of Sir John and it would come back to haunt me in the defeats to come. My decisions that day may have won a battle but they also may have lost us the war.

In fact, we should have lost the battle, if only the French had acted decisively. If the French had continued their barrage of cannon and so blasted holes in our defences, they could have charged in and slaughtered us. If they had brought forward their hundreds of crossbowmen first, they would have softened us up further. But the Scots could not control themselves, as usual, and the French had lacked the will to finish us off. Ever since the days of Edward III, the English armies had been protected by an invisible cloak of invincibility. It was a cloak that existed in the hearts of Frenchman and Englishman alike and that magic had turned dozens of battles that should have been English defeats into English victories.

But it would not last for much longer.

For unknown to me, or to any of us, that very day in a place far to the east, a young girl was begging for permission to meet the Dauphin. Claiming to hear the voices of angels commanded by God, Joan of Lorraine swore in front of witnesses that the Dauphin's arms had that day suffered a great reverse near Orléans.

When news of the victory that I had wrought reached the court of the Dauphin, the girl Joan was finally invited to his presence.

After convincing him that she was indeed divinely inspired, she was given leave to lead an army to the city of Orléans and so defeat the English.

At her side as she approached the city was a nobleman from Brittany named Gilles de Rais.

4

Castle Tiffauges

May 1440

"THIS IS A TERRIBLE IDEA," Stephen said as we approached the gatehouse of Castle Tiffauges. "The priest will not be within."

Rob and Walt rode behind us in silence, prepared to do violence, should it come to it. Rob had even strung his bow in preparation and held it low and ready. Our three valets rode behind them as I hoped that a larger party would make a grander impression on whoever I found within the castle.

One of the Marshal's servants was a priest who I had two interesting pieces of information about in the few days since arriving. Firstly, he had stayed his master's hand when a fellow priest was threatened with murder, and second, it seemed he had attempted to flee from his master's service some months before. I believed that he might possibly be an unwilling participant in whatever was going on in the castles and manors of the Marshal. And if that was true then perhaps he would be willing to make a statement himself. Or at the very least, perhaps he would provide information on the other servants, such as who they were, what they were up to, and where they might be found.

My men disagreed.

"You did not have to come, Stephen," I replied, leaning forward to pat my nervous horse's neck. "If you truly think this such a terrible idea."

"I am not one to shy away from danger," Stephen said, clutching his satchel to his chest and hunching over in the saddle, his face pale beneath his hat.

"And the priest is here," I said. "The Marshal's choir remains in this castle to practice their singing, day and night, and so the priest will be here, also."

"Hmm," Stephen said, for although we had this information from more than one local, he suspected half of what was spoken was rumour. "It is whether the Marshal's soldiers are here that concerns me."

It concerned me, too, but I was never going to admit it. "We are not going to assault the place, Stephen. Why would the soldiers bother us, even if they are here?"

The castle was powerful indeed and commanding, built with enormous blocks of sandstone and tiny, narrow windows dotting the towers and the curtain walls. The strength of the place bore down on us evermore the closer we got.

"What is with this damned weather?" Stephen complained, rubbing warmth into his arms as he rode. "The calendar approaches summer and yet winter's cold has not passed. Will it never be spring?"

"Cursed land, ain't it," Walt called from behind.

"Don't be ridiculous," Stephen said.

The ramp up to the gate tapered until it constricted to the width of a cart or two horses riding abreast. Attacking the place would indeed take an army and I forced down the nervousness rising in my throat.

"The Marshal is not in residence," I said aloud. "Other than the choir and our priest, the place is practically empty."

"Who are trying to convince?" Stephen said as we came to the gatehouse. "Me or yourself?"

The outer gate was open and the portcullis up in the darkness of the ceiling above when we passed into the gatehouse. A castle's gate was rarely closed, whether the lord was in residence or not, for few men would be desperate or fool enough to attempt theft or mischief when they knew that retribution would be swift and terrible. Even so, I half expected the inner and outer doors to magically slam shut but we rode into the courtyard inside the gate, the hooves from our horses loud on the cobbles and echoing from the four walls. Looking up, the windows all around were black like the narrowed eyes of a snarling wolf.

An old porter came out striding from a side door, still chewing something and wiping his greasy hands on his apron as he came forward.

"The lord is away," he said. "What business have you here?"

"I have come to see the priest," I said, confidently. "Please take me to him."

"Priest?" the porter said, scratching his nose. "What priest? Who are you, sirs?"

"We serve the same master, you and I," I said, lying. "And so I need not answer to you. Bring me to the priest, or our master shall be sore disappointed."

He squinted at me and I felt certain he was about to summon guards. From what I had heard about the strange goings on at Castle Tiffauges, the rumours of comings and goings in the darkness, I had hoped to bluff my way in with vague assurances.

"I will have your name before I let you within," the porter said, finally, before pointing to me. "And you shall come alone, without your men. Not a one of them. And you shall come unarmed."

"My name is Le Cheminant," I said, which meant the Traveller. It was as good a false name as any and it was not an inaccurate moniker to assume. "And I agree to your terms."

My men grumbled at me as I dismounted.

"You must not enter this place unarmed and alone," Stephen muttered, rushing over and grabbing my arm before I went in.

"Stay here and do whatever Rob and Walt tell you to do," I replied as I removed my weapons and handed them to my valet.

Stephen was outraged because he was far more ancient than they and had been my companion for longer, and he considered himself to be above them in every sense. However, he was naive to physical dangers in a way that my soldiers were not.

Walt and Rob moved to take positions by the outer gateway and also by the door I was to enter by, so that they could watch for approaches and warn me and also so that they could quickly come to my aid, should I require it. All this was done without words and even without much in the way of glances.

"Le Cheminant, is it?" the porter said, frowning. "My name is Miton. I shall escort you to the chapel. Dominus Blanchet will be there or in his quarters."

"Very well, Miton. Lead the way."

While the exterior of the castle was severe and brutal, the interior was remarkably different. In my experience, castles were poor places to live. They were always cold, the chambers small, and it was ever dark and smoky. What is more, when the lord was not in residence, a castle would be quiet and miserable. Tapestries would be taken down from walls. Rooms, towers, entire wings would be closed up. Fires would not be lit. The caretakers would keep to their own quarters most of the time and the rest of the place would be left to the spiders.

But not Castle Tiffauges.

It was like walking into a dreamland. Ornate decoration adorned every wall and surface in a riot of blue, red, and yellow painted patterns, and intricate carving embellished with gold and silver leaf bordered every doorframe. Open courtyards resounded with the tinkling of beautifully carved marble fountains and passing from one wing to another I found every chamber lit with wax candles in silver holders and enamelled oil lamps, even in rooms with no people within. Servants walked to and fro, going about their business. I saw a priest in his full raiment hurrying along with a young servant behind him carrying a handful of books and I expected that the porter would call out to him that he had a visitor. Instead, he said nothing and we continued on and I realised this meant there was more than one priest in residence. Four soldiers lounged in a small inner courtyard drinking wine and playing dice. They glanced at me as I passed but made no move to stop me. Manic laughter echoed from a tower window. The castle was full of life. I found it profoundly disturbing.

I wanted to ask Miton the porter, strutting along beside me, to confirm that Gilles de Rais was not in residence but he was suspicious enough of me so I held my tongue.

"When is our master due to return?" I said instead, thinking I was being cunning.

"You don't know?" he said, squinting up at me. He shrugged, flinging his arms out. "But who knows with him? He comes, he goes. No warning. One day he's in Machecoul, the next he's here. Then he's off again, God alone knows where." Miton shook his head and broke off muttering.

"Were you a soldier, Miton?" I asked him suddenly.

He glanced up. "Course I was."

"Did you serve with our lord? At Orléans?"

He sniffed. "I was there."

"Did you see her?" I asked. "The Maiden?"

Miton jerked to a stop. His face clouded in darkness, glancing around us but no one was near. "Speak not of her." His hand was on the hilt of his sword. "Speak not of her in this place."

I raised my hands. "I apologise, sir. I shall not speak of it again."

Miton hesitated and nodded, striding past me in his jerky gait. I hurried after him, wondering at the reasons for his outburst.

Was it moral outrage? Or fear? Did he have deep love for the Maiden or did he regard her as a heretic?

Clearly, I would get no more from him on the matter.

Distant singing echoed through the castle and it grew stronger as we entered the most distant wing, resonating from the walls of the chapel there. There must have been dozens of choristers and the sound was like Heaven had come down to Earth.

Inside, the chapel was lit by hundreds of tall wax candles, illuminating the golden rails, golden crucifixes and candle holders and the vivid colours of the painted statues seemed to glow with inner light. The boys of the choir had fallen silent and were making their way from the chapel when I entered. It seemed as though the walls yet echoed with their beautiful song. One or two of them eyed me warily and it seemed as though those ones pushed forward through their fellows to get away from me more swiftly.

"There." Miton stabbed his finger at the priest. "Do not leave this chapel. I will wait until you are done."

The priest wore his full priestly vestment. A bright white alb showing at the wrists and the hem at his knees, long amice around his shoulders, an embroidered maniple of thick silk and golden thread draped over his left arm, a crimson stole hanging around his neck and heavy and intricately embroidered chasuble. He was a small man of about forty years with an open, kind face. When I drew closer, though, I saw his eyes were filled with a profound fear and he shook beneath his robes.

"Is this it?" he asked me in a small voice. "Is it time?"

"Time for what?" I asked, brightly. He simply stared at me,

confusion playing in his eyes. "My name is Le Cheminant. Are you Dominus Eustace Blanchet?"

He blinked and spoke warily. "Yes, that is who I am."

"How delightful to meet you, brother. I hoped to speak with you about what happened at the church during Pentecost."

Blanchet's eyes flicked around all over the chapel and finding that we were alone, turned back to me. "Why? Who are you?"

"I told you my name. Allow me to tell you something else. The Marshal went with armed men to the church at Saint-Étienne-de-Mer-Morte during the Pentecost Mass. He and his soldiers entered with their weapons drawn. The Marshal bore an axe in his hand and he seized the priest, threatening him bodily, forcing him to his knees. And then you, Gilles de Rais' personal priest, came to the rescue of the threatened man and stayed the Marshal's hand. You saved the priest le Ferron from a bloody death at his own altar and instead the Marshal dragged him off to the dungeons of Machecoul where he remains. Is this all true, brother?"

He looked around again, eyes flicking about. "Where did you hear such a thing?"

"Brother, there were scores of witnesses. A certain number of them were willing to give an account to agents of the episcopal and secular authorities."

Blanchet's eyes bulged and he swallowed twice before he could speak. "You come from the Bishop?"

As I was under strict orders not to reveal the Bishop's investigation, I could not confirm it outright. "I did not say that."

He shook his head in frustration. "What are you saying, sir?

Are you threatening me?"

I sighed and lowered my voice. "Brother, after I heard how you had saved that priest's life, I asked after you. I asked about you in Nantes and in other places. What I heard was that you are somewhat newly come into the Baron's service from elsewhere in Brittany, by way of the Order of Saint Benedict. What is more, I heard that you lived for a week or two in a village a few miles north of here, at the inn at Mortagne. You know what the innkeeper, Bouchard-Menard, told me? He told me that you were then brought back here by servants of the Marshal. Brought back against your will, so he told me, shouting at the men to leave you be while they carried you out of your room at the inn, tied up and bundled onto a cart and dragged back to Tiffauges in the dark of the night."

He swallowed and looked down, no doubt greatly ashamed.

"Now, a man like that," I continued, "a man who attempted to flee this place, and a man of God who risked his life by defying the will of his master to save the life of a priest, well, that is a man I wished to speak with, Dominus Eustache. Despite what my friends urged me, I believe you may be willing to speak to me in turn about certain things. Things that are said to happen in Tiffauges and Machecoul and other accursed places. Do not be so afraid, Dom Eustache. The Baron will never know that we spoke, you and I."

Blanchet coughed and whispered. "He knows everything." Then he crossed himself and then crossed himself again. "I will deny speaking to you."

"Very good," I said, clapping him on the shoulder. "I will deny it also. And so as far as the world is concerned, we never spoke at all. All I want is to know from you, brother, is what happens here."

He looked down at the floor and spoke so softly I could barely hear him. "I do not know what you refer to, sir."

"Oh, you know. What happens to the little boys that are brought here in the night? What is done to them? And who is it that does it?"

Blanchet shook his head. "I do not know all that happens. In truth, I know nothing at all."

"You know enough to be afraid."

"No, no. I am happy here. I am blessed."

"I shall tell you what I think," I said, leaning in and lowering my voice. "I think you did not know the nature of your lord until it was too late to flee. But you are still a decent man and that is what drove you to save the priest on Pentecost. And so I think that you, as a decent man, will want to unburden yourself and help me to save others who might yet be saved."

He took a sharp breath and let it out slowly, glancing up at me once before replying. "He is violent. He drinks, now. Always. I was so blind, at first. Like a fool, I believed that because he was rich and powerful and devout that he was a good man. And I did not know that I was a prisoner until I fled and they brought me back. But nothing can be done. Whatever you are doing, whoever you are from, even if you are from the Bishop, nothing can be done. He is too powerful."

"Your lord holds his Barony from the Duke. And there is the King, who made him Marshal by royal command and can unmake him in turn. The Church is perhaps even more powerful than them both, and the noble Bishop of Nantes is the cousin of Duke Jean and what happens if they decide to work in concert, brother? No man is too powerful to escape his crimes, even on Earth, if there is a will to do something about it."

His eyes narrowed. "And is there such a will, sir?"

I had been commanded, on pain of terrible repercussions, to keep the investigation secret. The Bishop wanted no hint of an investigation to get back to Gilles de Rais, for what I imagined was a variety of reasons. And so I forced myself to hold my tongue.

"Listen, brother." I placed my hand on his shoulder and leaned in close. "Even the Marshal must know his actions will have consequences. He has abducted and imprisoned a vassal of the Duke, this priest le Ferron whose elder brother is also a powerful lord. Questions are being asked. But all the answers I want from you are about these other servants of your master. Who are these men who do his bidding? Who are the men who brought you back when you attempted to flee?"

"Very well. But you heard nothing from me, do you understand?" Blanchet looked around again. "The worst of them is Henriet Griart. An ugly man. Strong, fat. Sour. Not yet thirty years old. Just as bad is the one they call Poitou. His true name is Etienne Corrillaut but everyone calls him Poitou, I assume because he is from there. He is younger but balding on the top of his head at the front. His body is as thin as a stick but somehow his grip is like iron, strong enough to bruise me for weeks with no more than a grasp of his hand. He laughs often, at nothing. They are commoners who serve our lord as valets but they do whatever the Marshal wills."

"What does he command them to do?"

"I do not know, whatever the Marshal wills. And my lord also has two other servants who seem more like companions. Gentleman, I believe though I do not know what they are but they call the Marshal their cousin. One is named Sillé, a big man, older, and he perhaps rules over the others. He often carries a coil of rope that he uses to whip his horse but he carries it with him everywhere he goes and even hangs it on his belt when he sits down to eat. One other is Milord Roger de Briqueville, who is a knight. Tall and dark, like the Marshal. He is always drunk on brandy wine, just like the Marshal. He smiles and speaks well, like a lord, but he is frightening. There is a darkness behind his eyes. All these men go where my lord goes but they also do his bidding elsewhere. He sends them hunting but I never see them return with any prey."

Henriet, Poitou, Sillé, Briqueville. Hunters, are you? Soon, you shall all become the prey.

"What of this cleric I have heard so much rumour about? The sorcerer."

Blanchet's eyes almost popped out. "Prelati the Florentine. He is an alchemist but yes, they say he practices magic. He is always with de Rais now or else in his tower. Rarely seen."

"The rumours are that this Prelati summons demons for the Marshal."

"I know nothing of all that. It is probably peasant rumours, you know how the common folk like to gossip about such things. Prelati came here after me but what brought him and what he does, I do not know. Whatever it is, I believe he is a fraud."

"What brought you here?"

Blanchet sagged and held a hand over his eyes. "I was in Orléans."

"For the siege? Truly, brother?"

"No, no. Not for the siege, no. Sadly, I did not see the glory of the Maid. I mean after, when peace had come. I saw the Baron's pageant play."

I had heard of this extraordinary event but I still barely believed it was true. And if it was true, what did that say about whether Gilles de Rais was a mortal or not?

"Tell me about the pageant play, brother."

Blanchet took a deep breath and his eyes focused through me into the past. "It was years ago. Perhaps five years. It was a play but that is hardly the word to describe it. It was a festival. It began each day at dawn and ran all the way through until darkness fell. It was performed by a hundred and fifty people, each with spoken lines. And there were five hundred non-speaking parts. Twenty-thousand lines of verse. Twenty-thousand, sir! It was a re-enactment of the entire siege, you see. The expense of it cannot be calculated. No man in the history of the world has spent so much of his fortune on such a thing. For each performance, entirely new costumes were provided. Do you understand? At the end of the day, the costumes were thrown off, sold, tossed into the Loire, thrown on fires. And each morning over six hundred identical costumes were handed out to the players again. And, you must understand, these were not cheap costumes but true clothing. Robes that a lord would have been proud to wear, made from the finest cloth and embroidered and patterned and dyed with the utmost care. Even those who were dressed in the rags of the defeated English were made of fine, thick cloth and cut into jagged edges as if they were torn and dirtied. It was a wonder, a true wonder. The play began with the vile English making their plans in London, and at the climax there was the Maiden's victory. In between was her journey, and her battles against the enemy as she destroyed their forts one after the other. You saw her wounded and carried off. You saw her stand when others fled, and by her example, turn the tide of the battle. It was glorious. So many stages, all open to the air. Indeed, at times there would be simultaneous scenes being acted on two or three. On one, Joan would be haranguing the commanders to act while across the city the players would be acting out a raging battle. The crowd surged from one stage to another, following the action. And the wine, sir. You cannot imagine how the wine flowed. Barrels of fine vintages rolled out for every performance, all day, and every person in the crowd was filled with the wine. All free, of course. All rooms in the city were paid for by the Marshal. Enough wine and bread and meat to feed thousands, every single day. They say it cost eighty thousand gold crowns."

"A fortune," I said. "Enough to buy a duchy. And this disgusting display of opulence so impressed you that you sought service with the Marshal?"

He looked at me with surprise. "Because it was all for her. For her memory. To put right the lies they told about her. The Marshal wrote the play himself, all twenty-thousand lines of verse. To tell you the truth, as poetry goes it was not inspired. But it did not need to be when the tale itself was inspiration enough. You see, he told, and they showed, Joan tending to her work in her village when she had her vision that commanded her to go to the Dauphin. It showed her interview with the Dauphin, when she inspired him into believing in her. It even showed her return to the city after the great final victory against the vile invaders at Patay. It was for the glory of Joan. She was the heart of it. As she was in life. And at her side throughout it all was her most faithful captain, her brave and loyal bodyguard, the devoted soldier Gilles de Rais. And that is why I came to serve him. Because he served her. And she is here no longer, because the English burned her, and so I came. God forgive me, I came to this evil place. But I did it for her."

I placed my hand on his shoulder, for I believed I knew a good man when I saw one, and he seemed to be suffering greatly. Taking my leave, I swore I would not bother him again and reaffirmed that if anyone asked, I would deny ever having spoken to him.

"I swear to you, Dominus Blanchet, that one way or another, this will all be over soon."

"God bless you," he said, and went away shaking.

I went out to find the porter and told him my business was concluded.

Miton shrugged. "Thought you might have him with you."

I nodded. "You thought I was here to murder Blanchet. Yes. Of course you did. Not today, Miton."

He shrugged again and led me out through the decadent, beautiful interior of the castle. Before I left, I heard the distant sound of the choir starting up again and I thought about what the priest had told me.

Henriet, Poitou, Sillé, Briqueville. And Prelati the alchemist.

I had their names, their descriptions, and I knew they roamed the countryside hunting for prey and I meant to pick them off one by one.

In fact, I was to find that the damned porter or some other bastard told those very same men about a prying visitor calling himself Le Cheminant. And I would find out that, while I was searching for them, they were coming for me.

Two days after my visit, with his entire household, Gilles de Rais returned to Castle Tiffauges.

5

A b d u c t i o n

J u n e   1 4 4 0

TIFFAUGES WAS A DISTANT SILHOUETTE against the bone-white sky. I crept forward toward a cluster of jagged black rocks and behind wind-blasted scrub and sedge so the position was shielded from the main track heading northeast or southwest. There was also a good view on the track into Tiffauges village.

I whistled a couple of short trills, like a blackbird, and after a moment the replying tune came from deep in the rocks. I crawled forward and settled in next to Walt.

"Bring any wine, Richard?"

"You will find barrels of the stuff back at the inn."

"Bloody chilly again, is it not? Did you not bring any wine for yourself? Miserable cloud and damp all day long but it's clearing up now so it'll get real cold tonight, real cold and you'll wish you had it."

"Drinking wine on watch is utterly foolish. Once a man gets comfortable, he may as well give up and go to bed, for sleep is certain."

"Oh yes, is that so?" Walt said, looking me up and down. "Why you got that nice fur-lined cloak with you, then?"

I laughed. "What happened today?"

Walt's face grew serious. "Thought you might have heard tell of it at the inn by now. He's come back. Our lord of Rais."

"Dear God. When? What did you see?"

"Started early on. Stream of riders coming in, one or two at a time from the west. About the middle of the day came about fifty soldiers, all in their finery. Shining armour like each one of them was a prince, with pennants on their lances and streamers on the horses' tales."

"Yes, the Marshal has a penchant for ostentation."

Walt raised his eyebrows. "Does he, by God? These debauched barons, eh. Well, like I was saying, they were all done up fancy but they rode smartly, too. Like they was parading before a king, only there was no one to see them but I. They came up the road, tight together, two-by-two and nose to tail. Pages and squires came up behind and they was not far off in neatness, neither."

"Fifty soldiers, you say?"

"First group was fifty or so. Then came up the lord himself, riding in a party with fine horses. I swear to you, each horse was a walking fortune. Beautiful creatures, they was. His lordship rode beneath an unfurled banner in black and gold, great big thing like a war standard. Behind him was men playing trumpets and banging drums as they rode. And up after came more soldiers. Seventy, maybe. Same as the first lot. Fanciest fighting men you ever saw, all trotting on powerful big war horses. Later on comes wagon after wagon, some full of servants, most of them with barrels and sacks. Few people still coming in, here and there."

"By God, that is a large household."

"If I hadn't known better, I'd have sworn it was a king coming home from war. Or going off to one."

"Anything since then?"

"Nothing much and I doubt you'll see anything now. They just arrived after a day or two on the hoof so they'll all be pissed up by sundown. Might as well come back to the inn and sleep in your bed, sir, not sit in this dank hole and shiver in the dark for no reason."

"I appreciate your concern but one never knows what might occur. If the Marshal or any of his men are in fact immortals then they may sneak out for blood. We must remain vigilant. Besides, I already slept today in preparation. No, you get back and get yourself to rest. It will be your watch again on the morrow."

"All right, I will go get my head down after a flagon or two of ale and a bit of that boiled beef, if they have it still. But you just promise me you ain't going to go in there and fight all them soldiers. Not without me and Rob, at least."

I laughed. "Have no fear of that. We seek only to nab a servant for questioning. Nothing more."

"If you say so, sir. Good luck. God bless."

After he scrambled away toward the horses behind the hillock,

I noticed the sounds of the place. The ceaseless wind rustling through the clumps of grass and whistling between gaps in the rocks. Buzzards wheeled overhead and already I could hear an owl screeching in the distance. Rooks cawed as they headed for their roosts, their black shapes sliding across the darkening sky. Goats cried their misery to each other across the plain. I pulled my fur-lined cloak closer about me and settled down further. It was sheltered from the worst of the wind but the rocks under me and at my back leeched the heat from my body even through the furs.

"Should have brought some bloody wine," I muttered to myself as the light faded. The moon was almost full and I prayed that the clouds would indeed blow right away before it rose, else I would be able to see nothing at all.

Stephen had complained about my strategy. He believed the best way to obtain the evidence we needed was a thorough questioning of the people from every village, hamlet, and farmhouse in the region and to do it thoroughly he needed my help, and Walt's and Rob's.

"They shall never speak to us," I had said. "My way is better. Swifter."

"How can it be swifter if all you do is huddle in the rocks and do nothing, day after day? At least by speaking to the people I am making progress of sorts. Collecting names."

"Hearsay from peasants," I said, scoffing.

"There is often truth hidden in rumour," he said. "And they are not peasants, Richard, as you would know if you bothered to speak to any of them."

"I have spoken to many of these good people," I said.

"Yes, to the physician's pretty daughter and to the innkeeper, while he brought your wine. What a dogged pursuit of the truth you have committed to, sir. If you would but listen to the stories of those who have suffered, you would be moved to act on their behalf."

"What do you think I am doing here?" I snapped. "Am I not taking action?"

"You mean to go charging in, as you always do. As you already have done, in fact and now you mean to do more. Illegally abducting a servant, Richard? It may undo our standing with the Bishop and the Duke and with the good folk of these parts. They have suffered for so long with no legal recourse. Despite having been so abused for so long, they are yet powerless to defend themselves but now we are here and we can represent them but first we must listen to what they have to say."

I had no interest in hearing them complain for days on end and I believed that I knew enough.

"For years they have able to submit a petition to their Duke," I pointed out. "And to the King. If they have not done so then that is their own fault."

"They are rightly terrified of repercussions!" Stephen said, almost wailing. "They are being preyed upon by the man who should be protecting them. Does it not outrage you, Richard?"

"I am here, am I not?" I countered. "I will find out if he is an immortal and slay him if he is. Otherwise, these people's troubles are their own. Now, while you go about listening to these peasants gnashing their teeth, I am going to illegally abduct one of his servants, beat the truth from him, and then we shall know what

71

is really going on here."

Recalling it again, I realised that I had spoken with unnecessary heartlessness. But Stephen always did have the propensity to nag like an old maid when the common folk were concerned.

Before the last of the day's light was completely gone, I caught movement at the base of the castle. A wagon came down the slope from the gatehouse and then went on rumbling and bumping along the track to the east. A lantern held aloft helped to show that two men sat up on it side by side, driving the single horse. It was a long way from my hiding place and they were wrapped up in cloaks and hoods but I fancied that one of the men was thin while the other was broad.

Could it be the valets Henriet and Poitou that Blanchet had told me about? It was surely wishful thinking on my part but I could not allow the opportunity to be missed. Keeping low, I slid back from the rocks and ran, stooped in half, behind the hillock to my horse. I had left him saddled so that he would be ready for just such an eventuality, the poor creature, and so I mounted him and headed out for the track. Night was falling fast and I had already lost sight of the wagon for some time.

My black horse was concerned by the strangeness of it all and went very slowly indeed until the moon came out. More clouds blew away until the world was illuminated once more and my horse picked up his pace. Following the track east, crossing the old stone bridge over the river, I thought I had likely missed the wagon. Perhaps it had turned for some house along the way. But then I saw the lantern glinting in the distance and I knew it was yet heading east. I thought it unlikely that they could see me on my dark horse but still I kept well away rather than scare them into flight before I could spring an ambush somewhere.

After a couple of miles they edged to the northeast, further from the river. I knew there were houses out there in the dark. Single dwellings, hamlets with three or four families, and larger villages, and I could smell the smoke from their fires and occasionally saw a flash of light from lamps through the edges of shuttered windows. But the wagon rumbled on by them all, deeper into the night. Every so often I stopped to listen, straining to hear over the wind. Once or twice I fancied I heard voices and perhaps a bark of laughter. Always the noise of the wagon banging over ruts and squeaking off in the distance continued and so did I.

The wagon stopped. Its lantern illuminated the driver and his passenger as they sat motionless. There was nothing in sight, not in any direction. Nothing but fields and plains edged in silver and shadow.

A light flashed in the east. A faint yellow glow winking on and off.

The wagon rumbled into life again, turning from the main track to head toward the light. Going slower than ever, I urged my horse forward. He was nervous but well-bred and he trusted me enough to obey after a moment's hesitation.

A house loomed in the dark, the moonlight showing a reed-thatched roof and another wagon sitting outside. Far beyond, squared lines and woodsmoke suggested a village of a few houses. I stopped and waited as the wagon creaked to a stop and the men called out a greeting. Another man emerged from the house, throwing a streak of yellow light across the scene, and muttered words were exchanged. A fourth man stomped out with a bundle over his shoulder which he threw into the flat back of the wagon I had followed.

That bundle was a boy, his limbs bound in some way and his head and shoulders covered in sackcloth.

He cried out as they tossed him down on the timber floor of the wagon and one of the men thumped the lad in the belly to shut him up. Another man jumped into the wagon and crouched by the boy.

I removed my cloak, rolled and tied it to my panniers, climbed into my saddle, and checked to ensure my sword and daggers were where they should be.

My intention had been to take and interrogate a single servant. If I intervened while there were four men, possibly more within the house, that made it highly unlikely I would be able to complete my mission. Alerting them to my presence would make taking them another night all the more difficult, perhaps impossible if they kept within the castle.

But of course, I could not allow them to take the lad to Gilles de Rais. He would go through the gates in the darkness and never see the light of day again and so it mattered not one bit what the consequences of saving his life might be. I resolved to take them on the road before they returned, perhaps while they crossed the bridge so that they could not easily flee. I would surprise them, bind them, question them and finally free the boy and take him back to his mother and his father, wherever they might be.

The boy cried out and I saw the men were pulling down his hose from beneath the sacking. One of the men stood over him, loosening his own doublet, pulling out his shirt tails, and undoing his belt.

Resolving to ride in, snatch the boy up, and ride away before they could react, I spurred my horse and he jumped forward, startled by my sudden command and tossing his head in protest. He was a good horse but I was asking too much of him to race toward that scene as if he was trained in war. Instead, he swerved away and snorted, stamping his foot on the stony ground. In the time it took to wrestle him back under my control, the men were alert to my presence.

"Who goes there?" an angry voice called out.

"Show yourself!"

I rode toward the light and stopped at the edge of it. "I am a simple traveller," I said, speaking slowly but clearly.

They had their hands on their daggers and two of them wore short swords on their hips. The boy squirmed on the back of the wagon.

"You alone?" the one standing over him said. He was thin, with a pinched, ratty face.

"Course he is," the fat one said, standing at the rear of the wagon with one hand on the boy's bound ankle.

"Get off your horse," a third man said from behind them. "Get off it and come here."

I laughed. "Why would I do that?"

"If you don't," the fat man said. "We'll make you."

A fourth man edged around to my flank in the shadows,

attempting to be silent.

"I think what I shall do is ride immediately to the authorities and tell them I have witnessed an appalling crime."

They stared at the boy and back at me.

The fat one recovered his wits first. "Crime? What crime? Ain't no crime. We're just returning this boy to his father."

"He run away," the thin one said, grinning.

"What is his name?" I asked. The fourth man edged further to my flank and I lost sight of him. "For that matter, what are your names, sirs?"

They laughed, first one and then all three of them chuckled.

"Don't you worry what our names is," the fat one said.

"Oh, but I do worry. Let me see if I can guess them, shall I?" I pointed at the skinny man clutching the bunched-up tails of his shirt in one fist. "You are the one known as Poitou." He gaped at me and I pointed at the fat one. "And you are called Henriet Griart." The two men looked at each other and back at me while I pointed at the third man. "I do not know your name, nor the name of the oaf stumbling around in the dark there, but I will have them soon enough. For now, simply hand the boy over to me and I will say no more about it."

They overcame their confusion rather rapidly when they knew what it was that I wanted and Henriet smirked and grasped the boy's leg harder, digging his fingers in. The boy whimpered and writhed.

Poitou grinned as he stuffed his shirt back into his hose. "He ain't for you," he said.

"Ah, I see," I replied. "He is for your master, is that what you mean?"

Poitou giggled. "Who's to say where he ends up, whether it's with the master or—"

"Shut up, you fool!" Henriet snapped.

The man creeping in the dark scraped his foot and I realised he was closer than I expected and I turned as he rushed toward me. He was coming to grasp my horse's bridle or reins to stop me fleeing while the others pounced on me.

I kicked out at him, connecting with his shoulder hard enough to send him sprawling with a shout. The others wasted no time in drawing their weapons and so I pulled my sword and rode forward, turning to come around the wagons. I passed by the first and into the light of the house where a fifth man rushed out with his sword drawn, screaming blue murder. It surprised me, I will admit, and frightened my horse. He came close enough to slash his blade down the back of my calf and I turned and speared the tip of my sword down into his throat. He dropped his blade and wheeled away clutching at the blood gushing from his neck and I knew that I had caused a mortal blow.

I turned to see Poitou jump from one wagon to the other, falling on his face as he landed. It was too great a distance for a mortal man to leap and I knew in that moment that he was an immortal. Rushing to kill him quickly, I found another man coming with his dagger drawn.

"He's killed Ysaac!" he cried. "He's killed him!"

"I'll kill the bloody lot of you," I shouted, and I leaned down and ran the man through his chest.

He fell to his knees and I swung my sword up to block a wild blow from Poitou, standing on the back of the second wagon. The swords rang and my arm was jarred from the impact. He was untrained but immensely strong and I was surprised that neither blade was damaged. I threw his sword back and stabbed him in the belly. He wailed and fell back, scrambling away. His wound could not have been deep but being stabbed in the guts is rarely a pleasant experience. I looked for the other two.

"Stop!" Henriet shouted.

He stood on the rear of the other wagon with the boy standing before him. The poor lad was about eleven years old or so. His face swollen and bloody and his hands bound. Henriet had one fat arm wrapped tight around the boy and he held his dagger to the lad's cheek.

"If you don't stop right there," Henriet said, "I cut his face off his head and eat it in front of you."

"And if you harm him," I said, forcing myself to be calm, "then I shall certainly murder every one of you."

Henriet grinned, his teeth brown and black in the lamplight. "You want him, do you, you bastard? You want this? Do you? Eh?" He took his blade and sliced into the boy's arm, a long, wicked, twisting cut down the inside of his elbow. The boy cried out in anguish and his legs gave out, though he was held where he was by the massive arm coiled about him.

"Enough," I said, my voice coming out as a growl. "Hand him over."

Henriet grinned and shoved the lad off the wagon. Wrists and ankles bound as they were, he fell on his face in the dirt, landing hard. He lay motionless in shadow.

"Best take him and go," Henriet said. "Before he leaks himself to death."

I rode to the wagon but Henriet must have guessed my intentions, or else he was a naturally mistrustful soul, for he jumped from the far side and loped off into the darkness. The other man likewise scampered away.

"Henriet?" Poitou wailed. "Samuel? He's killed me, he's killed me, he has. My guts be pierced. Henriet? I need blood, Henriet. Samuel, you come back here, you filthy bastard."

Jumping from my saddle, I stooped to pick up the boy. He was unconscious and drenched with blood from his wound and soaked from pissing himself. It seemed likely that he would die but while there was breath in him there was hope, and so I flung him over my shoulder, mounted and eased him into position in front of me on the saddle, holding him upright.

After a mile or so, I stopped to wrap my cloak around the lad. He was cold to the touch and his head bounced around alarmingly as I rode. The horse was tired after his exertions that night and I begged him, over and over, to have strength and keep riding.

There was a physician, Pierre Mousillon, in the village of Tilleuls. I prayed that this time he would be home and that the boy would still be alive when I reached it.

Through the moonlit landscape, I rode.

"Hold on, there, son," I said, over and over into his ear. "Just hold on."

6

The Physician's Daughter

June 1440

I BANGED MY FIST against the door again. "Please! I need help!"

The boy in my arms was soaked with blood and his skin was cold to the touch. He seemed dead already but there was the faintest whisper of breath coming from his nose and so there was still hope. But there would not be for long.

"Please, I need the physician," I called through the door. "I need Pierre Mousillon, the physician."

Shutters banged open on the floor above the front door, spilling wan yellow into the blue-grey night. "Begone!" the voice called, harsh and urgent.

I backed up, carrying the boy. "Who is that? Are you the servant? I need your master."

"Be off with you, I say," the servant hissed.

"I met you, sir. My name is Richard. Let me see, your name is Paillart, is it not? You were present when I met with your mistress."

"What's that to me? You need a physician, you got to go to Nantes."

Other houses in the village behind me opened their shutters at the commotion and the church door creaked open. Yet no one came to help.

I shifted the lad, lifted him slightly so the light fell on his face. "For the love of God, man. Look, see here? I have a boy. See this boy in my arms? He is dying, Paillart."

The servant was pushed aside by the young woman, Ameline. She held a lamp out of the window and peered down, her hair free and lit up like a halo.

"Open the door, Paillart," she said.

He stayed where he was. "It's a ruse, Ameline. A ruse. He's no good, that one, I can smell it on him as clear as—"

"Open the door," she commanded.

Grumbling, he moved off into the house.

"Thank you, my good woman," I said. "The boy is in need of—"

"If this is a ruse, I shall gut you myself," she said, and brandished a long knife.

"I understand."

The door was unbarred and opened.

"I'm watching you," Paillart said, pointing at me with his drawn sword.

"Out of the way, man," I said and I strode into the dark house.

"Put him on the table," Ameline ordered me and I obeyed, laying the boy gently down upon the dining table as she cleared away the surface. "Light all the lamps and bring them here," the woman ordered her servant. "Candles, too. I must have light."

"Forgive me, good woman," I said. "Is your father not yet at home?"

"He is home," she said, her eyes fixed on the boy as she peered into his face. "Yet he will not be roused until morning and if we could rouse him, I fear he would be insensible."

"Ah," I said, my heart sinking. "Is there anything you can do for him?"

"What happened?" she asked. "Where is this blood coming from?"

"His arm. A cut, see, here? There was a group of men who—"

"Cut away his clothing, all from his upper body," she ordered, then raised her voice. "Paillart, we must have clean water immediately and then hot water as soon as you can."

The servant came in with two lamps and a bundle of candles in his arms, speaking rapidly. "Yes, mistress. Lighting the lamps, cold water, then hot. Anything else?"

"The boiled cloth, my father's physic bag, and the needle and thread."

"At once, miss."

She pointed at me. "Take this one with you." She glanced at me. "If you wish to save this boy's life, you will follow Paillart's orders."

I nodded. "I will."

"And take off your belt. I need it."

While Ameline worked on the boy, I did as I was instructed and lit and tended the fire, and fetched and boiled water. When I was called back in, I found the room filled with light and the delightful smell of fresh blood. The boy was on the table, his upper body bared. He groaned, a low, mournful cry and twisted where he lay. My belt was tied about his upper arm just below the shoulder and Ameline was sewing together both sides of the long gash down the inside of his arm.

"Out of my light!" she snapped, and I stepped aside. "Hold him down."

"He lives," I said, placing my hands on the boy's chest. His skin was cold and damp. "By God, you have the skills of an army surgeon."

She blew a strand of hair away from her face as she worked, concentrating closely. "I think that he will die," she whispered. "And so we must pray to God."

Paillart came in. "The bandages, mistress. Clean and new."

"Out of my light!" she barked at him. She wrapped his wound up with practised skill and slowly loosened my belt before handing it back to me. "I apologise. I fear it is quite covered in blood."

"It is not the first time," I said softly as I tied it around my waist. "What now?"

"Now, we will see if he survives to see sunrise. Paillart, carry him to my bed, will you, please?"

"Oh, no, mistress. Dear me, no. Your own bed, mistress? I will not hear of it."

"Do as I say."

"Let it by my bed, Ameline. Don't sully your good clean bed with the filth of this peasant, I beg thee."

"It is because my bed is good and clean that the boy shall have use of it. Now, you will do as I command."

He sighed and scooped the boy up with a profound gentleness and bore him toward the stairs, whispering kind words as he did so. "There now, lad. You'll be alright now, you will. You just rest, son, and you'll be right as rain, you will."

Ameline stood and stretched her back, her hair falling about her face with the light falling on her from every angle and her dress straining at her chest. Her hands were bloody up to the elbows. She looked really quite wonderful.

"I will wash, now," she said.

"Thank you," I said. "For saving him."

"He is not saved."

"For doing what you have done, then," I said. "You were magnificent."

She scoffed, and yawned. "He will need watching," she said. "In case he takes a turn."

"I will watch him," I replied. "If you do not mind it."

She eyed me. "Who is this boy to you?"

"Nothing," I said. "I do not even know his name. There were men from the castle. I followed them. They met more men, at a house a few miles east of here across the river. They handed over that boy, who I assume was bound for the castle. I stopped them but they hurt the boy. I wanted to finish them all off but he was dying. I had to get him help."

Paillart returned, stomping down the stairs and into the parlour. "What's that he says? He assaulted the lord's men?"

"I stopped them from taking this boy, yes," I said to him.

"That's trouble, that is, miss. That's trouble, and trouble for you and for your father."

Ameline said nothing but regarded me with a strange look in her eye.

"I want no harm to come to you," I said to her. "No one will know I brought the boy here."

Paillart scoffed. "No one will know? You daft sod. Everyone will know, and know already. You've done it now, so you have."

"Whatever I have done, I have done with good intentions and for good reason. I will let no harm come to you, my lady." I looked at her servant. "And I will kill every man in that castle if I have to."

"Paillart," Ameline said. "Escort Richard to my room so that he may keep watch on the boy. Then go spread word that a boy has been found."

"Go?" he spluttered. "And leave you alone with him?" He jabbed a finger at me.

"Father will wake soon enough," she said, unconcerned. "And you must find the boy's mother and father and have them come. Before it is too late. Go and find who has lost a son about his age in the last day or two. Other servants in the village may ride out also to let the boys' parents know so that they can be here for his end, if that is what God wills. We must do that for them, at the least."

I sat alone in the bedchamber, on a low stool, watching the boy breathing beneath the sheets. Every breath in seemed a miracle, and every breath out seemed as though it would be his last. The lamplight played across his grey face, making it seem as though he twitched and grimaced where in fact he lay as if he was dead. The only sign was that breath in and the shuddering breath out. Over and over. In and out. I grew tired and my head nodded.

"Here," Ameline said, nudging me with her knee and handing me hot wine. Grey light shone at the edges of the shutters. I must have fallen asleep. In fear, I looked at my charge.

The boy yet breathed.

"God bless you," I said as I took the warm cup in both my hands and breathed in the spices. "Some watchman I turned out to be," I said. "My apologies."

"It is well," she said softly, and placed a stool beside mine. She had her hair tucked away beneath a simple cap. "He has passed the most dangerous hour. And you had a long night, full of adventure."

I smiled into my cup. "Not compared to some nights I have had, my lady."

"You must call me Ameline, sir. Your work must be quite remarkable, if saving a boy's life is not a thing out of the ordinary."

"I snatched him away from danger but it was you who saved him, if saved he is."

She looked at me, a slight smile on her lips. "Unless you wish to argue further, sir, shall we agree that we both saved him?"

I smiled and nodded. "Let us so agree it. And you must call

me Richard."

She flashed a quick smile at me and looked once more to the boy. We shared a quiet, companionable silence while we sipped our hot spiced wine. It roused me.

"But you are wounded, Richard," she said, looking at my leg.

"I am?" The hosen over my calf was torn and drenched in dried blood. I recalled that the man who had sneaked up on me in the darkness had cut me there. "Oh yes. Well, I am sure all is well now."

"But your wound must be cleaned before the corruption begins." She moved to one knee and reached for my leg, poking a finger into the sliced fabric to look beneath.

I had little doubt that the wound had already healed and so shifted my leg away. "A scratch on a branch, nothing more. The blood is not mine."

"Is that so?" she asked, disbelieving me. The sharp tear was clearly caused by a blade and the wool was dark and stiff all around where my blood had gushed out. "Very well." She sat back and frowned.

I thought perhaps she had noticed there was no wound to be seen on my flesh and I spoke quickly to distract her from what that might mean.

"Is what your servant said true?" I asked. "That I have caused you danger by coming here?"

She reached out a hand and grasped mine firmly where it rested on my knee. "I am thankful that you came here. I would not have had you go anywhere else. Whatever the consequences, that shall remain the way that I feel."

I squeezed her hand back and she let it linger on my knee for a moment before withdrawing it.

"How much like Jamet he looks," Ameline said softly, tilting her head to regard the sleeping boy. "If only someone could have saved him as you did this one."

"Forgive me but he was taken in this manner? By men in the night?"

She sighed. "We told him. We all told him. Never go off with anyone. Never, not for anything. Stay within sight of the church at all times, never once lose sight of it. I wonder what cunning they employed to get him away. They said it was La Meffraye who took him."

"The Terror," I said. That was La Meffraye in the Breton dialect.

"That is what they call them," she said. "And they are well named. The old woman from the castle who wanders from village to village with her evil familiar at her side, tempting the children away with her sweets and promises and dark magic. But no one knows what happened with Jamet, not truly. Perhaps it was not La Meffraye after all and instead it was the men, and they snatched him up in a sack. Not knowing how it occurred is perhaps the most awful part. Is that appallingly selfish of me? How conceited I must sound."

"Not at all," I said, as gently as I could. "Surely, nothing could be further from the truth."

"Ever since my brother and my mother, my father is almost never at home. He attends to the sick for miles all around. When he does come home, he does not stay. When he is here, he drowns himself in brandy wine. I think that his heart cannot bear it."

"I can understand such actions," I said. "People stay away from pain, like an animal fleeing attack, or a child flinching from a hot candle. But we are also drawn to places where we once felt strength and love. And no doubt that is why he returns to his home. To you."

She scoffed, though there was a surprising lack of bitterness in it. "Strength and love, or even to the illusion of such things. As can be found in a bottle of brandy wine."

No matter the pain her father felt, he had a duty to his daughter, the only member of his family still alive. Despite all her evident ability and the strength in her heart, she needed him.

"Perhaps, in time, he will find the strength to be your father once more."

She sighed at that, almost gasping at the sudden emotion of it. "Forgive me," she whispered. "I do not know why I burden you with such nonsense."

Ameline had lost her brother, and the grief had taken her mother in turn. And her father's misery had driven him away while only she remained, all alone with no one but a grizzled old servant for company. And no one to share herself with.

I reached out and took her hand. "It is no burden. But if it was, I would bear it gladly if it meant easing yours."

Our eyes met and her look was unwavering, latching onto mine with a fierce scrutiny. I could have drowned myself in her eyes but I sensed it was she who was drowning and she saw in me the strength that she needed to pull herself free.

A loud voice burst in on us, filling the room with outraged

surprise.

"What is the meaning of this?"

Her father loomed in the doorway, his hair wild and shirttails flapping. His eyes were red and unfocused as he blinked all around, leaning on the wall. I could smell the drink on him from across the room.

Ameline snatched her hand away and jumped to her feet. I stayed seated.

"Father. It is nothing. This good and decent man brought the child in the night, grievously wounded and in need of a surgeon." She lowered her voice. "And so I attended to the boy myself."

The father's outrage dwindled into shame and he hung his head. "Ah. I see. Well, get off with you, now, girl and fetch my water. Where is Paillart, for the love of God?"

"Gone to send word to the boy's family to come and collect him," Ameline said. "He will be back soon."

Her father stuck a finger in his ear and wiggled it around. "Well, what is all that blasted commotion that roused me? Is it Sunday already?"

As he said it, I noted the swell of voices outside, several of them, speaking softly but incessantly and growing all the while in volume. It did indeed sound like folk gathering for Mass at the church across the square.

"It is not Sunday, father," Ameline said and crossed to the window. She pushed open the shutters and then stepped smartly back, crossing herself in the morning light.

I stood and looked out, edging forward to lean on the sill.

There were a dozen people outside, men and women both,

drifting closer to the house from all directions. Some led horses behind them. When they saw me at the window, the men pulled off their hats. Beyond the group directly below, more people approached in ones and twos from both sides of the street. Horses clopped in at the edge of the village.

"God bless you, sir," one of the men said. "I heard you found a boy in the night and we was wondering, me and my wife, if it's our little Michel?"

Another man shuffled forward and bowed, before looking up. There were tears in his eyes. "Is it my Jean, sir?" he sobbed, sucking in a great big gulp of air. "Is it my fine boy, Jean?" He sank to his knees and held up his hands in supplication.

All at once, they all began speaking, asking questions, begging me for answers.

"Dear God," I said, turning to Ameline. "We must go down to them."

7

Oaths Sworn

June 1440

MY ARRIVAL THE NIGHT BEFORE had woken the whole village and Paillart had told them what had occurred and to send word out to the neighbours. And so word had spread as quickly as lightning and parents from all around had come in as quickly as they were able to in the mad hope that it was their child who had been found, even if theirs had disappeared months or years past.

Their hopes were quickly dashed, of course.

The boy's parents were an old couple from just a few miles to the east, the father a cartwright named Pierre le Charron. Their boy was named Guillaime and had been missing for two days.

Both fell to their knees by the bed and wept and thanked God.

I turned to leave but the mother cried out.

"You saved him, sir. You saved my sweet boy. God love you, sir, God keep you and watch over you."

Their gratitude was almost more than I could bear but far worse was the sight of the other parents outside turning to leave when the boy's name and parentage was confirmed. It was heartbreaking to see their hopes crumble but I had an idea that I might have caught them at just the right moment. At least, perhaps, it was worth a try.

"Wait, please," I called out. "I beg you."

After much cajoling and pleading, I had them come into the church. The priest was wizened and sickly but kind enough to allow the use of his nave, though he was suspicious of my intentions. They all were.

The sun had come out stronger that morning and the light shone through the narrow windows high up on the walls of the nave and poured in through the open door, along with the faint smell of spring.

Standing by the altar, I noted that the parents were angry and fearful. They did not know me and so they did not trust me but I had won a certain level of renown from my rescue of young Guillaime and they came in, clutching their hats and hoods to their chests and crossing themselves. It was a small church and was soon filled with scores of local people, from Tilleuls and the neighbouring villages. Their anger and disappointment were palpable but the fact that they came at all suggested something else.

It suggested that they felt some hope.

Perhaps, I thought, I was imagining it. That it was wishful thinking on my part. But they were there and they stood to listen to me address them.

I could bellow words of inspiration at a company of unruly soldiers before battle but standing before the eyes of those grieving families I found my words dried in my mouth.

"Thank you, all." I coughed and cleared my throat. "I am sorry that I rescued just one boy last night. I wish that I had found and brought back all of them. But I suspect that is not to be. What is worse, I suspect that can never be. You know in your hearts that this is true." At this, I saw many heads drop and many sighs sounded. I glanced over to catch the eye of Ameline, who returned my look. She nodded, a tight, determined set to her lips. "You all have suffered. For many years, you have suffered, and you have had no justice. And no hope of justice. Until now." At that, a few heads lifted. "Some of you may know me, or my colleagues. We have come from Nantes with orders to take sworn statements from those who would bear witness against the man who has committed these crimes against you."

"It is not a man," a voice called out. "But a monster."

Many called out their agreement.

"A monster, yes, indeed," I said. "A monster who is served by monsters. But they must be arrested and tried as men, in court, and when they are found guilty they will be hanged."

"That's too good for them," a woman shouted. "They need to be burned!"

This brought another chorus of agreement.

"I wish it also," I said. "But there will be no trial." I looked around, letting my words echo.

They muttered in confusion and I let them feel baffled for a moment.

"There will be no hanging. And none will burn." They stared back at me in disbelief for offering hope before snatching it away. "There will be no justice at all for those you have lost until the good people of these lands come together and bear witness to these crimes." They began muttering to each other again. "All those who lost their children, I ask that you make your sworn statement. A statement sworn with your names and entered into the records of the official investigation. Once we have enough of these statements, a warrant will be issued and the criminals will be arrested."

"That will never be done!" a man cried out.

"You ask us to risk all," another said. "Add our names? Accusing him, in public? It will be the end of us, sir. The end!"

A woman wailed. "We have other children. Who will care for them when we ourselves are carried off?"

They erupted into endless objections.

"Who are you, sir?" someone called out, and then repeated until the others quietened. "Who even are you to come here and speak thusly to us? Where do you come from? Who do you serve?"

Another man answered. "Pipe down, Gerard. You know he saved Pierre le Charron's boy? Give him his due."

"He saved one boy and I'm supposed to bow down at his feet? I ask it again, who do you serve, sir?"

I held up my hands. "It is a fair question." The muttering died down. "I say, it is a fair question. You do not know me. We have arrived in your midst and we are asking the world. Now, I will tell you. But before I tell you, I ask you to listen. We were brought here, myself and the lawyer Stephen who some of you have met, along with our men who have gone with us to guard us. We were brought here under the strictest orders not to reveal the full nature of our employment to anyone because to do so would risk the success of the investigation itself." They grumbled but I held up my hands. "Have I not said I will tell you?" When they calmed themselves I continued. "And I will tell you because I trust you. I trust that you will today do what is necessary and you will add your voices together with such force so that nothing can stand in your way, no matter what the monster Gilles de Rais hears about it. So, I will tell you. It is the Bishop of Nantes who directs this investigation. It is he, along with his dear friend, Milord Jean the Duke of Brittany, who will issue the warrant for the Baron de Rais' arrest. It is the Bishop of Nantes who will sit in judgement of his crimes. Our demonic Baron de Rais will be finished. And this will happen. But only after each of you sits down with me and my lawyer to make your sworn deposition." I waited for them to digest what I had said. "Now. Who here is willing to step forward?"

Silence.

Feet shuffled on the floor and people glanced left and right. At the back, I saw someone duck out and then another two, and I was certain the trickle would turn to a flood and I would be left standing alone with the priest. Assuming he stayed.

I sighed. It had been worth a try but I was expecting too much from them. They had been subjugated by terror for years and now

I was asking them to throw off their caution for a stranger's promise. It was too much.

"I will do it."

Turning, I found the one who had spoken and stepped forward.

"Ameline Moussillon," I said and bowed my head. "Truly? You wish to make a sworn statement? Are you certain?"

Her gaze did not waver. "I am."

"Well, then, mademoiselle, you have my sincere thanks."

"No," she said. "It is I am who am thankful. You have come and you have shown through your actions that you mean what you say. Because you are here, you have saved Guillaime le Charron from a fate he would have shared with my dear brother. His name was Jamet and he was taken and I know in my heart that he is dead now. He was murdered. Murdered, like so many others, by the Marshal. He was murdered by the Baron Gilles de Rais of Tiffauges. We all know it but none of us can speak it aloud. Well, I shall speak it. I shall swear it, in writing, and I shall speak the words in a court or anywhere else required of me so that the Marshal is punished for his crimes. You have my word."

I nodded to her, struck dumb by her bravery.

Beside Ameline, her father stood looking down at his daughter, leaning on his stick. He seemed astonished and horrified in equal measure and I was sure he would berate her and order her to know her place and send her away. The physician looked around at the villagers, who all were staring at him also, waiting to see him quash his daughter's reckless courage.

Drawing himself upright, he hobbled forward half a step. And then a step further. Lifting his chin, he looked around at the entire congregation.

"Some weeks ago, I went to see the Bishop of Nantes. He sent some scrawny little episcopal lawyer to speak to me in his stead. I told that young man I wished to make a statement. To give evidence. To bear witness to the crimes and to name the criminal. But my courage failed me. I did not make the statement." He cleared his throat while the villagers muttered in surprise. "But I will do so now. My daughter has shown me today what courage is. And for that, I am grateful. So yes, sir, I will make a sworn deposition. I will do it, yes. I will do it."

As he stepped back, he wiped his eyes with his spare hand before wrapping that arm around Ameline's shoulders. She patted his hand and glanced at me.

That was all it took for more of them to step forward and offer their support. At some point during the meeting, Walt appeared and he came forward while people were giving me their names.

"You had an eventful night then, I take it?" he said, grinning and jerking a hand over his shoulder. "By the way, I just see someone hanging around that I reckon you might—"

"Find Stephen," I snapped. "Get him here immediately before they change their minds."

I was right glad that morning by what had transpired. With a mountain of witness statements, it seemed certain to me that the Bishop and the Duke would have to act in issuing the arrest warrant for Giles. And then even his private army of two hundred expert soldiers could not save him.

But it would not be so simple.

And what is more, there was someone else watching from the shadows that morning in the church in Tilleuls.

Someone small and hooded and all-but unnoticed, keeping expertly to the darkness, who would soon scurry back to Castle Tiffauges and report on everything that had transpired.

If only I had given Walt a moment to speak, we might have avoided so much of what later occurred. But such is the way of things and sometimes all we can do is regret terrible events and missed opportunities. And to move on from regret we must somehow come to terms with what happened and our part in it.

My regrets, my guilt and my sense of failure, stemmed from the day the Maiden of Lorraine arrived at Orléans and began undoing all that had taken a century of war to achieve.

8

The Maiden at Orléans

April 1429

IN MAY 1429, ELEVEN YEARS EARLIER, we were with the English army outside of Orléans. Our siege around the city was not one of continuous trench lines ringing the walls. We never had anywhere near enough men to undertake such works nor could we have hoped to man them, even with the army of Burgundy in support. Instead, we had constructed a series of small forts that covered strategic approaches. We had seven strongholds on the north bank and four on the south and one on an island in the river.

From the start, we had meant to assault the city from the south across the bridge that led into the middle of the city but the garrison had defended well and we had fallen into a strategy of grinding them down over weeks, months, and years.

I was not there but I heard well from the grumbling of the soldiers that building the series of forts, the siege outworks had been bloody difficult. The garrison sallied out endlessly to assault our men and tear down what we had made whenever they could drive us off. But our men were veterans of such warfare and could not be resisted for long. Because we did not have enough men to stop the flow of enemies entirely, they could still get some supplies in and men out but that could not be helped.

On the south bank, covering the bridge into the city, we had a huge defensive complex, made up of linked forts. Guarding the approach to the bridge from the east was a fort, while to the west of the bridge complex was another fort which also guarded the bridge to the island of Charlemagne, which had yet another fort to protect it.

On the north bank, to the west of the city, was the great fort of St. Laurent, the largest of them and where the commanders resided. I made sure that was where me and my men lived also, to be close to the heart of the English command.

In hindsight, I should have tried to take effective command of one of the other forts instead.

North of that, ringing the city were a series of others that guarded the approaches. These were wittily named, London, Rouen, and Paris, because they sat across the roads that led ultimately to those places. The massive forest that supplied the city's wood and charcoal lay to the northeast and we had no forts there but we moved freely there in force. Far to the east, about a mile from the city, we had our final fort named St. Loup. This covered any approaches from upriver, however, it was almost totally isolated from the rest of the forts and would struggle to receive reinforcements, should it be attacked.

And attacked it was. But not yet. Not until she arrived.

"It's only a matter of time before the garrison surrender," men told me when I arrived at the forts with the supply convoy and our remaining barrels of herrings.

"Is that so?" I asked them, after touring the forts myself. "What makes you so certain, friends?"

"The Earl of Shrewsbury Sir John Talbot is in command now," they said, "and he knows his business well enough, does he not?"

"I suppose he does," I replied.

"Mark my words, lads," one old soldier named Simon cried out. "I been doing this for close to thirty years, now, so I have. I know my business even better than Shrewsbury and I know that the city will certainly fall by this coming summer."

"Perhaps even before the end of spring," another soldier said.

"Any day now," another claimed.

"Summer," Old Simon said to me. "Mark my words, you lads, mark my words. We'll be in there, raking the silver and gems into our purses, by the end of summer."

"The fall of the city is not the objective of our efforts," I said to them. In return, they scratched their chins and frowned. "It is the gateway to the south, is it not? You men surely know that when Orléans falls, it will secure the northern half of France above the Loire for the English and will so open the way for us to assault and crush the forces of the Dauphin Charles in the south."

"Course, that be true enough, and all," Old Simon allowed. "But first, they'll surrender and we'll get rich. Right, lads?"

They cheered his witless confidence but even a fool could see that the stakes could hardly have been higher, especially for the French in general and for the Dauphin Charles in particular.

It was not only the general soldiery who were convinced that they need do nothing other than sit on their arses for a few months to achieve victory. Indeed, how confident were the lords of England also that Orléans would fall, and how resigned the city's denizens and leaders were to that very thing.

In March, the Bastard of Orléans offered to surrender Orléans to Burgundy. The terms were incredibly generous. Humiliating, even. The enemy proposed that Burgundy would be able to appoint the city's governors and half the city's taxes would go to the English. The other half would go for the ransom of the imprisoned Duke of Orléans, they would pay ten thousand gold crowns to Bedford for war expenses, and the English would be allowed to pass through the city, and so our army could assault the Dauphin and win all of France for England, forever. All of this, France itself on a platter, in return for lifting the siege and handing the city to the Burgundians.

The regent, Henry V's brother, the Duke of Bedford said no.

He was convinced that the city was about to fall anyway and so he would have all the plunder and possession of it for the English. Why on earth, I am sure he thought, would he hand it over to the damned Burgundians?

Not only was the opportunity thrown away, it naturally annoyed the Burgundians so much that they took their army away from Orléans.

While all this was occurring, we began to hear hints about a witch who was coming from the east.

I did not know this at the time, but it seems that vague prophecies had been circulating in France concerning an armoured maiden soldier who would rescue France from destruction by feat of arms. Many of these prophecies foretold that the armoured maiden would come from the borders of Lorraine.

It just so happened that this witch was coming from Domrémy, on the borders of Lorraine.

"It's nought but a barrel-load of arse pimples," Walt said, spitting.

It was finally a warm day and we sat on fresh grass with the sun on our backs supping beer with a few hours to spare in between our duties. I would rather have enjoyed the day in silence but soldiers are the world's greatest gossipers, save old women and new mothers.

"Perhaps it is the truth," I replied.

Walt scoffed. "What, some little girl marching with soldiers, dressed as a page boy, is going to save France?"

Rob looked up at the sky, as if seeking inspiration. "They say she is no longer dressed as a page but now wears full plate armour and helm. Just as it is foretold in the prophecy."

"Prophecy," Walt said, spitting again.

"I suppose it does seem rather unlikely," I allowed.

"Do you believe in prophecy, sir?" Rob said. "That events is preordained by God?"

"I have been assured by a number of priests and monks, including dear Stephen, that mankind is given free will, to make what choices we will. If this is the case, how can there exist such a thing as predestined actions?"

Rob frowned. "Can't God do what He wants?"

"I am sure He can. I believe this is what we would call a miracle."

"This whore from Lorraine ain't a miracle," Walt said. "Some cunning sod has tarted up his little piece in fancy armour and is dragging her here hoping we take fright and run away. Won't work, Richard. Look around you. Look at the miserable, hard-faced bastards we have here. All they want is to get inside them walls over there, finally, and have at the wine and the women therein. Ain't no sodding witch going to turn these sons of war from them there walls, no, sir. You wait and see."

I thought he was probably quite right about all of that.

We soon knew, as did the citizens of Orléans, that this maiden from Lorraine had been brought before the Dauphin himself. Reports were confused but by the end of March we heard that she was marching in a suit of plate armour, mounted on a warhorse, flying her own banner while attended by pages, heralds, servants, and high-born knights serving as her bodyguard.

It was fantastical. We could not quite credit the rumours we were hearing.

And then her first letters arrived addressed to our commanders.

Begone, or I will make you go.

The missives were signed, La Pucelle, which meant the

Maiden.

It was all so strange. A peasant girl, by all accounts, addressing great lords and giving them ultimatums. The men jeered and cursed her and mocked the French for falling for the ruse. But underneath it all, I sensed a disquiet among the English. Perhaps it was only I who felt such anxiety but, knowing what later occurred, I do not believe I was mistaken in noting the rising apprehension.

At the end of April, a messenger arrived at the fort of St. Laurent, his horse shuddering and the man himself sweating. I rushed over to the commander's position in the hope that I would hear of what was occurring.

"My lord," he said to Sir John Talbot, speaking with all urgency. "A great supply column approaches from Blois. From the south, on the other side of the Loire."

"Indeed?" Talbot cried and turned to his men with a smile on his face. "We shall send word to the bastilles guarding the bridge to intercept them."

His knights smiled also, for if we stopped the convoy, as we had done to many others, it would mean additional supplies for the men and quite possibly additional wealth for the lords.

"Begging your pardon, my lord," the messenger said, catching his breath. "I must also report that the convoy is escorted by five hundred soldiers."

The grin fell from Talbot's face. "Five hundred? Are you certain, man?"

"It is five hundred, my lord, at the least."

"And..." the messenger continued, then paused.

"And?" Talbot cried. "Out with it, man."

"And they say that the Maiden of Lorraine is with them, my lord. The Maiden what has been sending letters, I mean, my lord. The Maiden who they say is beloved by God and who is destined to—"

"We know what damned maiden you speak of," Sir John Fastolf snapped. "Be silent."

"By God," Talbot muttered, turning to his men. "We shall allow this convoy to pass. It is a shame but it cannot be helped. On the next occasion, assuming they are not so well defended, we shall take the supplies."

"Are you mad?"

They turned to me as one and I realised I had spoken aloud without thinking.

"Hold your tongue, sir!" Sir John Fastolf roared. "How dare you?"

I stepped forward toward the group of outraged lords and addressed Talbot, the Earl of Shrewsbury, directly. "Forgive me, my lord. But surely we must make every effort to stop these supplies entering the city? It otherwise might extend the siege beyond the summer and into the winter and who knows what might occur if we tarry here another year?"

"Tarry?" Fastolf said. "Control yourself, sir, or I shall have you removed from my presence."

Talbot was quiet, though, as he regarded me and when he spoke it was with condescension. "Our only soldiers on that side of the river are the ones manning the bastilles that guard the bridge. If I order the men out of those forts, the garrison from the city will assault the bridge and with no men to defend them, we will lose them. What is more, taking such action is unnecessary, because there will be no way for this convoy to cross the river and so they will retreat, just as so many other convoys have done in previous months. Now, young man, I know it may be difficult for you to understand but this is the best course of action. You, Richard, are an able commander of a small company and carry out your duties guarding the perimeter and escorting messengers perfectly well. But you will allow your betters to dictate matters of strategy, will you not? You are dismissed, sir."

I scoffed and looked at him, at Fastolf, and at the furious knights all around them.

"Thank you, my lord," I said, bowing.

Later that day, the supply column came at the city from the south just as the messenger had warned. Unable to approach our forts at the bridge, they instead made to cross the river by boat opposite our fort of Saint-Loup on the north bank.

And from afar we watched upriver and heard reports as they came in. While French skirmishers kept the garrison of Saint-Loup on the north bank contained, a fleet of boats from Orléans sailed down to the landing to pick up the supplies, and the soldiers, and the Maiden.

"You must stop them, my lords," I urged Talbot and Fastolf. We watched the events from afar, on the north bank. "There is yet time to stop them before they embark."

"Remove this man," Talbot muttered, watching the fleet sail upstream to where the small army and the wagons waited as the sky darkened toward nightfall.

No one moved to do so but I fell silent. They would not listen to reason.

Walt edged forward at my elbow. "Do you see the Maiden, sir?" he whispered.

"Do not be absurd," I said. "I can hardly make out one man from another at this distance."

"I can't see her, neither," he grumbled.

"The winds blows east," someone nearby said, with excitement in his voice. "And so they will not so readily return to the city against the wind."

There were murmurs as the men all around concurred. Some even went so far as to celebrate the fact that the supplies would remain stranded on the south bank as night fell.

"Perhaps a limited number of companies might raid the convoy in the night," Fastolf suggested to Talbot. "Take some for ourselves and help drive them off."

Talbot nodded. "Raise the signal before dark," he ordered.

But then one of Joan's reputed miracles occurred. The wind which had brought the boats upriver suddenly reversed itself, allowing them to sail back to Orléans smoothly under the cover of darkness and there was not a thing we could do about it.

It was no miracle, of course. The wind often changes as night falls, and though no man can say why it does, all men know that it is the most natural thing in all the world. No man alive has not noted the fact of it and yet the French were convinced that the Maiden had intervened with her prayers and then God had answered.

Either way, the long-awaited Joan of Lorraine had arrived.

The people of the city celebrated the arrival of the prophesied Maiden, who was destined, so they said, to save them all.

"It's a barrel load of arse-pimples," Walt said again as we watched the boats of the convoy, little more than black shapes moving on the black water, heading up to the landing places at the city walls. "All that stuff about the Maiden. Ain't it, Richard?"

"Certainly, it is," I replied, the dark shapes bobbing in the distance becoming lost in coal-black shadow.

Only later would I discover that sitting hunched down beside the young woman in the bottom of one of those river boats as it landed in Orléans, was a nobleman in the finest armour, named Baron Gilles de Rais.

None of us could know at the time but it was the beginning of the end for the English in France.

9

Illumination

July 1440

"THIS IS NOT ENOUGH," THE BISHOP SAID, looking at the list of named witness depositions. He rolled it back up and tossed it onto the desk in his audience chamber.

Stephen and I exchanged a look.

We had taken more than three weeks to record almost thirty sworn statements from bereaved parents and other local people who felt brave enough to go through with it. Each one had taken time to locate and Stephen recorded their words. Some had changed their minds and refused to speak to us after all and we had crossed back and forth from Cholet to Challans, fifty miles from east to west, and twenty north to south. A vast area and we had run ourselves ragged. Our valets especially were exhausted.

But I had driven my men hard, day after day, because those statements were the means of bringing Gilles de Rais to justice whether he was an immortal or human.

"Not enough?" I said, incredulous. "What in the name of God do you mean not enough? We did precisely as you wanted and now you say to us that it is not enough?"

The Bishop stared in astonishment and his clerks and servants muttered behind him. "How dare you, sir? How dare you speak to me in this fashion? I will have your apology, sir, or I will have your damned head on a pike."

I scoffed. "If you are going back on your word, my lord, then I will end this in the way I am used to."

"What in the world do you mean by that? If you are not careful, I will have you dragged from here and thrown in gaol."

The two guards at the back of the room stepped forward, ready to do the Bishop's bidding.

"Richard," Stephen said, warning me.

I smiled at the Bishop. "You may certainly try."

He scowled, his fat cheeks wobbling. He certainly had the authority to have me treated very badly, if he so wished. But after two and a half centuries of immortality, I was capable of quickly and accurately judging a man's character. And the Bishop, though he blustered, was at heart a kind and decent man and I knew I could face him down.

"You say these are not enough, my lord?" Stephen said, stepping forward to pick up our list. "I suppose we could find a few more who are willing to make their sworn statements but it was something like a miracle that we have secured so many as this."

"No," the Bishop said. "I am sorry, Stephen. Depositions from peasants are not enough for us to issue a warrant for the Baron's arrest."

Stephen and I turned to look at each other in shock.

"Your pardon, Milord Bishop," Stephen said, "but we followed your orders. You told us this was what you needed."

"I did," the Bishop replied. "And I have since spoken to the Duke. He is unwilling to act on this basis alone."

"Unwilling?" I said, still speaking with too much passion. "So he may be persuaded to change his mind?"

The Bishop looked me up and down, as if suddenly recalling that I existed. It seemed as though he would pretend I had not spoken but then he deigned to reply. "I misspoke. He will absolutely not issue a warrant based on the depositions of peasants, no matter how many of them there are."

"They are not peasants," I said, snatching the roll of names from Stephen's hand and brandishing it like a weapon. "Less than half are labourers, as you can see for yourself from the professions listed by the names. You have builders, embroiderers, fullers, carders, butchers, spinners, a cartwright, roofers, coopers, a herbier, potters, millers, a boat builder, and a physician, for God's sake." The Bishop had his hands up, palms facing me, to shut me up. "These are good and decent people who have bravely taken a stand for each other and for the sake of justice. I gave them my word that action would be taken if they spoke up. I gave my word that justice would be done."

The Bishop sighed. "You should not have done that."

He was right. I should not have done such a foolish thing. I had been caught up in the moment in the church and had wanted to give those desperate people the hope that they deserved. It was not even hope for the lives of their children but it was at least the hope that justice would be done and their murderers punished.

Right he may have been but still I was angry and ready to break the Bishop's writing desk over his head.

Stephen stepped to my side and placed his fingers on my arm. "Our intentions were good, Milord Bishop. Whatever we have done, we have acted only on your instruction."

"Oh?" he said, darkness clouding his expression. "Was it my instruction that led you to assault the Baron's servants?"

I snapped at him. "They would have killed that boy if I had not acted."

"It is a shame you could not have seized one of the servants. Perhaps if you had done so, we could have used him."

"Seized one?" I said. "What do you mean, seized one? It was all I could do to get the boy to safety before he perished in my arms, Bishop. And as for seizing one, I would have killed the bloody lot of them if I had the—"

Stephen grabbed my wrist to shut me up and spoke over me. "If we had one of the servants in our possession, my lord, if we had one and brought him to you. Would that be enough to have the warrant issued?"

The Bishop pursed his lips. "It might... if the servant was to make a deposition that directly accused the Marshal of specific capital crimes. The servant would have to describe the Marshal committing murder and conducting heretical acts. Yes, that would be enough to persuade the Duke to issue an arrest warrant." He sat back in his enormous, ornate chair. "But I fear you have by your actions quite ruined any chance of that. They will not venture from their castle now, I am sure."

"They will come out, alright," I said. "They have a need for blood that they will not be able to deny for long. And if they do not, well, I will simply storm the castle and tear the place down around them."

The Bishop sat upright and banged a palm on the table. "You will commit no crimes, sir, or I shall have you dismissed at once from my service. Do you understand?"

I stepped forward and leaned down. "I will bring you one of his men. You will get a confession out of him and issue the warrant. Do we agree?"

He spluttered. "I do not make deals with underlings, sir. You do as I command, do you understand?"

"Do we agree, Milord Bishop?"

He glared at me, no doubt expecting that the authority of his office would intimidate me into submission. When it did not work, he sighed and leaned back again. "Yes, yes. Bring one here to Nantes. I will speak with the Inquisition and we shall do the rest."

Stephen bowed and pulled me back. "Very well, Milord Bishop. We shall do so at once."

He pulled at me again and I stepped back, bowing before I left.

"That bastard," I said as we left the Bishop's palace and stepped out into a steady rain. "That lying, treacherous bastard."

Stephen glanced over his shoulder to check no one was in earshot and moved away across the courtyard, heading toward the gatehouse. "He has his hands tied as much as we do. His legal authority does not extend to arresting the Baron alone. Gilles de Rais is the Duke's vassal and so the Bishop must satisfy the Duke's requirements."

I stared at him. "Yes, I know that, Stephen. Still, he could have forced the matter and he would have done if he had a spine running through his body instead of a lump of wet cheese."

"So, how do we find one of the servants?" he asked, grimacing at the sky and pulling up his hood.

"Let us speak to the others."

Walt and Rob were waiting at our inn near the centre of the town and we found them with our valets drinking wine in the public rooms downstairs.

"Are we all set then, Richard?" Rob asked brightly as Stephen and I sat down, shedding rainwater from our clothes.

Walt elbowed Rob. "Look at them, Rob. You reckon those are happy faces? What's gone wrong now, Richard?"

"We need to kidnap one of those servants and bring them back here."

Our valets hung their heads, for no doubt they were enjoying their time in Nantes and were hoping they would not have to return to the wilderness near Tiffauges.

Rob and Walt looked at each other, then grinned.

"Can't we just murder the bastards?" Walt asked, swirling the wine in his cup and squinting into it.

"Not all of them. We must return to the castle and grab one

of the men when they leave."

Stephen leaned in. "I would agree with one thing the Bishop said. They will surely be too alert to leave their castle undefended, following your recent brush with them. They know we are watching and so they will be ready for us."

"He's got a point there, Richard," Walt said, raising his hand for the servant to bring him more wine.

"Two hundred soldiers in plate armour," Rob said. "The Marshal's got to be using them for something."

I drummed my fingers on the table. "I would not be so certain of that. The Marshal spends money even faster than does Walt." My men laughed at Walt's wounded expression. "Those soldiers are pretty as a picture, are they not? With their polished steel and bright pennants and fancy riding in formation but I saw a few when I went to see the priest. Drinking, dicing, lounging about and totally unconcerned with the sight of me, a stranger, in their midst. I have not heard of these soldiers harming any villagers, have you? Not in any of the depositions we have taken. No, I am quite convinced that it is for show, I tell you. To impress upon his people that their lord is a great man. He acts like a king, you said it yourself, Walt. These soldiers are how he dominates his people but by overt demonstration of his wealth, not through strength of arms."

Rob nodded slowly, pursing his lips. "Sounds like a most favourable employment. I wonder how much is their daily pay?"

"More than Richard pays, I bet," Walt said and they laughed, clashing their cups together.

"Very amusing." I turned to the valets. "Prepare our

belongings and see to the horses. We will leave today. Now, please." They knocked back their wines and stood to obey my commands and I waited until they were out of earshot before continuing. "It seems clear to me that Gilles de Rais and at least some of his men are surviving on the blood of these children. Certainly, the scrawny one called Poitou and the fat one called Henriet. Perhaps they are bleeding their living servants, as we do, but consider how many children that have disappeared over the years. How many would you say, Stephen?"

He sighed and shifted in his seat. "Very difficult to calculate such a figure. Based on the depositions we have taken, it is certainly over one hundred. Extrapolating over the years since the first ones disappeared and over the number of villages within his lands, I believe, although I cannot prove, that it is over four hundred children."

"Dear God," Rob said, crossing himself. "Four hundred murdered children from these accursed lands."

"Perhaps many more," I said. "It could be thousands. Who can say how far afield they have travelled over the last few years?"

"Dirty bloody bastards," Walt said, downing his wine and slamming his cup on the table. "Let's go find them."

∞

I did not wish to be without either Walt or Rob the next time I had a run in with the Marshal's servants and so we took turns on watch in the same place as before. The jagged rock formation on the plain north of Castle Tiffauges provided enough cover for us all but we could not move around without showing ourselves, should anyone be watching for us. While I slept in the daytime, wrapped in my cloak and wedged in the pile of rocks, Walt stood watch, peering through the light brush and sheltering from the sun beneath his wide-brimmed hat. Rob took over in the evening and first part of the night, while I took the later watch until dawn.

Stephen and our valets were safe back at our inn at Mortagne, not too far away. If we were forced to wait more than a couple of days, I knew I would have to send Rob and Walt back to get their supply of blood before they degenerated into the blood sickness.

The first day, we saw nothing but ordinary castle business. Supplies of wood and fresh food were trundled up through the gates. During the night, I was sure I would see the servants slinking out to find another child to feed on but the night was still and silent and none emerged and I settled down at dawn, feeling irritated and spoiling for a fight.

In the morning of the second day, Walt shook us both awake and we crawled forward while he jabbed his finger at the castle. Peeking over the top of the rocks, I watched as around three score of the Baron's soldiers rode out of the gate in their exquisite armour on their powerful, shining horses.

"They've spotted us," Rob said, sending a chill through me. He grabbed his bow and slipped an arrow out of his bag.

But the great mass of soldiers turned their magnificent beasts onto the main track and headed west, throwing up a cloud of dust into the morning sun.

"The Baron's escaping," Walt said, peering out from his hat.

"Sneaky bloody bastard."

"Shall I get the horses?" Rob asked, tugging his hood closer about his face.

"The Marshal's banner is not flying over them," I said. "He is going nowhere. It is just the soldiers."

"Could be a trick?" Walt said. "Keep his banner over the castle here while he flees with his soldiers?"

"Could be," I said. "And yet he seems like a man obsessed with declaring his own position to the world. I do not believe he would skulk away anywhere in such a way."

"You might be wrong," Walt said. "Maybe I should follow those lads, just in case."

"No, it does not matter what they are up to. Even if the Marshal is with them, we do not want him. We want one of his men, that is all."

"That must be a quarter of his strength," Rob said as the riders thundered away. "More, even. Why would he send so many men away?"

"To the west is his other favourite castle at Machecoul. They must be headed there for some reason. To protect the prisoners that he is keeping there, no doubt, the priest le Ferron and the men the Duke sent to bargain for his release."

"There are soldiers enough at Machecoul already," Rob said.

I sighed, because I did not have any answers though I needed to pretend certainty. "Some other important reason, then."

"What could be so important?" Walt asked.

I snapped at them. "Whatever they are doing, it is of no concern. We will stay here and remain focused on finding a single servant to take. Wake us if you see any such man emerging, otherwise I am returning to sleep."

It was almost dark when Rob shook me awake and hissed in my ear. "They are coming out, sir. The servants are coming out. A wagon with four men. Heading east."

I crept to the top of the rocks and watched the light of a lantern bobbing along the road as the wagon banged and squeaked

"Just as last time," I said. "Well done, Rob."

We scrambled for our horses and followed the wagon at the longest distance we could. There was not much cover in the landscape and much of it was flat. But we had experience scouting enemies from horseback and keeping a constant watch on one's target is not necessary, especially when they are driving a wagon along a track. However, the sun soon set and the moon was waning. With the sporadic cloud cover it became very dark indeed and I had to rely on my men's enhanced night sight. If I was right and Gilles de Rais' men were revenants, created by ingesting his blood, then their vision would likely be even better than Walt and Rob's but I prayed we would not be spotted before we could close the distance and attack them.

The wagon soon stopped by a large farmhouse. We saw it in the distance, as light from inside spilled out from the open windows on the top floor, as if the very building was a beacon.

"Not exactly ashamed of themselves, are they?" Rob muttered as we observed from afar.

"The people are so cowed that they do not care who sees," I said. "But they shall find their confidence is misplaced tonight."

"Ain't going to be easy, Richard," Walt said. "Forcing our way inside that place with four of them in there."

"What do you want to do?" Rob asked me.

"We will ride up fast," I said. "Go through the front door and grab the closest or the smallest or the quietest man. We will truss him up and throw him over the spare horse. If the others resist, we will kill them."

Rob cleared his throat. "Stephen said we should try not to murder anyone."

"We'll murder the lot of them if need be," I said. "Come on, let it be done."

Quickly, we divested ourselves of our cloaks and stowed them and other unnecessary items on the horses and prepared our weapons. We rode up to the house. It must have belonged to a wealthy franklin and the outer walls on both the ground floor and the one above were covered in pale blue painted plaster between the timbers of the building's frame. The shutters were thrown open to the night and the lamps within threw yellow light from all four windows.

If anyone happened to look out of those windows as we approached, they would have seen us illuminated in the glow. They had even left the lamp alight on the wagon outside. The horse stomped his foot and snorted at ours as we approached, and Rob hushed him after we dismounted and threw our horses' reins around parts of the wagon.

Steeling myself, I lifted the latch and threw open the front door with my dagger in hand.

The room was empty.

On the ground floor was two rooms. One large and one small and I stood in the larger of them, occupied by a table with two lit lamps and five good candles throwing out light, a pair of benches, and a large hearth and chimney at the far end. A small fire burned in the hearth, rapidly going out. Stairs at the rear, by the back door, led to the floor above.

Otherwise it was quiet.

I nodded at the stairs and we rushed to the rear and charged up to the next storey, ready to fall upon the Marshal's servants.

There was no one upstairs in either bedchamber. Again, those rooms were lit with multiple lamps, stood on the bed frame, on a storage chest, and others placed on the floor by the open shutters.

We looked at each other blankly but I was beginning to feel a twisting in my guts.

"Maybe they went out the back way," Walt said.

"That must be it," I said.

"There was a cellar," Rob blurted out.

We clattered down the stairs and Rob pulled back the hatch in the floor by the back door. The hinges creaked and so, any remaining chance at surprise gone, I jumped down the steep steps into the cellar.

It was empty. Again, they had lit the cellar with a lamp but there was nothing within other than barrels on one side and sacks of dry goods on the other.

"What's with all the bloody lamps?" Walt muttered.

"There must be a passage from here," Rob suggested. "A passage leading away underground to some secret place where they bring the children t0—"

"Oh, don't be a plum, Rob, for God's sake," Walt snapped. "They done sold us a duck, have they not?"

"We must flee," I said. "Immediately."

Even as I spoke, there came the sound of hooves drumming outside. A sound that grew and grew until it seemed as though an entire army was charging up on us.

"Dear God," I said. "Up, up!"

We charged back up the steps and I threw open the front door to see dozens of the Marshal's soldiers swarming outside in their steel armour with their weapons drawn, glinting in the lamplight. Our terrified horses were already surrounded, with soldiers grasping their reins, and there was no way through.

I slammed the door shut, swung down the bar, and turned to my men. "They outwitted us, the bastards." We drew our swords and looked at each other.

"Worth trying to talk our way out?" Rob suggested, as the shouts of the soldiers grew.

I almost laughed and he hung his head. Each of us knew that we faced what might prove an insurmountable challenge and I felt death's presence lurking near. "Bar the door," I snapped at Walt. "Let us be away through the back."

The men outside called orders to each other, and many laughed as they did so, for they believed bringing us down would be no more than sport.

By the time I ran through the back door, there were already a dozen mounted soldiers riding down the wattle fences surrounding the kitchen garden. They charged at us with their swords and maces raised and I pushed Rob back inside and shut the door behind us. We dragged the table across the room and pushed it against the rear door, then threw a bench and a chest against it.

Walt backed away from the door as the soldiers tried to force it open.

"The windows," I said, nodding at the nearest one. There was one in each room, on the south side like the front door, and each large enough for a man to climb through. Sure enough, a helmeted head poked through the one I had indicated as the soldier it belonged to tried to climb in. Walt grabbed the man's helm and twisted it off. His shocked face looked up as I cleaved his skull in two with my sword and pushed his twitching body back outside again where his comrades cried out in anger.

A crash from the smaller room next door alerted us to more men climbing in through there and I left Walt to guard the window while Rob and I went to deal with the intruders.

Three men were already within and helping a fourth in through the window. All were armoured in steel and with helms down. There would be no breaking through such fine armour and our only chance was in slipping our blades into the gaps between pieces. I knew from experience that seeing through such helms as they wore would be difficult and I rushed them before they noticed my approach. One man I threw back off his feet into the shelves against the wall and the next man I wrestled off his feet. Rob, with his archer's strength enhanced by his immortality, pushed one man back out of the window and then pitched another one off his feet right out after him. We fell on the downed men, flipped open their visors and ran them through

127

their terrified faces.

Walt shouted a warning from the other room and I ran back to find him grappling with an armoured soldier while another pulled himself through the window. Blood soaked one of Walt's arms.

Guiding the point of my sword with my free hand, I slipped the blade under the soldier's aventail and speared him through the back of the neck and he fell straight down. Together with Walt, we forced the other man back from the window.

Both the front and back door resounded with hammering while outside the soldiers shouted orders to each other. The furniture across the back door shifted as the men pushed and shoved and heaved their way through.

Rob came running back from the other room with a group of soldiers after him that I checked with a wild cry and the swinging of my sword. But they were not to be held at bay for long, not by an unarmoured opponent, and they rushed us with full-throated cries of their own. I grabbed the arm of the first one and heaved and swung him across the room with considerable force and he crashed into one of the lamps, knocking it to the floor where it broke and threw oil across the floor, which burst into flame.

Never one to miss an opportunity for destruction, Walt grasped the other lamp and threw it at the feet of the attacking soldiers. The flames flashed up and drove them back.

At the back door, the soldiers finally pushed their way in and we found ourselves heavily outnumbered and attacked from both sides.

"Up!" I ordered, and we bundled our way up the stairs.

From there, we held them off at the top. A few brave souls rushed us and we seized each of them in turn and killed them, one after the other, and threw the bodies back down the steps. We held them for long enough that the flames spread in the room below, catching on the furniture and the beams in the walls and floor, driving them away from the base of the stairs.

They clambered in through the windows upstairs and I killed them as they came in. One man I smote with a single blow through his helm and I quickly sawed his head clean off and threw it down to the men below, shouting at them to come and share the same fate.

All three of us were wounded and bleeding and the next man I tore off his helm and sank my teeth into his face and savaged his cheek. He screamed like a woman and I held him in the window before tearing off half of his face in a jagged big streak and throwing him down to his fellows. I sucked the blood from the chunk of flesh and tossed it out with the blood streaming down my chin. The fire below flickered out of the building to shine on me and the heat was growing with every moment.

"Come and die!" I shouted through the smoke and flame. "Come and die, cowards, and I will drink your blood! I will feast on your flesh and wear your skin. I will devour your souls. Come and die! Come and die!"

Instead, they remounted their horses and rode away into the darkness, their collective will shattered by the horror that we had sown.

We had killed a score of them and wounded more so their trap had failed. But so had our plan to lure them out and seize them. Instead, they had outwitted us and played me for a fool. We had our lives, to be sure, but we had nothing else.

Bloodied, battered, and coughing out smoke, we calmed and mounted our horses and slipped carefully through the darkness to our inn as the sun turned the sky red in the east.

There would be no warrant for the arrest of Gilles de Rais.

10

Summoning Demons

August 1440

"RICHARD!" STEPHEN THREW OPEN the door to my bedchamber before dawn and I sat bolt upright, heart racing, and grabbed my sword from beside the bed.

"What is it?" I asked, grasping one of the bedposts in one hand as my head swam, brandishing my sword in the other.

"Another child has been taken."

"Dear God. We must act swiftly. What has happened?"

"We had a local man ride through the night to tell us," Stephen said. "Bone tired and his horse will never be the same."

"I hope you paid him well for bringing us the news."

For weeks, we had spread word everywhere we travelled to take depositions, that we would pay handsomely for immediate news of lost children. We stipulated that it must be genuine information and it must get to us swiftly, so that we might catch the servants in the act. Perhaps yet on the road.

"Of course, I tried, but he would accept no payment, saying he was cousin to the missing boy's mother. He said the blacksmith in Saint-Georges-Montaigu had lost his son. The father is named Jean le Fevre, his son they call Little Jean, aged about twelve or so."

"Where is the rider now?"

"Drinking spiced wine in the public rooms below."

"I must speak with him."

"You suspect a trap?"

"Trust me, Stephen, if you had been with us in that burning house last week, you would suspect it also."

I shouted for the valets to prepare our gear and the horses. Walt and Rob stumbled, bleary-eyed, from their rooms and came down with us to speak to the rider. He was younger than I had expected, little more than a boy himself and just a little, narrow-shouldered thing, he was.

"You can save Little Jean, can't you, sire?" he said, jumping to his feet as we approached. He swayed on tired legs and Rob helped him to sit once more on the bench. The innkeeper, Bouchard-Menard, lit a candle on the table and I watched the young man's face as he spoke it all again. His cousin's boy went on an errand and did not return. Little Jean had ever been a dutiful boy and had never tarried before.

"He is twelve, you say?" I prompted, looking at Stephen.

"Twelve years, yes, my lord, or perhaps eleven. Thereabouts."

It was the most common age, Stephen had found, when collating the many witness statements. Almost all of those lost were boys aged between eight and fourteen and most of them were aged twelve.

"It seems," Stephen said, "that even demons have preferential tastes."

"Thank you," I said to the exhausted young man. "For bringing this to us so swiftly. You must rest. The good innkeeper here will take care of you until you have strength enough to return home. We shall do everything we can to find young Jean."

"Believe him, then?" Walt asked a little while later as we made for the stables.

"Don't you?" Rob asked, hoisting his arrow bag onto his shoulder.

Walt shrugged. "I suppose he's too simple-minded to make a good liar."

Rob grinned at him. "Takes one to know one, eh?"

Despite himself, Walt laughed. "A truer word never was spoken, sir."

I laughed also but then shook myself. "We shall have fewer jests and more alacrity," I reminded them. "A boy's life is in peril."

All of us together, along with Stephen and the valets, hurriedly rode south, beyond the immediate environs of Castle Tiffauges, toward the village of Saint-Georges from where the boy had vanished. Something about the abduction had brought the reality of it into sharp relief that morning and I was filled with emotion. He had been taken the day before, perhaps only half a day since he was a happy young lad going about his business. And I knew that he might be suffering even as we rushed to his aid. Suffering by having his blood drained from his body and who knew what other horrors being inflicted at the same time. Baron Gilles de Rais had created those horrors, he had made his servants into blood-mad revenants and the whole nest of the bastards had been growing fat on the children of the lands he was supposed to be protecting.

"I will kill him," I said to myself as I rode, twisting the reins in my hands. "I will damned well murder him and every bloody one of them."

It took half the day to get to Saint-Georges-Montaigu. By the calendar it was the height of summer but it had never really begun on the ground. The crops were stunted and the best that could be hoped for was a miserable harvest and at the worst, the rain and damp would continue and there would be no harvest at all. If that happened, and they could not import grain from elsewhere, people would starve.

And while the crops remained stunted, the weeds grew amongst them as wild as ever, winding their way between the stalks of wheat to choke them until they were torn out by hoe and by hand. People laboured in the fields as hard as they ever did but their hearts were sick with the thought that their efforts might be for nought.

Saint-Georges-Montaigu was a decent-looking village on the side of a small, low valley, with buildings of stone and a fine, if small church.

The people there were out in the street as we rode up and many recognised us from our traipsing back and forth collecting witness statements. Some, I thought, had even been in the church when I had promised them justice and two of them I recognised as they had provided sworn statements about their own stolen children.

I had expected that these people would be anxious and afraid. In fact, they were furious.

The men and women gathered outside the church swarmed us even before we could dismount. Our valets were frightened. And not just the valets.

Walt muttered a warning. "How about we ride right through them?"

I did not want to hurt them in an effort to get away but it certainly seemed that they wished to inflict harm on us.

"You promised us!" the blacksmith swore as he stomped toward me, waving a wide-bladed short sword over his head. "You stood before us and gave your word. And now this!"

"Aye, Richard," Rob said. "Let's ride on through."

"It would be sensible to do so," Stephen said.

The crowd called out curses and named me as a betrayer.

"False!" a woman cried. "He is false!"

Mobs are perhaps the most dangerous thing in the world and it is always prudent to flee from them as you would flee from a bear or a rabid dog. Instead, while my men hissed and swore at me, I dismounted and went to the blacksmith with my hands spread wide. I hoped he would not behead me.

"I came to you," I said. "I came as soon as I heard. I came to help. Help you, I say, help to find Little Jean."

"Help?" the boy's father said, eyes bulging. A tall man, and lean, he seemed half skeleton in his anguish. "It is too late for your help, sir. You must go, before I do something I regret."

"When did they take him?" I asked them.

"Yesterday," a woman said beside me. "In the full light of day."

"What happened?" I asked the crowd. "Where was he?" I asked the blacksmith. "The rider who came to us said your boy's name is Jean? What happened to Little Jean?"

The man seemed to suddenly deflate and his shoulders slumped. "I cannot keep him in my sight every hour. I cannot. I have business. He was sent to fetch the charcoal in the morning. And he..."

When he could not find the words, the women clinging to him filled in the details.

"He never returned with the charcoal, sir."

"But he was seen, he was."

"Seen with them."

I grabbed the woman who had spoken. "His servants? The ones they call Henriet, Poitou? Sillé? Roger de Briqueville?"

They replied all in a jumble, half speaking over each other.

"No, no. No, sir."

"It was her."

"Her and her familiar."

"The old woman and the young."

"La Meffraye and her girl."

"La Meffraye's granddaughter, a little demon spawn."

"She teases the boys in, so she does, with smiles and sweets and promises."

"We told them not to listen but..."

136

"They was seen, leading him away by the hand towards his place."

I turned to the one who had spoken last. "To Castle Tiffauges?"

They crossed themselves as they nodded in confirmation.

"Why did these witnesses not stop them?" I asked.

"It was from far away," one woman said.

"They was children themselves, sir," another said. "They was afraid."

I could certainly understand that. "You say that Jean was taken by La Meffraye and this young girl who assists her and they led him away by hand. You mean they travelled on foot from here to Tiffauges? No horses or carts?"

"They walk always, La Meffraye and her familiar," a woman said, to much nodding from the others. "Horses and other beasts will not allow them near."

"Smell the demon blood," another confirmed.

I had to hold up my hands and raise my voice to speak over their peasant nonsense.

"I shall go to Tiffauges at once," I said. "If Jean lives, I shall bring him back."

They stared at me like I was mad, silence settling over the crowd at last.

"You?" the Jean the blacksmith said, breaking the spell. "You alone?"

"Me and my men," I said, jerking my finger over my shoulder. "It will not be the first time we have stormed a castle."

Shaking their heads, they wept and cried, for they knew then that I had lost my mind and that there was no hope for Little Jean le Fevre.

"Leave, leave," the women said, pushing me. "Be gone."

"Not only will I find your boy," I said. "But I shall kill Gilles de Rais and his hellish servants when I do it."

It only made them wail louder and heave against me. I stepped back toward my men as the crowd surged forward.

"You are a liar," his father said, his face contorted in anguish and his voice breaking and raising to a wail as he ranted. "A liar and a deceiver. You gave us hope and then you snatched it away. Go! Never show your face here again or I swear I shall murder you myself and the law be damned."

Swinging myself into the saddle and turning my frightened horse around, I looked back at the crowd.

"I will return. With your boy or with his murderer's head."

We rode away, with their angry shouts and curses ringing in my ears.

∞

Gilles de Rais was not at Castle Tiffauges.

For the first time since he had arrived there, his banner was not hanging over the battlements of the tallest tower.

We took our usual position a mile away across the plain in our rocks by the hillock.

"Gates are shut," Rob said, unnecessarily nodding at the castle. "Portcullis down. No banner. That's that, then."

138

"Doesn't mean he's gone," Walt pointed out. "Could just be pretending. Skulking inside."

I still thought that was not the Marshal's way of doing things but then I had been recently outwitted to such an extent that it had almost cost us our lives. So I said nothing about that.

"Ride to the village," I said to Rob, jerking my finger northward. "Find out if they saw him leave. Saw his person, that is."

While we waited for his return, the rest of us sat in our saddles and watched the great mass of the castle, squatting like a great stone beast upon its rock.

"If the Baron has fled," Stephen asked, "surely the boy is not within."

"Perhaps Jean was taken for the benefit of revenant servants who yet remain. See, the smoke rises from that tower."

Stephen covered his eyes with his hand and slumped against the rocks. "You promised those poor people that you would bring back their boy. You swore you would storm that fortress, Richard."

"I did," I said. "And I stand by it."

Stephen scoffed and for once, Walt seemed to agree with him.

"Come on, sir. Can't fight our way into that, anyway, can we," Walt said, chewing on a piece of sausage. "Not a hope."

"Some of the walls are old." I gestured. "See, on the northwest tower? And on the eastern wall."

Walt stopped chewing. "Was hoping you hadn't noticed."

"How could I not? The mortar is crumbling and lichen growing on them. They may not have been repaired in all the years since they were built."

"Probably still younger than you, though."

I grunted. "Probably."

Stephen glanced between us. "Surely, you do not intend to scale those walls? But you would need ladders. Or ropes and iron stakes, at the very least, hammered into the gaps between the stones and the rope wrapped around them."

Walt snorted a laugh. "That'd be nice."

"If we are to save the boy, we cannot delay."

Stephen's expression plainly suggested that he considered the boy long dead. But he had sense enough to not say so aloud in my hearing.

After some time, Rob came galloping back and came running forward, hunched over at the waist. "He is gone. East, on the road to Machecoul. Yesterday at dawn, he left with his army, flying his banner aloft."

"Dawn yesterday," I said. "Before Little Jean was taken by La Meffraye and her girl. Perhaps there is hope after all. See for yourselves, it is as I said. Smoke from more than one fire rises from within the walls. There is life there. If it is as the last time I was there, it could be fifty or a hundred men within. One or more of them requiring blood."

Stephen rubbed his eyes and summoned courage enough to confront me. "Surely, Richard, you know there is no hope. If Gilles de Rais has indeed gone, I will agree that perhaps his servants are still within. But if that is true then they would have had the boy all last night and all the hours so far today. If they use boys for the purposes which we suspect, the poor lad is surely drained white and long dead by now."

"All the same," I said, speaking slowly and keeping my voice as low and steady as I could. "I am going to find him. If he died within, his murderers are still there. And it is they who will be drained white and dead before long. You stay here, Stephen. Hold the horses."

"I will send the servants home," he said, jerking his head to them.

"No. They stay with you at this position. We may need them."

He realised I meant that we may need their blood if we are injured in the attempt on the castle. "Very well. God be with you all."

"Fortune favours the bold, Stephen," I said.

As I spoke it, I thought of the disasters at Orléans and the lost battles afterwards. Joan the Maiden had been bold and she had been so favoured by fate. But had it ever truly been Joan or was it Gilles de Rais who had been the bold one? Inspiring the French with his cunning employment of a prophecy about the Maiden saving France.

"I believe those were Pliny the Elder's last words," Stephen said.

"Truly?" I asked. "I take it he was a great knight?"

"Well, Stephen began, furrowing his brow. "I believe he was a soldier in his youth."

"Fine words," I said.

"Load of nonsense," Walt said. "Boldness gets you killed. Fortune favours the cautious, more like."

"And will those be your final words, Walt?" I said.

Walt wiped his mouth. "I'm going to live forever, Richard. You ain't never going to shut me up."

We laughed together and Stephen stared at us, confused. He did not understand that soldiers must make jests at such times. We were about to risk our lives in a perilous stratagem and a man either laughs at fate or is crushed by the fear of what may come. Indeed, I have come to understand in centuries since that the ancient aphorism should mean that fortune favours the bold in spirit, not necessarily in deed. Although, if you have one, you tend to find yourself risking the other.

"It is not too late to return to the inn," Stephen said. "Or even to Nantes, to reconsider our strategy. You promised the villagers, the blacksmith, yes. But you need not abide by it in these circumstances."

"Stephen, I am disappointed in you. We must go. We are knights, we three, and we have sworn to protect the innocent."

We stripped ourselves of whatever we did not need and walked through the wind-blasted clumps of sedge and scrub toward the castle. It was late in the day and the shadows were long. Night would soon fall but in the meantime if anyone was keeping a close watch of the approach, we would be seen.

But none came and we closed with the castle without any warning cry or trumpet or bell sounding and without soldiers coming to stop us. I almost hoped for it, and prayed a group of horsemen would ride us down. For we could kill them and take their horses and ride in through the gates instead of risking our necks in a mad climb.

And it was mad. The closer we got, the more absurd it seemed.

The lowest wall, on the east, was atop a thirty feet high rockface and the wall itself was another forty feet above that. A fall of such a height was not survivable by a mortal man and would perhaps even be enough to dash one of us to pieces.

With a chill, I recalled the story about Joan the Maiden. When she had been captured and held by the Burgundians in Castle Beaurevoir in the north, she leapt from a tower and fell seventy feet. Somehow, she did not die. It was one of the key pieces of evidence that led me to believe Gilles de Rais had made the girl into a revenant by forcing her to ingest his own blood, for how could a mortal girl survive such a height?

I looked up at the wall, impossibly high overhead, and imagined the fall from the top. They said Joan lay crippled at the bottom and was unable to walk but then somehow she recovered in a few days and was soon as fit as she ever was.

And so it was impossible to avoid concluding that she had either been a revenant or she had truly been blessed by God's own hand. And if it was the latter then what did that mean for God's judgement of England?

Walt nudged me. "Come on, don't just stand there gawking. It ain't going to get any lower."

And we climbed.

Hand over hand, clinging to the crumbling facing stones. The blocks were almost half a man's height and so it was a stretch each time to reach up a hand and drag up a foot. Searching always for a secure hold, enough to bear my weight.

My hands were soon raw and my knees scraped bloody.

Joan was ever on my mind. Surely, she had been given blood

after her fall. Or perhaps she had taken it from someone against their will. But I could not imagine such a thing would not have been reported at the time. Joan of Arc, savaging the neck of one of her gaolers?

They said that she had landed on the muddy ground of the drained moat but even so, it was not possible to fall the height of seven floors and make a swift recovery. If I were to fall from the wall, I thought, I would have no moat, drained or otherwise, but a steep ravine with hard stones and a rock floor. A fall onto a stone would crack my skull open like an egg and my brains would be dashed out.

My foot slipped and I grasped a handhold, missed it and my fingers slid down the side of a block before I could arrest my fall. I lost the nails from both middle fingers of my left hand and I had to stop and clutch at the wall, shaking, with tears running down my face from the pain. I have been stabbed, sliced, and shot with arrows and balls and bullets more times than I can recall, and I have even been set on fire, but there is a particular agony to losing one's fingernails. Especially when dangling on the side of a castle wall.

Rob was far above me and Walt, much closer, looked down and cried out, alarmed. I hissed at him to keep going and forced myself up. It would not do to be so outdone by my men and I hurried up and up, being driven by the pain and the blood and the anger that Gilles de Rais had defeated me, had defeated England. His old castle wall would not defeat me.

I pulled myself up over the battlements at the top soon after Rob and ahead of Walt. We sat on the other side, breathing deeply. It was almost completely dark in the shadow of the battlements and the sky above was dark blue on its way to black.

"We should have tried," Walt said, "knocking on the front door."

"Come," I said, pointing to the doorway that led from the covered parapet walk along the wall into the nearest tower. "Let us go down."

Rob nodded and drew his sword.

"Put it away," I said, to confused looks. "Almost every soul within is a servant. I would avoid starting a mass panic, which we will surely cause if we charge in like soldiers."

Walt scratched his head. "Can't we just kill them all?"

"We're not killing anyone unless they are a revenant," I said. "Knights cannot slaughter at will, like barbarians, our oaths will not allow it. Our oath to the Order of the White Dagger is to kill the spawn of William de Ferrers."

"Yes," Rob said, sliding his blade back through his belt ring. "You are right, of course."

Walt shrugged. "If you say so. What if we're in danger?"

"Defence of one's self and one's companions is a separate matter. If anyone attempts to harm us, we will kill them as usual."

"Oh," Walt said, brightening. "That's alright, then."

The castle was lit up all over, just as it had been on my first visit. Empty stairwells and chambers were lit with beeswax candles and lamps in the walls and fires burned in rooms with no people. Even if Gilles had been present, it would have been a mad waste of money. Who was the display for? The servants? It was they who were employed in all the cutting and fetching of wood and lighting and refilling of lamps, all day and all night. Who was it supposed to impress? All I could think was that it was for God, for who else would be watching? Perhaps it was some strange expression of guilt that he felt for his crimes, I thought, or perhaps I was assuming that he was a man and not a demon in human flesh, for if he felt guilt at all then why would he continue as he had?

On the ground floor we found two servants carrying empty serving trays and they froze in surprise when they saw us approaching.

"Where is La Meffraye?" I asked them.

"Eh?" they asked, both gormless.

"The woman," I snapped. "The old woman servant."

"Old woman?"

"Come on, man," Walt said, grasping a fistful of the man's clothes at his chest. "Can't be many women servants here."

"Yeah there's the old one and the young one," he said, eyes flicking between us. "But we ain't allowed to speak to them, nor even to go near them, sir, not for no reason at all, sir."

"Specially the young one," the other man said, glumly.

"Quite right, too," I said. "Now, where can I find their quarters?"

They blew out of pursed lips. "Can't be saying, my lord. Can't be saying. Not allowed, is all. Not on our lives."

I grabbed the free one by the neck. "It'll be your damned life if you don't tell me where they are!"

He gulped and pointed a shaking hand. "You go down by the lower hall, through the outer yard, past the guardhouse toward the chapel but then you gots to go through—"

"Take me there!" I said and shoved them both forward, tossing their trays to the floor. "Now! Faster!"

They all but ran through the castle and we hurried after them.

"Thought we weren't hurting no one innocent," Walt observed behind me.

Other servants we saw drew back in confusion to allow us to pass until we came out into a vast courtyard.

"That tower?" I asked the servants, pointing to the nearest one, which had smoke drifting from the chimney.

"Oh, no, sir!" they said. "We ain't allowed in there, sir. That's the magician's tower."

I turned on them. "The what?"

"The magician's tower. The sorcerer."

His idiot companion shook his head. "Alchemist, my lord. He's the master's alchemist."

"What goes on there?"

They both turned white. "Can't say, my lord."

"Forbidden."

"Not to go near."

"Not never."

I drew my dagger and forced the nearest one to his knees, placing the edge of my blade against his throat. "Do they take the children in there?"

The servant pissed himself and wept, tears welling and quickly spilling down his cheeks. "Yes," he whispered. "Yes."

Throwing the servants down, we raced toward the base of the tower and threw open the door. I took the stairs two at a time and wound up and around to the first chamber, which was lit up and had a table with the remains of a recent meal but no one else. There were noises above. A man's voice echoing through the floor. Up and round and up again until I threw open the door to the room where the noises came from and there I froze in horror.

Before me was an unholy scene.

A man in white robes with his hands outstretched stood in the centre of a five-sided star painted on the wooden floor. At each point burned large candles and there were bowls of blood beside them. At the feet of the white-robed man was a naked boy, whose arms and belly had been crossed with cuts, bleeding freely. He writhed against his bonds but his mouth and eyes were wrapped with black velvet cloth and a well-dressed brute held him down by the shoulders, leering at his victim as he did so.

Across the room at the slit window, looking out at the night, stood the third and final man. He was tall, wearing very fine clothes, as a rich lord might wear.

They all turned as I burst in, their eyes filled with surprise and fear turning quickly to anger.

The alchemist jabbed his finger at me. "Begone from this place! I shall cast you out with the power of the demon Barron, with the power of Satan, with the power of—"

I rushed him and drove my fist into his guts with such force that he was lifted from his feet and driven back before collapsing into a ball, his white robes settling around him.

The man on his knees leapt up and backed away, holding his dagger back by his hip, ready to drive it into me. On his belt hung a coil of rope, such as a herdsman wore. "You made a mistake," he growled, lip curling into a malicious grin. "The last mistake you will ever make."

He darted at me with incredible speed. Immortal speed. His dagger flashed low and then up toward my neck, twisting and flicking the blade like an expert cutthroat.

I leaned away, grasped his wrist and whipped my sword down to take his arm clean off at the elbow. I tossed his forearm, somehow still clutching the dagger, over my shoulder. He wailed and fell, clutching the stump of his ruined arm and scurrying back on his arse toward the wall while blood gushed from his terrible wound.

The third man had not moved from his spot by the window. There was a short sword at his side with an ornate hilt, in a scabbard decorated with gold.

"Are you him?" I said, stepping slowly toward the window. My toe kicked over a bowl of blood on the floor and it splashed across the floor in a dark, shining fan. "Answer me."

He faltered, shaking, looking at me and at my men behind me. "I am... I am Sir Roger de Briqueville."

"You are him," I said, drawing closer still. "You are the Marshal. Do not lie to me."

"No," he said, raising his chin and holding my gaze. "You are mistaken. You will not find him here."

I stopped. For some reason, I believed him. "Where is Gilles de Rais?"

Briqueville hesitated. "Not here." I tilted my head and he hurried on. "That is to say, sir, that he has relocated temporarily to his castle at Machecoul, to better protect his noble prisoners."

"He knows the Duke is coming for him?"

"Ah, yes. Indeed, he does. At least, he suspects that it is so."

I looked around to see that Rob had scooped up the boy, Little Jean, in a cloak he had found somewhere and was removing the blindfold and bonds, all the while whispering gentle things to him. Walt stood over our other two prisoners with his sword drawn. I knew it would be taking every ounce of self-control he had to resist murdering them both.

"You are an immortal?" I asked Roger de Briqueville.

He glanced at the man with the dismembered arm before drawing his eyes back to me. "I know not of what you speak."

I sighed. "It is a shame that you are not honest with me. All your deceit means for me is torture for you, sir. You should know that I will take off your fingers and your eyelids and your ears and at some point as your body is taken from you, piece by piece, you will tell me it all anyway. So why not avoid the bloody and agonising part and simply tell it all now?"

Walt spoke over his shoulder. "Seems a shame. Maybe we should do it anyway? I'll do it."

"Perhaps you are right," I said. "I would enjoy seeing justice done."

"Please," Briqueville said, his calm demeanour beginning to waver. "I am an innocent man. A mortal man."

"Be silent, Roger," the one with the missing arm said through gritted teeth.

I turned to regard him. He was a well-built man of forty or so, with a big jaw and a low brow like a shelf over dark eyes.

"And who are you?" I asked him.

He spat at my feet. "You will soon die. All of you will die."

"Who is he?" I asked Roger de Briqueville.

"Sillé," he said. "His name is Sillé."

"Ah!" I said, brightly. "I have heard of you. Yes indeed, you are one of Gilles de Rais' most faithful servants. You are one of those men who journeys out into the villages and homes for a hundred miles east and west to bring home young boys and sometimes girls, using your rope there to bind them up. You bring them back here and your master drinks their blood and murders them. And so do your comrades, the servants Poitou and Henriet. I have met them, sir. I saw how their strength and speed were much increased. I know what they are. And I know what you are, too."

"And we know what you are!" Sillé said. "A traitor and a betrayer of the true master!"

"The true master?" I wondered if he meant my brother William, who was perhaps considered by these servants as the master of Gilles de Rais. "Tell me about the true master."

Sillé scoffed.

Walt laughed his mirthless laugh. "Seems like we got another one who cares nought for his fingers and his eyelids, Richard."

I nodded. A whimpering behind me brought my attention and I spoke over my shoulder without taking my eyes away from the captured men. "How is the boy, Rob?"

"Freezing, exhausted. Cuts ain't deep, though. Reckon he'll be right as rain, God willing."

The alchemist groaned and shuddered and crawled to the wall. I wondered if I had fatally ruptured his entrails. "Are you one of the blood drinkers?" I asked him. "I know who you are. You are Prelati the Florentine alchemist and sorcerer. Did the Marshal give you his blood to drink?"

Prelati looked at me with tears in his eyes. "No."

"Is he telling the truth, Roger?" I asked. "Or are you all three here for the boy's blood?"

"No, by God," Briqueville said. "Not I. I would never stoop so low. It makes a man's seed dry and I have a noble name to pass on. I will take a wife and make a son and that will be the only everlasting life for me."

I resisted the urge to explain to him that he would hang before he made a son and merely nodded. "What of these others?"

Sillé, clutching his stump to his chest, roared at him. "You are a betrayer! The master will cut your heart out. You will burn in Hell."

"Can I shut him up, sir?" Walt asked.

"Please do."

Walt kicked Sillé in the belly, then he aimed a second kick in the man's face which drove the back of his skull into the wall with an awful, wet crunch. He fell unconscious, his chest soaked with the blood from his wound and the arm itself now flung out and leaking everywhere. Sillé was not long for the world.

"Well?" I asked Briqueville.

"He is one," he said, pointing to Sillé. "He and Poitou and Henriet."

"Oh? Not Prelati? And you truly expect me to believe that you are not one either?"

He shook his head. "Never. It is evil."

"And yet you are willing to partake in child murder," I said, confused. "How can you speak of evil?"

He lowered his gaze. "I never killed a child with my own hand and I never knew what this place was until it was too late. You see, I was deceived, sir. Snared. I wished to flee but was trapped from fear of my lord, who would never let me go nor let me live if I fled."

It sounded so similar to the excuses of the priest Dominus Eustache Blanchet that it made me doubt not only Briqueville's words but the priest's also.

I sighed. "And what about you, Prelati? Let me guess. You are a victim, also and were forced against your will to sacrifice children and summon demons?"

On his hands and knees, he crawled forward along the floor toward me, knocking over a candle that rolled into a pool of blood and was extinguished. "You are as he is, are you not? The master is afraid of you, my lord. He knows you. From a long time ago, he knows you. A century ago, he said, confiding in me one dark night. You are an ancient one, of great power. Greater even than the true master and your blood will make me more powerful than the others. Please, please, my lord, hear my words and know that they are spoken from the depths of my heart. I beg you. I will serve you. I will serve your every whim. I can perform transmutation if only you provide the materials and I can make you rich, my lord. Richer than any king since Croesus. All I ask in return is that you make me one of you, like your good men here. Give me your blood this night and I will create mountains of gold and I will summon demons to serve your every whim for millennia, until the Last Judgement."

He fell upon my legs, grasping them and reaching up with one hand. With my knee, I struck him in the face and he fell back, wailing, spilling another bowl of blood across the floor and further soaking his white robes.

"I would never give the Gift to a creature as pathetic and useless as you. And it seems that even Gilles de Rais, who gave his own blood to odious, witless fools like Poitou and Henriet, thought you unworthy of it."

Prelati wailed and covered his face with his robes as he scuttled away on his side toward the wall, like a wounded spider.

Sillé stirred and pulled himself upright, clutching his arm once more. His face was grey and his eyes glazed.

"Sir?" Rob said. "We should get the lad away, now."

He was right and not only for the boy's sake. For all I knew, there could be half a hundred soldiers gathering outside the tower, alerted by servants.

"Sillé?" I asked him. "Do you deny that you were changed by ingesting your master's blood?"

He lifted his chin. "Why would I deny such a thing? I am honoured by the blessing. I am brought closer to God by the gift of the blood and I have done their bidding. Such an honour can never be taken from me, not by you and not by death."

"My Order is sworn to unmake all beasts such as you, Sillé." I showed him the blade of my sword. "Kneel, and prepare for your death."

He tried to spit but his mouth was too dry. "You will never unmake the master."

"Lean forward," I commanded, and struck his head from his body with a single stroke. His head rolled toward Prelati, who thrashed it away by kicking his legs, and scurried back across the room.

"Your turn," I said to Briqueville.

He tore his gaze away from the headless corpse twitching within the pentagram. "I swear to you that I am not what he was. I swear it."

"You certainly deserve death anyway for the crimes you have done."

"I do," he said, sobbing. "I do."

"Your only hope," I said, "is to submit a full confession of those crimes and the crimes of your master to the Bishop of Nantes and the Duke of Brittany."

He cried out and sank to his knees. "I will. I will do it. I will."

"Give me your sword," I ordered, and Walt moved to my side in case Briqueville attempted to use it on me instead of surrendering it.

Behind me, a door banged and I jumped about to see Prelati fleeing through a door, his robes billowing out behind him.

"Sneaky bastard!" Walt cried and ran after him.

But I called Walt back. "We have tarried too long as it is. The murdering sorcerer will get what is coming to him but now we must get the boy to safety and drag Briqueville to Nantes."

I looked down at Little Jean as Rob held him like a baby in his arms. The boy was deathly pale and shivering, eyes flicking about beneath their lids.

"All will be well now, son," Rob said to him. "All will be well."

∞

There were no soldiers waiting for us, and the servants I had accosted earlier had long fled, along with every other soul in the place, or so it seemed. Once we made our way through unchallenged, we roused the porter and ordered him to open the gates.

"These men are good friends, Miton," Briqueville said. "Let us out at once."

"In the dark?" Miton said. "Anyway, how'd they get in?"

"You know me, do you not?" I said to him.

Miton's face clouded. "You said you was one of my lord's men but you was a liar. I should never have let you in before."

"Oh, but I am a faithful servant, am I not, Roger?"

"Indeed he is, Miton. Would I be in his company if it were not so?"

Miton eyed the injured boy in Rob's arms and hesitated. My patience long gone, I grasped Miton and lifted him against the wall. "Open the damned gate. Now."

Stephen and my servants met us on the plain and we rode away from the evil place, though it left a filthy stain in my soul. I felt contaminated by the evil and executing one servant and taking another had only served to deepen the feeling that no amount of killing could undo the malevolence that had been done.

At least we had recovered the child while breath remained in his body. We brought him at once to Tilleuls where the physician

Pierre Moussillon treated the boy's wounds and put him to bed. Ameline and her servant Paillart had opened the door willingly, this time, and managed to rouse the old man.

"Your father is in good health," I said softly to Ameline, by which I meant that he was not pissed as a newt. "I had thought you alone would be capable of attending to the boy."

"Yes," she said, smiling. "He has been entirely himself these past three days. I think you have given him some hope, perhaps. Not for Jamet, of course, but for the people here. It is like a curse is being lifted."

"Surely, that is not my doing," I said, smiling at her.

Seeing Ameline's face smile at me in return made me feel as if I was at home.

"You saved another one, sir," she whispered to me. "Surely, you are working miracles."

"I wish only that I could have come last year," I replied.

She took a deep breath and placed her hand on my arm, looking up at me through her lashes. "I wonder, now that you have come, whether you put any consideration in staying longer."

I was saved from having to answer by her father bellowing for her from upstairs and she went to attend to him. The servant Paillart came in with an armful of wood which he dumped by the hearth and began tending to the fire.

"I hope you ain't playing on her heartstrings," he muttered with his back to me. "She be an honourable girl, who deserves to be treated so."

My instinct was to tell him to mind his own damned business but I sensed no malice in his words. It was more like an old soldier offering advice to the younger man he perceived me to be.

"I will not dishonour her," I said, softly.

He peered at me over his shoulder, as if wondering if I meant I would not lay with her or if I meant that I intended to marry her. In truth, I wished I could have either, or both, but such a thing could surely never be.

The next day, Jean le Fevre came to claim his son. He fell to his knees at his boy's bedside and his happy weeping sounded through the house. When he came down, his throat was too tight to speak and all he could manage was to shake my hand with both of his while he looked me in the eye, tears flowing from his.

"You must rest longer," Ameline said. "Stay and eat with us. I know my father would like it."

"Nothing would give me greater joy," I said. "But we have rested the night through and now I must get the prisoner to Nantes. With his confession, we can take Gilles de Rais and truly put an end to this nightmare."

Poor Ameline. Her nightmare was far from over.

Two weeks later, on Tuesday 13th September 1440, we went to arrest Gilles de Rais.

11

The Arrest of Gilles

September 1440

WE RODE SOUTH UNDER THE black banners of the Bishop of Nantes, for it was on his authority that we finally acted, in partnership with Jean the Duke of Brittany.

Roger de Briqueville had confessed all.

I was not present for his questioning but I am told the words spilled from his mouth faster than the Inquisition could record them. He told a tale of continual murders, depravity and sinful lusts, and worse even than all that he told of heretical acts of worship and demon summoning and the invocation of Satan himself. And all throughout Briqueville's long, desperate confessions he named the deviant, the criminal, the heretic, as his lord Gilles de Rais.

It was to Castle Tiffauges once again that we rode. The Marshal had returned to his most favoured home and fortress just days before from Machecoul. The Bishop believed he was attempting to confuse us as to his true whereabouts but we had enough agents by then watching his nests and reporting back to Nantes to know where he was at all times.

And yet to me it seemed less like a cunning ploy and more like desperation. It rang of the frantic oscillations of a beast caught in trap that it does not understand. We were coming for him and he did not know what to do about it.

Our company was a large one, almost eighty men. Some were soldiers, all were armed, although Stephen and the other lawyers were armed with writ and warrant rather than brigandine and blade.

"It is not enough!" I had said to the Bishop. "His personal army is two hundred strong. Less a score or two, perhaps. They will outmatch us in number and in skill."

"God will protect you," the Bishop had insisted, raising a soft, fat palm to the sky. "And anyway, there are no more men."

"The Duke can raise thousands," I replied.

"And if you find that thousands are required," the Bishop said, "then he will raise them."

"That will be marvellous for you and the Duke, my lord, but in the meantime me and my men will be long dead."

"I have every confidence in you all."

We purchased what additional armour we could from the best merchant in Nantes. I found a new coat of plates in Nantes made from the finest steel plates riveted between two layers of thick linen. Somehow, he knew that we were associated with the Bishop in some way and constantly attempted to entice us into purchasing absurdly overpriced nonsense instead of the robust forms we required.

"That piece is of course excellent," the armour merchant said as I tapped the rivets and plates all over with my knife. "But it is rather heavy and unrefined. For a man of your obvious taste and means, I would recommend this remarkable item newly arrived from the armourer in Milan. The steel is lighter and the outer layer is this splendid red velvet and the rivets are well gilded, as you can see."

"I would rather suffer the extra weight for the added protection of the thicker steel," I said. Rob was rapping his knuckles against a series of helms behind me and I had to raise my voice. "And the Milanese piece is hideously gaudy."

"I'll take it," Walt said, grinning.

"No you bloody well will not," I said. "I will not have you at my side all tarted up like a whore on May Day. You shall have that coat of jacks from Nuremberg and you shall be grateful, sir."

I got for myself an open-faced sallet which left my face exposed but would enable me to see, while Walt and Rob made do with a pair of old bascinets that had the long, pointed skulls which had been popular thirty or forty years earlier.

"I always liked these," Rob said, grinning at the helm that he held in his hands.

"Only because they add four inches to your height," Walt grumbled.

For all our new armour and dozens of companions,

approaching Tiffauges across the plain that September day, I found my heart was in my mouth. If our company of soldiers, palace guards, bailiffs and lawyers clashed with the Marshal's army, our side would collapse and flee, and they would be cut down.

"Wait here while we go on ahead," I said to Labbe, the Duke's captain of arms, who was in command of our troops.

"It is I who must serve the warrant," Captain Labbe replied. "Personally."

"You will serve nothing if you are lying dead on the field," I replied and galloped off with my men, Stephen included.

"I been thinking," Walt said as we approached, slowing our horses to a walk. "Has anyone considered that this Marshal, the Baron Gilles de Rais, might be your brother William in disguise?"

The wind grew colder every day and it cut into every inch of exposed skin and between gaps in my armour. It was turning to autumn without ever being summer and the crops all around were stunted and diseased and I knew none of the sheep and goats scattering at our approach would live to see Christmas.

"Of course I have considered it," I said. "But I saw the Marshal in battle, at Orléans and at Patay. It was at a distance but I would have recognised my brother even so. It is not him."

"Besides," Stephen said. "William promised to leave Christendom for two hundred years and it has been merely a hundred and fifty."

"A hundred and eighty years," I said, correcting him. "And I never believed he would commit to the letter of the agreement. I have often doubted whether he would keep to the spirit of it either, come to that, and yet he seems to have done so. We have had no word of him ever since."

"Perhaps he died," Rob said. "In the East."

"Perhaps," I admitted. "Though I somehow doubt that we will be so blessed. He will return one day soon and when he does, we shall kill him. But first we will take this lord and if he is one of William's, we shall see him destroyed."

I spoke with complete confidence but I still wondered if it could be true. Certainly, I would not put such a thing past William. He could certainly have taken the identity of one of his immortals and then ruled the land in his name. The depths of depravity had the ring of William's evil to it. Indeed, the first horror that I had seen him inflict was when he murdered my half-brother's little children and consumed parts of them.

Will I soon see William again? I wondered. Is he almost within my grasp once more?

There was no army drawn up and waiting on the plain before Tiffauges. There was no one at all, in fact, and the gateway to the castle was fully open and the Marshal's gold and black banner hung from the tallest tower, declaring to the world that he resided within.

"That's a trap," Walt said, pointing up at it.

"Nonsense," I said.

"Got to agree with Walt, Richard," Rob said. "Too good to be true, ain't it?"

"I think not," I replied, though I could never have explained why. It was merely a feeling that Gilles had given himself up.

"But where's his army?" Rob insisted. "Waiting within?"

"Perhaps he has dismissed them entirely."

"Why in the name of Jesus Christ and all His saints would he go ahead and do something as stupid as all that?" Walt said. "Don't make any sense."

"What about this man's actions makes sense, Walt? Nothing he has done has any reason to it. His magnificent play in Orléans that was so lavish it almost ruined him. The needless murdering of this great host of children when he could have quietly supped on living men's blood, undiscovered and safe for centuries more. Charging from one castle to another with no pattern nor reason. They are the acts of a man who has lost his mind and lost his will besides. He seems already defeated, does he not?"

From the corner of my eye, I saw Rob and Walt raise their eyebrows at each other.

"Whatever you say, Richard. After you, then."

I cleared my throat. "Perhaps we will allow the Duke's captain of arms to go in first."

In spite of my confident words, I was still on edge as our party approached the gate. We all watched the narrow slits of the windows in the towers flanking the gatehouse and in the walls. Every loud clop of a hoof on the cobbles caused me to flinch, expecting a crossbow bolt to come shooting down right after. I watched Captain Labbe's men file in through the gate passage and half expected boiling water to be dumped down on them through the murder holes or for the Marshal's soldiers to rush out from the courtyard.

But all was quiet.

In the courtyard, with the walls and towers now on all sides, I wished that I had a shield to raise over my head because surely it was the most perfect spot on earth from which to murder a company of men.

And yet the stable hands took our horses and we were shown in through the main door by the porter as if we were expected and escorted through the castle to the main hall.

"I bloody well knew it, you lying sod," Miton the porter said to me, wagging his finger in my face before strutting off. No servants scattered from our path and the place was no longer illuminated throughout as it had been.

"Where is everyone, Miton?" I asked the porter.

"Dismissed," he said, miserable. "Dismissed and sent home, never to return."

"What of the soldiers?" I asked. Just behind us, Captain Labbe and his soldiers listened closely for Miton's reply.

"Dismissed also," he said, shaking his head.

"He lies," Captain Labbe said. "They are here, lying in wait to protect their master, are they not?"

"If they are then no one's told me nothing about it," Miton said, glumly.

I did not know what to think. It certainly seemed as though the Marshal was capitulating but that may have been part of the ruse.

"Make ready," I said to my men. "String your bow, Rob, and have a good arrow ready."

Miton paused by an enormous set of doors and spoke before heaving one of them open and stepping aside. "My lord the Baron of Rais awaits you, sirs, in the lower hall."

The lower hall was very grand in scale but quite spare in decoration. The floor was paved in stone but it was rather rough and no rushes had been spread. The walls had sconces for suspending tapestries and yet the walls were bare. Open doors on both flanks and a gallery showed just darkness beyond and I wondered what was lurking there.

But we filed in and spread out and approached the far end.

For there he was. Finally, I saw him in person.

It was not William.

Gilles de Rais stood raised above us all on the dais at the top of the hall, dressed in a magnificent black and gold samite robe, with long sleeves and an elaborately embroidered hat upon his head, woven with bands of red silk and cloth of gold. The Marshal was tall and slim, with wide shoulders and black hair. At his hip, he wore a sword with silver inlay encrusted around the hilt in chevrons and knots, and the scabbard was covered in shining black silk with rubies around the top and a line of them all the way down to the point, like shining droplets of blood.

Rarely have I seen kings so majestically attired.

His face, though, was drawn and miserable. Around his eyes, his skin was pink and raw as if he had been awake for days. Those eyes cast around over us as we trooped in and advanced on him up the hall.

By the Marshal's side were his servants Poitou, Henriet, the priest Blanchet who I had met weeks before, and the sorcerer-alchemist Prelati, who had fled from us when we had rescued the boy. They each of them looked terrified, and well they might, for we were two score angry soldiers and bailiffs bearing down on

166

them and their master, it seemed, was offering them no protection.

"Gentlemen," the Marshal said, his voice remarkably loud and clear and commanding. A magnificent voice, truth be told, and one used to being obeyed. "No need to be so fearful. You may approach and state your business without threat or hindrance."

Other than Stephen, who was at the forefront, my men and I kept somewhat back and to one side, watching the doors for sudden assault. It was again a most perfect place for the Marshal's soldiers to ambush us from all sides, surrounding us with their greater numbers before cutting us to pieces. Above, the gallery was dark and I imagined a score of crossbowmen hiding up there, crouched with their bows ready.

I nudged Rob and nodded at the gallery. "Use the door and find a way up that gallery. If it is clear, keep watch on us with your bow. If not, raise the alarm. Walt, go with him."

They slipped across the hall and through the door.

As my men left, the captain at arms stepped up to the base of the Marshal's dais, pulled off his armet and lifted his chin before raising his voice so that it echoed even from the shadowed timbers of the ceiling far above.

"My name is Jean Labbe, Captain of Arms for Jean V, the Duke of Brittany. I come to deliver this warrant to you, my lord."

He glanced behind him and beckoned Stephen forward.

Stephen wore only robes and was practically unarmed and so when he stepped in front to become the foremost of our party, I was unsurprised to hear his voice wavering slightly as he spoke. Still, his voice was clear and loud and none in the hall would have missed a word.

"We, Jean Labbe, captain, acting in the name of my lord Jean V, the Duke of Brittany, and Stephen le Viel, lawyer, acting in the name of Jean de Malestroit the Bishop of Nantes, do hereby enjoin upon Gilles, Comte de Brienne, Lord of Tiffauges, Machecoul, Pouzages, and so on, the Baron de Rais, Marshal of France, and Lieutenant-General of Brittany, to grant us immediate access to his castle, whichever castle that may be, and to surrender himself to us as prisoner so that he may answer according to due process of the law to the triple charge of murder, and of witchcraft, and of sodomy, which is laid against him this day, the thirteenth of September in the year 1440, by the order of the Duke of Brittany and the Bishop of Nantes."

Stephen's voice echoed in the silent chamber.

All eyes were on Gilles de Rais. This man had been committing his crimes for years. Many of them in my company had friends or family who had lost sons or daughters. But still, it had only ever been whispered of in the darkness, about kitchen tables after children were abed, and in the dark corners of alehouses. All those who whispered had known that the Marshal was beyond the reach of the law. It did not apply to such men. The distance was too great between the ordinary folk and the lords above them. Only when one lord crossed another, or acted against the king, would they find themselves in trouble.

But there it was. The long-awaited warrant read aloud in the demon's presence, and the crimes named not in the darkness but in the full light of day.

The Marshal seemed to hardly react at all. I seemed to detect a small sagging in his stance, as if he had breathed all the air from his chest and but had not yet decided to breathe in once more.

Beside and behind him, however, the servants reacted. The priest, Blanchet, crossed himself repeatedly and prayed under his breath. Prelati the Florentine alchemist held his hands up to God as if beseeching him directly and personally, wailing softly in his mother tongue and in Latin. His Italian theatrics were quite repellent in their falsity. The scrawny monster Poitou sneered at me, glaring at me out of everyone in the crowd, because he knew that I was the main instrument in his destruction. His fingers grazed the dagger at his hip and I watched, ready in case he decided to throw it at me. Henriet hugged his arms about his fat body and rubbed himself up and down, as if trying to comfort his flesh.

"I deny the charges," the Marshal said smoothly, his eyes narrowing.

"Of course you do, my lord," Stephen replied, looking up at him. "And you may defend yourself against them in court."

Gilles grinned at him before looking up and fixing me with the full force of his gaze. "I knew you would come for me again, one day. I knew it. And now it is that day. The day that I have imagined. For many years, I feared you would creep into my chamber and slit my throat as I slept, or perhaps you and your companions would assault me as I travelled or besiege my castles. Never did I imagine this." He laughed. "Writs and warrants? Surely, all this does not become the likes of you, sir."

The men in the hall were confused and I am sure that they assumed the Marshal was speaking to Stephen or to Captain

Labbe.

"I only wish I had come sooner," I said, drawing surprised looks from everyone in the hall. "And seen to your end before all this."

"A shame for you, then, that I shall be free and safe once more," the Marshal said. "In time."

We stared at him, all of us confused by his mad confidence.

"Surely, my lord Marshal," I said, "you understand that this warrant spells your imminent death? You are to be taken into custody and then you shall stand trial for your crimes and they are crimes that you cannot escape from, even if you deny them. No, you cannot wriggle free of this, sir. Not for all your wealth."

He grinned again, pulling the pale skin of his face tight over the bones of his skull. "You have no conception of my rights as Marshal of France. The King himself will intervene to free me, by his command. Oh, you shall see it happen, sir, yes you shall. You know, do you not, that the Duke and his cousin the Bishop, stand in opposition to our King, who loves me dearly?"

I was astonished and felt a knot of disquiet forming in my guts. The politics of the French court were a special kind of insanity and for all I knew, he spoke the truth and the King of France would personally ride in and free his beloved Marshal with his own hand.

But we had a duty to perform and I said as much. "Even if all that you say is true, my lord, you shall still come with us, now."

"Shall I, indeed?"

I could not help but glance up to the gallery. To my relief, I saw Rob and Walt's faces up there, looking down. I always felt better knowing Rob's bow was in his hand.

"Us, is it?" the Marshal said, a knowing smile on his face. "You say us, as if you yourself have not engineered this entire sham."

The Duke's and the Bishop's men looked at me in even more confusion.

"You have it wrong," I replied. "It is no sham. The lords and the people of this land have long recognised you as a monster and finally they have moved to end your crimes. I have done nothing but facilitate them and am here now to protect these men, should you, in your madness, decide to resist by force."

"Ha!" he cried, dramatically throwing his hands into the air. Many of the men flinched. "And you would stop me, would you?"

"You know that I would," I replied.

And yet, I was far from certain. The Marshal was certainly quite ancient himself, having survived two centuries or more as an immortal and had clearly been gorging himself on far more blood than I had in that time. His strength could have been greater than mine, and he was an experienced soldier and a knight. He had defeated me once before, when he commanded the forces that had slaughtered mine.

"If you are so strong, sir," he said, smiling a knowing smile, "then why did you not save your people when you had the chance? Did you men know that there is an Englishman in your midst? They all are. All of his men, also. As English as King Henry."

"Nonsense," I said, not daring to catch the eye of Captain Labbe or the others. "We are Normans. Now, hand over your sword to the Captain, give yourself up into his custody, and let us be done with this."

"Me alone?" he spoke lightly, as if it were a small thing. But he seemed tense as he waited for the response.

Stephen spoke up. "The warrant names also as your accomplices Etienne Corrillaut the one they call Poitou, Henriet Griart, Prelati the Florentine, and Dominus Eustache Blanchet. Also, the woman they call La Meffraye."

Casually, he nodded, and yet it was as though that great tension had gone out of him. "Oh, very well. If you insist." Sighing, as if it were little more than an irritation, he unbuckled his sword and held it so that Captain Labbe could take the hilt. I expected the Marshal to suddenly spin it about, whip the blade free, and begin cutting his way through the mortals. Or still I was ready for the hidden soldiers of his army to descend upon us from all sides and so free their master.

But the sword was taken.

Gilles stepped down from the dais and Captain Labbe's soldiers surrounded him, ready to escort him from his own hall. I could imagine the sense of unreality that those soldiers felt. It was unheard of, literally an unknown event, for commoners to arrest a noble of anything like the Marshal's standing. He was a great baron and rich beyond any commoner's conception. For all Stephen's whining over the years that the common folk needed the legal means to challenge their overlords, in his heart every man knows the powerful are supposed to rule over the weak and to witness something different is to see the natural order being undone before one's very eyes. The profundity of the moment seized every soul present, of that I am certain.

Up at the top of the hall, the Marshal's men became greatly

anguished and Henriet and Poitou, I am sure, strained to resist their arrest. They could certainly have killed the bailiffs, if they chose. A handful of them, at least. Perhaps they feared me and my men and knew they would ultimately fail. Or perhaps some other reason stayed their hands.

Henriet, eyes darting around the room, jerked into action and cried out.

"I cannot, my lord! I cannot do it! Forgive me!"

Even as he spoke, he drew his knife and began to saw at his own throat. I was already rushing forward before he acted and managed to grasp his wrist and pull his hand away from his throat so that only a little blood was spilled and before he was able to cut through the great veins. He was stronger than any normal man, of course, but I was stronger still. As I held him, the bailiffs prised the blade from his hand before he could do himself mortal damage. We clapped the irons on him while he wept in despair.

"Why did you stop him?" Rob muttered, coming down with Walt as the bailiffs rounded all the Marshal's servants up and prepared them for the journey.

Walt nudged Rob in the ribs. "You want him to get tortured to death, that's it, ain't it, Richard?"

Rob ignored him and looked at me strangely. "Are you perhaps not taking this legal approach a little too far?"

Why had I stopped his attempt at self-murder? Partly, yes, I wanted him to suffer before he died but there was something else nagging at me. His cry to his master that he could not do it. Clearly, he meant that he could not give himself up but the way he spoke it, intoned the word it, seemed to suggest it was something he and the Marshal had discussed before our appearance. Had Henriet agreed to give himself up peacefully, only to give in to despair? Or was there something more to it? Was there something else he had promised?

"I want him to confess, that is all," I said. "And so condemn his master with his words. He cannot do that if he is dead."

"As long as he dies eventually," Rob said.

We took them all back to Nantes where they were to be tried. All the lands we rode through belonged to the Marshal. Every field, every village, tree, and beast were his. His lands stretched for miles beyond the horizon to the east and to the west and brought him vast incomes that made him fabulously rich. Yet, he had not fought to protect them. There were over a hundred soldiers in his private army and yet he had not used them. In fact, he had perhaps even dismissed them from his service. Why had he given himself up?

He sat straight-backed in his saddle, wrapped in his gorgeous sable cloak with his head held high beneath his hat, as if he were simply out for a ride. As if he were perfectly content with his life and with where he was in that moment.

I felt that disquiet again, that I was missing something obvious, something before my eyes and yet I had not the wit to make note of it.

But were his actions so suspicious? Very little he had done for some time made any sense, so it seemed likely that the man had simply lost his mind and could not accept that he would soon hang for his crimes.

Either way, I was sure, riding behind the arrested men in grim silence, that it was over. That not the King nor God Himself could now save Gilles de Rais from his fate.

He was the man responsible for our defeats nine years before, at Orléans, but soon I would make amends.

12

Siege of Orléans

May 1429

WE HAD NO IDEA OF THE DANGER we were in. After Joan came to the city of Orléans in April 1429, we still thought it was laughable. There was some nonsensical old myth, some confused prophecy, that said a maiden would drive away the enemies of France. It seemed to be utter nonsense.

Inside Orléans, Joan acted like a holy woman or even like royalty, parading herself around the streets of the city handing out food to the people as if she had arranged and brought it herself, rather than simply accompanied a convoy that was coming anyway. But the people did not care. And the garrison received their long-awaited salaries that the King had sent. But Joan, with her natural cunning, made sure they believed that it was her who had been responsible for the issuing of the coins.

She began sending messengers to each of our forts, demanding our departure. These messengers were cursed and jeered by all. Some of the commanders of the forts threatened to kill the messengers, accusing them of being emissaries of a witch, and they were driven off.

Unbeknownst to us at the time, Joan was even engaging in discussions of tactics with the lords in Orléans. According to what I heard later, she urged nothing but direct and immediate assaults on all of our forts, one after the other or even all at once. Those commanders would not hear of it. The French had not properly attacked the English for decades and they were afraid to do so. Most had never participated in an assault. Their most recent attempt, at the Battle of the Herrings, had once again resulted in their defeat. They knew, in their bones, that attacking the English, when we were prepared and ready, with stakes and archers, would always end in failure. It had been that way since Crecy, since Poitiers, since Agincourt.

And yet, somehow, Joan's utter conviction was infecting even those weak men. Her assertion was that all the French had to do was try an assault to be successful. Her madness poured out of her and into them.

One of the commanders left the city in the night and ran for the forest, along with a sizable bodyguard. They were spotted and I was ordered by Talbot to chase after him and to stop him. I took Rob, Walt, and a score of other veterans on good horses and with spares and set off. We tracked them down river toward Blois, but they had too long a lead and we could not catch them before they reached the city.

When we returned, I discovered that the Maiden had come out of the city and personally surveyed our fortifications.

"She was dressed in full harness!" the men told me. "Shining polished armour, all over. Like a man!"

"What did she look like?" I asked them.

"Ah, she was hideous," Old Simon assured me. "Like a deformed dwarf, she was."

"You are mad!" another said. "She was tall, with long, flowing blonde hair."

"She wore a cap the entire time," another man said, cursing the others for their ignorance. "But one could see she was a great beauty."

Half the men howled in derision.

"Nonsense," Old Simon roared. "She was pinched in the face, with a turned-up nose like a fat skeleton."

None of us could understand it and Walt and Rob put it down to the typical ignorance and argumentative nature of the English soldier on a long campaign. But I felt some disquiet. How could they have seen such different things? It hinted to me of some vague unnaturalness. Perhaps, I thought, she was a witch after all. And I was not the only one.

Seeking clarification, something solid I could cling to, I asked Talbot what she had looked like, seeing as he had exchanged shouted words with her over the palisades.

"What do you care what the witch looks like?" Talbot snapped when I asked him. "Who are you to ask me such a thing? Mind your duties, man, or I will have you shipped back to England in chains!"

I knew he did not like me and was threatened by my expertise, but I was shocked by his open hostility.

Rob attempted to explain it. "You don't know your place, Richard." He hurried on, when he saw my expression. "That is, your place as he sees it. You have no lofty position here, you are merely a lowly captain with a handful of men. You have no land, no income. And so the likes of Lord Talbot ain't ever going to listen to you."

Walt gestured at me with the nub end of a loaf of dry bread. "And you scare the wits out of most men, sir. Give men the jitters, so you do. You have a right nasty look in your eye, half the time."

"I do not," I said, offended. "I am the most civil man in the world."

They glanced at each other and said nothing.

A couple of days later, our scouts rushed in to warn us that a reinforcement convoy was coming up from Blois in the southwest. And somehow, there were other convoys converging on us from Montargis and Gien. It was early in the morning of the 4th May when the Blois convoy approached on the north side of the city, close to the fort of St. Laurent.

"We must meet them," I urged Talbot. "Form up and stop them outside the fort."

"Be silent," Talbot snapped. "Someone silence that man, there!"

No one moved to silence me but I held my tongue for a moment while Talbot stared out at the enemy forces.

"They are too many," he said. "If we pull men out from the

forts, the garrison in the city will rush out and take us at the rear."

I suppose it was a sensible precaution. But war is not a sensible business. It cannot be undertaken successfully without taking risks. Talbot was more afeared of losing the forts than he was of allowing the enemy to go unchallenged in their approach of the city.

The best commanders understand that battles are won in men's minds as well as in the force of arms. More so, in my experience, and as the English would soon discover. Sadly, Talbot was not one of the best commanders. And as we stood down and watched the French reinforcements riding between our forts and heading into the city, I saw her for the first time.

For Joan the Maiden rode out to escort the convoy in.

She seemed small to me, although she was mounted on an enormous destrier. She wore a helm with a closed visor and held aloft a great banner flapping and snapping in the wind overhead. That banner was one I would come to know and to hate by sight. A great white banner sprinkled with fleur-de-lys all over. On one side was depicted the figure of Our Lord in Glory, holding the world and giving His benediction to a lily, held by one of two angels kneeling on each side with the words Jesus Maria besides. On the other side of the banner was the figure of Our Lady and a shield with the arms of France supported by two angels.

But that day, Joan and her banner were far away and hidden, on and off, by the mass of men around her.

"She ain't all that," Walt observed. "They just strapped a harness around some little harlot from Lorraine. She ain't even got a weapon, has she, what's she going to do with that banner?"

"Her presence is the weapon," I said, seeing how the French soldiers swarmed her and cheered her very presence.

"Eh?" Walt asked. "How's that then?"

I said nothing in reply as the enemy paraded in through the walls to Orléans, cheering and singing.

Watching Talbot, he seemed pleased to have avoided a battle but he was too ignorant to know he had just suffered a defeat. And it would not be the last suffered that day.

∞

It was no later than midday when the enemy launched an assault on the fort of St. Loup. That was the most easterly and the most isolated of all of our forts. The fort was there to ward against supplies arriving from the east by land and by river and that was the exact reason the French decided to take it.

Provisions convoys were coming from that direction and our four hundred men in the fort there would have stopped them.

Defending is all very well, and it makes men feel secure and it is simple for less experienced troops to know what to do.

But in such a siege situation, where our forces were divided into groups, it was possible for the enemy to overwhelm a single defence point. Talbot and the other commanders were complacent but they were not incompetent. Most of the forts on the north bank of the river were close enough to support each other and St. Loup was the only fort that was too far to receive such reinforcement.

And so our four hundred men in St. Loup found themselves suddenly assaulted by almost two thousand French soldiers.

"We must relieve them," I shouted at Talbot, who seemed stunned by the moment. Fastolf was speaking in his ear and he turned on me as I approached.

"Be quiet," Fastolf snapped. "Of course we must. But we cannot risk the other forts falling."

"Risk?" I said to Fastolf. "This is an opportunity, sir. Look at them, out the walls. Their backs are to us. Mount the cavalry, pin them in place, and bring up the men on foot."

"Do not think to teach me my business," Fastolf snapped. "You are not in possession of the facts." He pointed at the attack. "Our scouts tell us that French reinforcements are converging on St. Loup from the east, coming in from Montargis and Gien. It is our garrison who are pinned in place."

"That is grim news indeed, sir. But all the more reason for us to commit now."

Fastolf chewed his lip and looked to Talbot, who was in command. "My lord?"

I held my breath.

"Send word. Order the garrison of Paris to attack the French."

When he said Paris, he was using the vernacular name for the fort of Saint Pouair which was the closest to St. Loup.

"Is that it?" I blurted out. "One garrison? My lord, if we bring out every garrison, we can wipe out the French and end the siege by the end of the day!"

"Remove yourself from my presence, sir. If you wish to throw your life away, feel free to charge headlong into death."

I pulled my helm on my head and shouted at Talbot. "It will not be the first time!"

With Walt and Rob and a few brave souls who felt as we did, we rode out of St. Laurent around to the northeast to join the garrison. In truth, it was hopeless. In the wasteland north of the city, we three hundred men assaulted two thousand French.

And we were thrown back. Again and again. At one point we came close to coming around their flank to the north but a sortie from the French blocked us.

By nightfall, St. Loup fell.

We lost a hundred and fifty soldiers and forty were taken prisoner. Some of the English defenders of St. Loup were captured in the ruins of a nearby church. The rumour was that their lives were only spared at the saintly Joan's request. The thought made me sick to my stomach.

When St. Loup fell, our purpose for assaulting them was over and so we retired our northern assault and trudged back into our forts as night fell. It was not an unrecoverable failure but already I sensed the momentum turning in favour of the French.

"We must take the fort back," I said to my men. "Take it tonight. Or at first light. Before it is too late."

"You reckon Talbot will listen?" Rob asked.

I slumped. "No."

The next day, there was no French attack. Whether it was the fact it was the Feast of the Ascension or if they needed to rest their men after the assault the day before, they took no action. It was the perfect opportunity for us to regain the initiative.

Instead, we sat in our forts and fretted.

In the morning, the French crossed the river from Orléans on boats and barges and by a makeshift pontoon bridge. I watched from the north bank along with hundreds of others. They came out in a great mass of soldiers and armed citizenry but of course our garrisons on the south bank were waiting for them. It was a hard-fought struggle and the French were forced back.

Joan was wounded in the counter-attack. Panic set in amongst the French and they retreated back to the river, dragging Joan back with them. Seeing the witch on the run and her spell broken, our garrison burst out to give chase as the men fled.

I did not see what happened next because the city walls hid the events from us but we all heard the story soon after. With the French in full flight, Joan, at the rear, stopped. Standing completely alone as hundreds of furious English soldiers charged her, she turned around on them, raised her holy standard, stamped the foot of the pole upon the earth and cried out.

"In the name of God!"

For some reason, this was enough to check the English pursuit. Why they did this is difficult to understand and many said that she used magic on them, either from her spell or by some magic inherent to her person. Whatever the reason and whatever really happened, it was enough to send the English back to the safety of our fort on the south bank and the fleeing French troops turned around and rallied about her.

At her side through it all, Gilles de Rais persuaded Joan to immediately resume the assault which he led in person.

His military brilliance with Joan the Maiden providing the inspiration, their attack carried the day.

With the Augustins fort in French hands, our Tourelle's garrison was blockaded. That same night, what remained of our garrison at St. Privé evacuated their outwork and went north of the river to join our strongest garrison, where I was, in St. Laurent. The last garrison on the south bank Glasdale was therefore isolated but there were eight hundred good men ready to throw back whatever came their way.

Despite her wound, Joan rallied the cities within the city and they joined the attack the next day. They bombarded our men for all hours and attempted to undermine the walls of the fort and setting fire to whatever they could. And still our experienced men were unconcerned.

All of a sudden, La Pucelle appeared with her great white banner held aloft and charged the front walls of our fort herself. As she charged by the cowering French soldiers, she grabbed a ladder and threw it up against the wall, calling out to them as she went.

"All is yours! Go in! Go in!"

The French were much stirred in their hearts and they rushed in after her, throwing up dozens of ladders to storm the walls alongside her.

One of our brave archers shot Joan with an arrow.

She was spitted between the neck and shoulder with a yard-long, thumb-thick arrow with its wicked iron point. She was thrown down from the wall and carried away. Our men knew they had won when the French assault faltered and fell back. Everyone knew that such a wound was fatal. There was no way that a man could survive such a terrible blow and the word quickly spread, even across the river, that Joan the Maiden was dead.

We celebrated in every fort and felt that the tide had turned back in our favour.

And then she emerged from the city. She was walking, leaning on her companion Gilles de Rais.

"Take heart, good soldiers of France," she called out. "Take heart and feel good cheer, for God knows that a final assault will carry the day."

We heard the cheering from a mile away and they renewed their attack like the Devil himself was at their heels. Our men fled and the fort, burning all over, fell just before night came.

It was a true disaster. In all the assaults, we had lost a thousand men and six hundred had been taken prisoner. With the south bank of the Loire lost, there was no point in holding the north bank because the city could be resupplied from the south until Judgement Day.

And so, just a week after Joan's arrival, the siege was over.

Lord John Talbot ordered us to demolish our forts and siege works and we drew up our army.

The French came out and drew up before us to the west of the city.

"Attack," I urged Talbot and the other commanders. "We can undo all that has been done if we just attack them. Our soldiers are better than theirs."

Talbot's eyes were fixed on the white banner of Joan the Maiden.

"They will attack us," Walt said. "Look at them. Roaring for it."

For a time, it seemed as though he was right but in the end they simply stood watching us for an hour and Talbot ordered us to retreat. The enemy were so close, I was certain they would fall upon our rear and rip us to pieces. But they were still afraid of us and they let us slink away.

The last thing I saw before I rode over the hill through the trees was Joan's banner flying over the massed French army.

Beside hers flew the golden and black banner of Gilles de Rais, but I thought nothing of that at the time. It was just one more banner amongst dozens.

It need not have meant the end of the English war on the French but their aggressive use of artillery and frontal assaults influenced French tactics for the rest of the conflict.

Joan and Gilles were far from done with us.

13

The Trial Begins
September 1440

THE TRIAL BEGAN IN THE GREAT HALL of the castle, arranged carefully to conduct a tribunal. What a grand hall it was, with enormous, modern windows with glass panes so that the lofty interior was filled with light all the way to the rafters and beautifully carved ceiling high above.

At the head of the hall on a high dais almost the width of the hall, was the chief officiating judge, the Bishop of Nantes in his purple robes. Directly behind him and above him, on a table covered in white cloth, was a great, golden crucifix, encrusted with rubies and emeralds and sapphires. Beside the Bishop of Nantes were his fellow assessors, the Bishops of Le Mans, Saint Brieuc, and Saint-Lo, along with the Chief Inquisitor of Nantes and other assessors I did not know. Serving them and the court were the typical functionaries in their gowns and caps, hunched over their tables with quill in hand to record every word spoken during the proceedings.

Also there, at one side of the hall below the judges, was the public prosecutor in his gown, my dear comrade Stephen Gosset, going by the name Stephen le Viel. He appeared composed but I knew him well enough to know by the set of his head and the way he held his shoulders that he was nervous. And why would he not be? For the hall was filled with members of the public, many of them the families of the victims of Gilles de Rais.

On the opposite side of the hall to Stephen, was the witness stand and beside it a huge iron cage with a bench along the rear. Empty, for the time being.

And between the judges and the public, also empty, was the huge chair reserved for the accused himself. He would be seated with his back to the public, facing the Bishops.

I sat near to Stephen, at the front of the public gallery, where I would be able to look across and see the side of the Marshal's face during his trial. I wondered how long it would take for the tales of the blood drinking to come out. My men, including Stephen, fretted somewhat that our secrets would be revealed yet I was not concerned. No one would believe in the blood magic and instead it would serve only to emphasise the satanic nature of the crimes and the men who committed them. Whatever accusations Gilles made against me and my men, we could throw off, I was sure of it and Stephen was prepared with clever responses.

The Marshal had been provided with a small suite of rooms in the castle of Nantes where he was awarded all the customary privileges of a nobleman who had yet to be proved guilty of any crime. It was disgusting, of course, but that was simply the way it was and there was no chance of having him clapped in irons in a dank dungeon cell.

"Do you reckon they'll declare him innocent in the end?" Walt had said, on hearing that the Marshal was held in such comfort.

"Of course not," I replied. "Already they have an enormous amount of evidence and the Inquisitors will obtain more from the servants. Do not concern yourself."

But I was concerned. I told myself that, if the people of his lands were denied proper legal justice, I would simply find Gilles de Rais and cut off his head. The same went for his servants, those that were revenants and perhaps even those who were not. Though they were guarded by soldiers of the Duke and the Bishop, I was sure I would be able to find a way.

In many ways of course I would have preferred to do the deed myself but it was important that I stay my hand unless there was no other choice. There were thousands of good men and women, fathers and mothers, brothers and sisters, who needed to watch their master hang before them for the monstrous evil he had done to them if they were to have any hope of satisfaction. I knew this because they told me. They had come to see the trial in their hundreds, from miles all around, and the inns of Nantes were full to bursting and I met with them before the trial

"I got to see him hang," some said. "With my own eyes."

Others had similar reasons. "And he needs to see us before he dies. To know it was us what did for him."

"He must burn," others replied. "Burn and be destroyed so that come what may he has no body to use on the Day of Judgement."

For their sakes, I hoped the trial would prove swift and satisfying.

Certainly, I had high hopes, for the Inquisitor of Nantes would personally apply their tried and tested methods to extract the necessary confessions from the accused persons.

Back in 1252, Pope Innocent had issued a papal bull authorising torture for the express purpose of obtaining a confession. The accused was first threatened with torture in the hope and expectation that the threat itself would elicit a confession. And it certainly was enough for many people, as I have often found in far less formal and less legal circumstances. If the threats failed, the Inquisitors would bring the accused to the torture chamber and show them the instruments to be used. It was oftentimes at this moment that the accused would decide to speak and in practice, many in the Inquisition moved immediately to this step because it was more efficient that way.

"Men are afraid of pain," I said to Stephen as we watched the Inquisitors preparing their assigned room in Nantes while the tribunals were likewise being set up in the halls. "It is a simple thing to frighten them into speaking to avoid it."

"Oh, no," Stephen said. "That is not it at all, Richard. It is far more deeply and accurately reasoned that that."

I sighed. "I suppose I would have to spend years in Paris

listening to doctors of theology explain it to me before I could hope to understand."

"No, no, it is perfectly straightforward. You see, the Inquisition knows that deception, the lies themselves reside in our tongues but the truth lives within the flesh. It is the body that is required to be examined in order to extract the truth from it. Lies, spoken by free tongues, are ephemeral and meaningless. Flesh and blood, however, cannot be denied."

"I suppose so," I allowed. "Still, these Inquisitors must enjoy hurting people."

"In fact they often do not need to touch a person at all. And when they do, it is done with the utmost reason and care. They inflict pain only to draw out the truth, nothing more."

"Come, Stephen," I said, lowering my voice lest they overhear me, "look at them. I have seen men with eyes like that in every army I have fought in and against. They love twisting the knife."

"You see a man like that every time you look in a mirror, you mean," he said, tutting. "They are learned men, practising the application of perfectly clear reasoning. Only through torture can we satisfy the demand for truth because it is so deeply hidden in the flesh. Hidden so deeply that the accused may not even be aware of it until it is drawn out. And how can truth be drawn from flesh, like water drawn from a well, or like a knife drawn from flesh? Pain, Richard. Pain is the conduit for truth, as I am sure you well know. It is distillation of the pure substance, that is to say truth itself which is another way of saying nature itself or God, if you like, lodged in the impure flesh. Pain betrays the truth by exposing it to view through the sounds and gestures it produces. Pain causes the accused to speak involuntarily, without his own volition, and so what emerges is uncorrupted by the lies of the tongue and the wits of a man."

"I am no expert of course but this theoretical complexity has the whiff of the alchemical, do you not think it so?"

"No, I do not think it so."

However, seeing the Inquisitors at their business, it was clear enough that the ones before us at least took no joy in their work. It was simply that. Work.

While they began to organise the evidence, the trial itself was begun.

Rather, it was two trials, running in concert with one another. The ecumenical tribunal was presided over by the Bishop of Nantes, and the civil court was presided over by Chief Justice Pierre de l'Hospital, Chancellor of Brittany. The Bishop's court would try the man Gilles de Rais for satanism, heresy, unnatural vice, sacrilege, and the violation of ecclesiastical privilege. The civil tribunal would deal with the charges of murder and of rebellion against the authority of the Baron's liege lord, Jean V the Duke of Brittany. Although one might assume the civil court would have precedence due to the utmost seriousness of the crimes of murder and rebellion, in fact it was the ecclesiastical court that would lead matters. For one thing, it was under the Bishop's authority that most of the investigations had taken place, led by Stephen's guile and my rather brute force approach. And for another, what more serious crime could there be in Heaven and earth than heresy?

"Are you well prepared, Stephen?" I asked him, while the hall was filling with officers of the court and members of the public. It was noisy with talk and the scuffing of feet. Stephen sat at his table to one side of the hall near to the front. "Chief Prosecutor, eh?" I said to him. "The Bishop certainly has faith in you."

Stephen sniffed. "As well he might, sir. I have prepared the arguments carefully and have full confidence in them."

"Then why do you look so nervous?" I asked, grinning.

"I am not nervous, Richard," he said, primly. "I am merely concentrating on my arguments regarding the charge of sodomy."

"Why?" I laughed. "Briqueville stated he witnessed the acts himself. Many acts, in fact."

He lowered his voice and leaned in. "That is just it. We cannot enter Briqueville's statements into the record of evidence. He confessed fully only on those terms and the terms are being agreed to due to the fact that he's a damned noble."

"Barely," I scoffed. "But what does it matter? You can skewer him with the charge of heresy alone."

He ignored me and muttered almost to himself. "We can but hope the other servants confess to this charge also. Only then will his conviction in the ecclesiastical tribunal be unquestionable."

"Surely, you cannot mean that sodomy is a greater crime than witchcraft? Than heresy?"

"Well," Stephen said. "Sodomy is a form of heresy, in the eyes of the Church. Perhaps the greatest form."

"What nonsense."

He tilted his head. "Why do you think it is a crime at all?"

"Well," I said. "It is unnatural, I suppose. Not that it stops men who feel compelled to do the deed."

Stephen all-but wagged a finger at me. "No one is compelled to sin. We each make the choice of whether to sin or not."

I sighed. "You have never been on campaign, have you, Stephen. There is often a man or two out of every hundred who do not mind sharing a bedroll and who venture alone together into the woods every once in a while. No harm in it, truth be told, as long as it does not interfere with a man's duty."

"How can you say such a thing?"

I was surprised at his vehemence, especially as I had often wondered whether Stephen engaged in an occasional sodomising himself. He liked women, that much I knew, but there was always the whiff of the degenerate about him.

"Come, Stephen, you are not innocent of these matters. You were a monk, for God's sake. Half the lads in the priory are there because they prefer the warmth of a hairy backside to the smoothness of a woman."

"How can you joke about such things? The law is very clear. Sodomy is a deliberate sin against God. It is an act of defiance against God's law. An act of rebellion, if you will, even more serious than rebellion against one's earthly lord."

"And yet all sins are acts against God, are they not?" I was proud of myself for recalling that one from my youth. I had such lessons beaten into me quite thoroughly.

"Yes, yes, but this base self-gratification is against Nature itself. It is wholly avoidable and so it is especially malicious. You see, a man's soul and his body are provided by God and so both are inherently good, as God is. But of course because of original sin, our bodies are also corrupted to one extent or another, and it is these lower, base parts that drag the goodness of our souls down to Hell. And it is our soul that restrains our base urges and leads us to salvation. And so the act is a sin against Nature and also a sin against the grace of God. There is no act which is so sinful, so against God, than sodomy."

"Not even murder?"

"Well," Stephen said, shifting in his seat. "It would be a bad Christian who considers a crime against the soul as lesser than a crime against the body, would it not?"

Exasperated, I sighed. "I do not know, Stephen. It seems to me that you can apply too much reason by far to such things. Of course murder is worse than arse thumping, man. What are you talking about? You have spent too much time at the college of the Sorbonne, that is what I think. You need to get back to the depravity of London, where you belong." I shook my head in wonder at his holy nonsense.

It was not that I necessarily disagreed with him but one does not need reason to know whether something is right or wrong. We feel the truth of it in our guts and then afterwards apply reason to one degree or another in order to justify our feelings. And for all their clever words and arguments, all moral philosophy is no more than this. Whether they be noble and courageous as Socrates and Nietzsche, or depraved and deluded as Sartre and Marx, their life's work is simply the elucidation of and justification for feelings that emerged unbidden and uncontrolled from their guts, heart, and balls.

Stephen frowned. "If only you would consider continuing your formal education, Richard. It might serve to help our greater cause if you were able to understand the nuances of—"

I was about to explain the nuances of my fist to his face when the crowd's hubbub grew suddenly in volume and emotion and I turned to see the Marshal's servants being led into the iron cage by the witness stand.

The priest Blanchet, the alchemist Prelati, and the two revenants, Poitou and Henriet. Both of these last two looked very ill indeed. Green and pale in complexion, and weak and gaunt. The lack of blood was turning them into beasts. I wondered if they would turn on the mortal priests inside the cage and savage them in full view of everyone, bishops and butchers both.

What a noise the people made. First one man shouted a curse, and then more began jeering and calling down the fury and the hand of God, until the place was in an uproar. The Bishop ordered them to be quiet and had the court bailiffs march into the public galleries and threaten and shove the people down.

"I will have silence or I will have every one of you removed for the duration of the trial!" the Bishop said, in a surprisingly powerful voice that echoed down from the ceiling, as if the Lord Himself had spoken.

The fear of missing the tribunal drove them to control themselves.

I wondered how they would react when the Marshal was brought in.

"Call the accused to appear before us," the Bishop said to the Clerk of the Court.

"Call Messire Gilles de Rais to appear before the court!" cried out the Clerk.

And the public, rising in a great wave, muttered and cried out and then roared, as the Marshal himself marched in from the side of the hall with four soldiers escorting him. He was dressed in red and black velvet, with red velvet boots and a red silk sash across his body. Though the crowd were baying for his blood, he did not so much as glance their way and instead wore a small smirk on his face as he stopped in front of his ornate chair and turned to the array of bishops, thus showing his back to the audience.

The Clerk was shouting down the public and the bailiffs were shoving the crowd back. The Bishop raised his hand and the thunderous look on his face was enough to remind them of his earlier threat to expel the lot of them and they managed to calm down.

When it was quieter, the Bishop of Nantes nodded to Stephen who got to his feet and cleared his throat. A hush descended and it seemed as though everyone stopped breathing, or perhaps that was me alone.

"Thank you, Milord Bishop. If it pleases the court, I shall now read the charges against the accused and enter them into record. Messire Gilles de Rais is indicted for witchcraft, sodomy, and heresy." He crossed the hall and handed a sheath of parchment to the Bishop and moved back to his place.

"Messire de Rais," the Bishop said. "Have you anything to say in response to the grave charges levelled against you in this court?"

The Marshal bowed low before standing upright and thrusting forward his chin. "I have full confidence that I shall unequivocally prove my perfect innocence to the court in no time at all."

Behind me, the public growled at the preposterousness of his statement and no doubt many were shocked at the brazenness of the lie that he was innocent.

The Bishop sighed, for his life would have been much the easier if the Marshal had crumbled and admitted his guilt but of course that was hardly expected. "No doubt, Messire de Rais, you will therefore require the services of a counsel for your defence of these charges?"

Gilles grinned. "Oh, no, my lord. Why would an innocent man need to rely on a lawyer's tricks when the simple truth will do perfectly well?" This drew hisses and noises of revulsion. The smirk on his face only grew. It dawned on me that the Marshal knew he was doomed and was simply enjoying tormenting and outraging the public behind him. "You see, my lord, I am a perfect Christian in every regard. A perfect Christian, I say, and nothing will give me greater joy than to prove this to the court."

The crowd surged forward and someone threw a fist-sized hunk of cheese at the Marshal, which missed, and then from another angle came a walking stick, hurled with considerable force. It clanged off the back of the Marshal's ornate chair and clattered along the floor.

The public were soon cleared from the court by the bailiffs and though they were mad with anger, they were still rightly afraid of the Bishop, who was only a couple of steps removed from God Himself.

"Because the charges include heresy," the Bishop said when they were gone, "I must seek assistance from a representative of the Holy Office in determining the truth of this case. Therefore, I will formally request the services of the Inquisition."

The Chief Inquisitor nodded. "Yes, Milord Bishop. Messire de Rais will be brought before the Inquisition."

I watched the Marshal as his sardonic grin fell from his face. He swallowed, as if a great stone had appeared at the back of his throat.

"Let it be thus recorded," intoned the Bishop, "that Messire de Rais will appear before the Inquisitor of Nantes of the Dominican Order. Oh, I should say that the accused has the right to object to this, if you do so wish, my lord?"

The Marshal forced the grin back onto his face. "Object? Why should I object, my lord? As I am entirely innocent of the charges, why, I welcome the questions of the good brothers of the Inquisition." He swallowed again.

"Very well," the Bishop said. "Now, you have the opportunity to name your enemies. For we shall summon witnesses to testify and so you may register with the court those who would have cause to do you harm with their words."

At this, the Marshal faltered. No doubt, he sensed that he was in some sort of legal danger in that moment but he did not have the understanding of the procedure to head it off. If he had but taken counsel, they would have told him to name each and every one of his servants that he could, and also to name every one of his subjects. For then their testimonies would be formally doubted by the court. But Gilles merely grinned and attempted to bluff his way through with the mad assertion that he was innocent.

"But, Milord Bishop, I have no enemies to name." The Marshal frowned and cleared his throat. "Except, there is one who has betrayed me. A knight in my service, and a friend, who I fear has quite gone mad and fled from me some days ago. I know not to what ends his actions were taken but I fear he means me no good. His name is Roger de Briqueville."

I swore under my breath. By so naming the man, the Marshal had ruled out the secret testimony already sworn. The testimony that had spoken of murder, sorcery and demon-summoning, or heresy and sodomy. The testimony that the charges themselves were based on.

The Bishop's face fell. "Very well. The name shall be entered into the record that the testimony of Roger de Briqueville will be understood to be recusationes divinatrices, and any such testimony will be treated with the gravest suspicion of prejudice. We shall now adjourn this meeting to allow other witnesses to be heard."

At this, the Marshal turned and looked directly at me with a glint in his eye for a long moment before he was escorted out.

"I suppose this means I will have to find a way into his chamber after all," I said to Stephen as the bishops filed out. "I should have done so when first we came to Brittany and saved us from all this legal bloody nonsense. What was I thinking?"

"No, no. Do not be overly concerned," Stephen said. "Now, we let the Inquisition do their work. They shall find the truth by drawing it from the flesh of the monster's servants."

14

The Question

Extraordinary

October 1440

Being in the presence of the deceitful, child-sacrificing sorcerer turned my stomach. Watching Prelati as he was brought into the chamber for Questioning by the Inquisition, it seemed clearer than ever that I should have sought simply to execute all of them instead of allowing any to live a moment longer than necessary. As well as the monks of the Inquisition, and their clerks, two guards watched proceedings. Stephen and I stood at the rear, behind the prisoner, and observed in silence.

They strapped him, hands and feet stretched out and bound to the rack in the centre of the room. Within his sight was the array of all the other equipment that would be employed, should he prove unwilling to cooperate. His bonds were tightened and the mechanism employed only until it was taut. Prelati was not suffering any pain. Not yet. They would, however, use whatever torsion proved necessary to elicit answers.

The Inquisitors need not have worried, for he was a man willing to say anything if it meant surviving.

"Francois Prelati, cleric, examined and interrogated for deposition," the Inquisitor said. "He has previously stated that he originally came from the diocese of Lucca in Italy and received his clerical tonsure from the Bishop of Arezzo. He has studied poetry, geomancy, and other sciences and arts, in particular alchemy. He is aged twenty-three or thereabouts, to the best of his belief." The inquisitor looked down at Prelati. "This is correct?"

"It is," Prelati said. He appeared composed and radiated openness, as if he was willing to tell all and tell it gladly.

The Inquisitor read from a list of prepared questions in a manner that suggested he was almost entirely uninterested in the answers. "Tell me how you came into the household of the Baron de Rais."

"I was staying in Florence, about two years ago, with the Bishop of Mondovi when a certain Milord Eustache Blanchet, a priest, came to me, who made my acquaintance through the mediation of a certain master from Montepulciano. Blanchet and I, as well as Nicolas de Medici, saw each other frequently for a time, eating and drinking together, and doing other things. And one day Blanchet asked me if I knew how to practice the art of alchemy and of the invocation of demons. And I said yes."

"You said yes," the Inquisitor repeated. "But were your words the truth? Did you know of these things?"

"Oh, yes," Prelati said, licking his lips. "Most assuredly. I had studied these things both extensively."

The pen scratched away, taking it all down. "What then?"

"Blanchet asked if I wanted to come to France. He said there lived a great man named Lord de Rais, who much desired to have about him a man learned and skilled in the said arts and that if I went there, I would receive generous accommodations. And so I came, bringing my books on alchemy and invocations. First, we went to the Marshal's grand house in Orléans but he was not there. When we got to the border of Brittany, there came four men to meet us. Henriet Griart, Poitou, Sillé and Roger de Briqueville." That last name would be changed in the official record to say simply and another. "They all together brought me back to Tiffauges to meet Milord de Rais."

"What happened at this meeting?"

"The Baron presented me with a book, bound in black leather. Part paper, part parchment, having letters, titles and rubrics all in red ink."

"You are certain it was ink?" the Inquisitor looked up. "And not blood?"

"I am certain of nothing. The writing was in the colour of red. This is all I can attest to."

"Continue."

"After asking my opinions on various elements of the content, Gilles asked me to try out and test them, particularly the invocations. And I agreed. So one night soon after, in the large lower hall of the castle at Tiffauges, the lord and the others that I have spoken of, took candles and other things along with the black book with red ink. Using the tip of a sword, I drew several circles comprising characters and signs in the manner of the armoires, in the composition and drawing of which I was helped by Sillé, Henriet Griart, and Poitou, as well as Blanchet."

"The priest Blanchet participated in the invocations?"

"Actively," Prelati said, his eyes shining. "Until my lord sent them all out so that it was just Gilles and myself in the hall. We placed ourselves in the middle of the circles. I drew more characters on the floor with a burning coal from an earthen pot, upon which coals I poured some magnetic dust, commonly called magnetite, and incense, myrrh, aloes, whence a sweet smoke arose. And we remained in the same place for two hours, variously standing, sitting, and on our knees, in order to worship the demons when they appeared, and to make sacrifices to them, invoking the demons and working hard to conjure them effectively. We took turns reading from the book, waiting for the invoked demon to appear. But nothing appeared that time."

"This book with the red ink gives instructions on raising demons?"

"Not that alone. But yes. The book says that demons have the power to reveal hidden treasures, teach philosophy, and guide those who act."

"Tell us," the Inquisitor said, "by what words do you summon these demons, precisely?"

"One invocation goes thusly." Prelati's voice took on a commanding, powerful timbre. "I conjure you, Barron, which is the name of the demon, I summon you, Barron, Satan, Belial,

Beelzebub, by the Father, Son, and Holy Ghost, by the Virgin Mary and all the saints, to appear here in person to speak with us and do our will."

At this, everyone present crossed himself and most looked all around the chamber as if expecting a demon to jump out.

I was half hoping that it would. We collectively let out a breath and the questioning continued.

"What other methods did you and the lord of Rais employ in order to summon a demon?"

"Many things. We used a stone named diadochite, and we used a certain variety of crested bird. We did attempt to summon the demon in many places, inside and outside of the castle."

"Did you use murdered children for these rituals?"

This was the question I had been waiting for. Would he confess to the crimes that he had committed and so condemn his master with his words? Or would he attempt to deny it and so face the Question Extraordinary.

Prelati swallowed and cleared his throat a number of times. The Inquisitor waited patiently. "The servant named Poitou told me that the room given to me in the tower for the invocations and for my alchemical work was the same room in which our master Lord de Rais had killed young boys, or caused them to be killed. And also that Gilles had slaughtered boys in my personal chamber before it was given to me, and he killed boys in all the places where I worked."

"Why did he do this?"

"Poitou told me that the children's blood and members were offered to demons."

"You claim you did not take part in these crimes yourself, and were not witness to any of them?"

"That is correct."

I scoffed, loudly. "Ha!"

The Inquisitor and everyone else turned to me.

"Say nothing," Stephen whispered. "Or you endanger the evidence."

I cared little for proper legal procedure but as I was in attendance only by courtesy, and as I wanted to hear it all spoken, I held my tongue. I even bowed my head to the Inquisitor for a moment.

He returned to the questioning. "You heard only rumours of murders done in places of your work, before and after your work was done, while you were elsewhere?"

"That is correct."

It was absurd. I had witnessed his murderous crimes myself. Only through my intervention had a boy's life been saved. Prelati was not only aware, had not only witnessed, but had been a willing participant in child murder for the purposes of raising demons.

"In fact," the Inquisitor said. "The other accused have given sworn initial statements that claim you were witness to the victims of murder, at the very least. They claim that you saw physical remains with your own eyes. Now, we will of course put you to the Question to discover the truth. Unless you would care to correct your statement first?"

Prelati glanced at the mechanism of the rack and winced. "Yes. Yes. Once, I entered Sillé's chambers and he had the body of a very small child laid out on his floor. It had been opened down the front."

"What of the Lord de Rais?"

"Yes. Once, he brought to me the hand, heart, eyes, and blood of a young boy, all kept in a glass. And he gave this glass to me so that I could offer the remains to the demon when he was summoned."

"And who murdered that child?"

"I do not know. I did not ask and was not told. I assumed the Baron had caused it by his own hand or had caused one of his men to do so."

"What then of the parts?"

"They were used as the offering in the proper ritual. No demon was forthcoming in this instance, however."

"What happened to the parts and the blood after the failed ritual?"

He cleared his throat. "The parts were burned in the grate."

The Inquisitors paused for a few moments of whispered conversations between them before taking their positions once more. All but one servant who moved to the rack and began turning the crank at the head of it which began tightening the ropes.

"My lords," Prelati said, his voice quivering. "Sirs, brothers. I have freely answered every question that you have put to me."

"Oh, you have indeed," the Inquisitor said, smiling pleasantly. "And now we shall ask every question once more but this time we shall elicit the answers from your flesh as well as from your tongue." He nodded at the servant who rotated the crank. The machine turned and Prelati gasped and groaned as the ropes pulled at him. "Now, tell me how you came into the household of the Baron de Rais."

For a time, I revelled in Prelati's agony but his answers remained remarkably consistent, as far as I could tell. But the Inquisition would ask and ask again, searching for inconsistencies that they could then tug at like loose threads.

When they resolved to further check the truth by pouring water from a funnel into his mouth until he almost drowned, over and over again between each question, I stood and let myself out, unable to listen any longer to the depravities and the crimes and the weeping of the tormented.

"He lies so easily," I said to Stephen during the recess for lunch in our inn across from the cathedral. "Even with all the pain, he excludes the blood drinking without cracks appearing in his tale. He tells just enough truth to appear to be telling all but not so much that he might yet hope to avoid a sentence of death. Sneaky bloody bastard."

"You called him a charlatan," Stephen pointed out, gesturing with his cup of wine. "And such men make their way through expertise in deception. Besides, it suits our purposes that no tales of blood emerge in the trial." He lowered his voice and leaned across the table. "Already I have undertaken to alter statements and omit evidence. If any of them speak of blood drinking and we cannot cover it up, well..."

"Yes, yes," I said. "Even if they speak of it publicly, none shall think it truth, of course. It will be just one more vile part in the madness, rather than the cause of it all."

"Is it the cause of it all? The blood? Do you believe that,

210

Richard?"

"I do not know. Perhaps it is. What else could it be? These acts are not natural. They are the furthest thing from nature as can be. Which seems rather similar to us, does it not?"

"Far from nature?" Stephen asked, sighing. "I suppose it is so. And yet we others have not succumbed to depravity and evil. Not even Walt. Something else caused Milord de Rais to take this path. He was evil already, in his heart, and it was only the wealth he accumulated that allowed him the means to enact it in the world."

"He made pacts with Satan. With demons. Prelati said so. I saw the rituals with my own eyes."

Stephen crossed himself. "I will not believe anything that Prelati creature says. Even when racked, or given the water questions. But I agree that the Marshal's actions are evil. They are Satanic. But were these acts done with Satan's hand? Or a man's?"

I gulped down the rest of my wine. "I do not know where the strength of our blood comes from. My grandfather claims his mother lay with a god. The sky god, he called him. What if, in his pagan babblings, he and his barbarian mother confused this god with Satan himself? Walking the earth, mating with a human woman?"

Stephen crossed himself again. "That cannot be, sir."
"Why?"

"Because..." He sighed in frustration. "Because you are not evil. Nor am I. Nor Eva. Do you consider Eva to be evil?"

"She is no saint," I said. "You have not seen all the things she has done in her time."

"But is she evil?"

"No," I admitted.

"That is right," Stephen said. "And even if William is, and Priskos and his sons are, the ultimate origin of this power cannot be from the loins of Satan. For nothing so evil could become good."

"What makes you think we are good? We drink blood. Human blood. If you had to decide if such a thing was either good or evil, which would you choose?"

"Why must it be one or the other, Richard?"

"You know why. You yourself told me what it means to be orthodox or heretical. A thing is either natural, and so from God, or unnatural and so is evil. I ask you, how can drinking human blood be natural?"

"We do good, Richard. Good deeds, good acts. You saved the lives of children who would certainly have died otherwise. We put a stop to all this. Yes, we were late, but if not for us taking action, how much longer would this have gone on for? What would the world be like if we had not with our actions stopped such evil as we have found? Come now, we must return for the deposition of the priest Blanchet."

I scoffed. "That lying sack of horse dung. When I first found him, he had the balls to beg ignorance. Swore to my face he knew nothing. We shall see what he has to say with the rack threatening. I would not be surprised if he was a damned revenant this entire time. How can we catch him out?"

"I do not see how we can, not during the questioning. You are certain Prelati is human?"

I shrugged. "He begged to be turned into an immortal. It appeared genuine. And if he was deceiving me then and is doing so now, well, what does it matter if he ultimately burns either way? For surely he has condemned himself with his own words."

"I pray it is so. Summoning demons with children's body parts..." He closed his eyes and slowly shook his head at the wonder of it. "Humans do not need your family's blood to do evil, Richard."

I nodded. "True enough. Very well, then. Let us hear from this Blanchet, shall we?"

∞

The monkish priest, Dominus Eustache Blanchet, was a different man entirely to Prelati. He was brought in, hunched over and close to weeping, with all the appearance of being a broken man. He said please and thank you to the Inquisitors as they made him ready for the Question. He was strapped into place upon the rack, as Prelati had been, but Blanchet shook in his bonds even before the machine was tightened.

"I came from Mountauban in the parish of Saint-Eloi, in the diocese of Saint-Malo, originally. I was born about forty years ago, to the best of my belief. After my years in orders, I came into the service of the Baron. About five years ago, I would say."

The Inquisitor looked down his list of questions. "A previous witness, Francois Prelati, claims that it was you who fetched him from Florence. Is that the case?"

"It is."

"And did you know when you set out that he was a demon summoner?"

Blanchet licked his lips. "And an alchemist, yes. Summoning of demons is not forbidden by the Church."

The Inquisitor paused to look up from his notes. "It is if done in a heretical manner, brother."

He swallowed and then swallowed again. "Of course. Which is why I ensured Prelati was properly educated in the matter, as well as in alchemy. He came well recommended by Nicolas de Medici and on discussion with Prelati, I concluded that he had the necessary skills to conduct the processes my lord wished to undertake."

"And which processes were these?"

"Why, to create gold."

"And?" The Inquisitor looked up and waited.

"All was to create gold, sir," he licked his lips. "That was the purpose of everything, to the best of my belief. Prelati had knowledge of the Philosopher's Stone and other special substances necessary for such works."

"Did the summoning of demons not disturb you, brother? Did the notion not alert you to the danger of heresy?"

"Oh no, sir. That is, I am ever vigilant where heresy is concerned, my lord. Only, I knew that Francis, I mean that is to say Prelati, was a qualified cleric and the demons were only to be summoned for the purposes of the transmutation from base matter into gold. And they would never enter any agreement with Satan in order to complete the summoning and so it was only sorcery and not witchcraft. It would be entirely orthodox, you see, sir, and the demon would be employed only for transmutation. Not for any other purposes. I would never commit heresy. Never."

The words were scratched into the records and the Inquisitor looked up at Blanchet. "And how would the demons help? What would they do? Please explain it precisely."

Blanchet swallowed. "I am afraid that is outside the realms of my expertise, brother."

The Inquisitor inclined his head. "Ah, is that a fact? So you, in fact, were not completely confident that the activities would not be heretical?"

Blanchet frowned, unable to see where he had erred. "I had every confidence in Prelati's expertise. He came highly recommended. Highly recommended."

"Hmmm," the Inquisitor said as the priests words were considered. "And you later took part in these ceremonies to summon demons?"

"Oh, no, sir."

"We have sworn testimony that you were in attendance. Where there is disagreement in testimonies then all parties must be put to the Question." The Inquisitor nodded at the servant who moved to the mechanism of the rack.

Blanchet shook and spoke quickly. "That is, I should have been clear, sir, I should have been clear when I spoke that I was in fact in attendance at one or two of these conjurations but when events turned somewhat heretical, or rather they had a potentially heretical nature, I naturally removed myself from the hall and from the tower immediately and did not return."

215

For a moment, the only sounds were the scratching of pens on parchment and the shaking, laboured breathing of Dominus Eustache Blanchet. I fancied I could almost hear the sweat running down his face. Was he simply nervous, I wondered, or was he in shaking need of human blood?

"During these conjurations, before you removed yourself of course, did you hear Gilles de Rais call upon Satan?"

The Inquisitor waited.

Blanchet gulped and glanced across the room at me before looking down before speaking in a quiet voice. "Yes."

"What did he say, precisely?"

"It was not when I was in attendance, but I happened to overhear them speak. Prelati and my lord, I should say Milord de Rais. They entered into Prelati's tower together and I fear I followed them at a distance."

"Why did you do such a thing?"

Blanchet's words tumbled from his dry lips. "By this time, I was growing suspicious. Because, you see, I had seen Prelati making his grant experiments at alchemy only the one time when he first arrived. Ever since then it had been all secrets and conjuring and smoke in the night. And so I followed. I heard Prelati call out the words and my lord repeat them."

"What words were these?" The Inquisitor looked up. "Precisely."

Blanchet sobbed momentarily but when the servant reached for the mechanism, he forced the words out. "Come, Satan. And then they said it again, more forcefully. Come, they said. And finally, they said come, Satan, come to our aid."

The Inquisitor was silent for so long that Blanchet lifted his head as far as he was able in order to see what was happening.

"Did you confront them?" the Inquisitor asked.

Blanchet dropped his head back on the rack. "I did not."

"Did you go to the Bishop with this knowledge?"

"I intended to. I got as far as Mortagne, at an inn. But I was afraid, God forgive me. I was afraid if I spoke of what my lord had done then he would kill me. As soon as I left, he sent men to bring me back."

"Oh? The innkeeper, Bouchard-Menard, has sworn in a statement that you stayed with him for seven weeks. Is that not the case?"

"Seven weeks, was it? Yes, that is right. My lord sent Poitou to threaten me. I resisted. Afraid to return and face murder but afraid to go on to Poitiers or elsewhere to swear to what I had told. And they sent Henriet. His threats were terrible. My lord wrote me letters, begging me to return. His words were honey but I knew his intent was poison. I failed in my duty to the Church, to my Bishop and to God, I know that. It was fear. I have sinned and for that I seek forgiveness."

"And yet you returned to the Baron's service. Why?"

Blanchet sobbed once more. "They brought me back. In the night. With a sack over my head. Threw me in the back of a wagon, all trussed up, and they swore they were going to hang me that very night. I begged them not to. Whether they meant only to frighten me or if they had a change of heart, I do not know, but they brought me back to Tiffauges and I knew from then on that I was a prisoner. To leave would have been my death."

"Why were you so certain? Were you told this?"

"It was implied." He gasped. "I knew."

"Because your knowledge of the summoning might have led to excommunication for the Baron? Was that all you knew? All you wished to tell?"

Blanchet banged the back of his head on the rack, his face screwed tight. "I knew also of murders. Murders of children. Oh God. Please forgive me."

"You witnessed murders?"

"No, thank God. But I heard. Over time, I heard from Poitou and from Henriet. At first, they hid it all from me and then over time, over the months and the years, they would tell me things openly. They delighted in my misery and terror at hearing such things spoken. I believed them to be malicious fabrications meant only to terrorise me but slowly I realised it was truth."

"They confessed to murders? What murders did they confess to, brother?"

"I asked where Francis' page had gone. That is, Prelati's page. He brushed me off. But other pages had disappeared also, the nephew of one of the soldiers, and the son of a pastry chef employed at the castle. All around fifteen years old. All quite close together. It was Poitou who turned on me one night, quite drunk, and said that he had killed them all. He and Henriet and my lord Gilles de Rais. They had, forgive me, they had buggered them and murdered them. I was shocked, brothers, shocked, I swear it. Poitou is such a grubby creature, I gave it little enough credence. But then I noticed a number of other rumours."

"What rumours were these?"

"One was that several old women detained in the prisons of my lord the Duke of Brittany, in Nantes, whose names I do not know, led children to Machecoul and Tiffauges, and delivered them to Henriet and Poitou, who killed them."

"Why would they do that?" the Inquisitor asked.

Blood, I answered in my mind.

"I do not know the reason," Blanchet said, closing his eyes.

"You say there were several old women. Are you certain it was not a single old woman and her granddaughter?"

"You speak of course of Perrine Martin, who they call La Meffraye. She is a terror, that is true. I have seen her and her granddaughter bringing back children, little ones. When I was innocent, naive and unsuspecting, I saw nothing untoward in it. Two servants, one old and one young, going to fetch a new boy for the stable or the kitchen. Somehow, I did not notice there were never child servants in the castle. Not one. Those little children all disappeared but I thought that they were servants and so I did not notice. Not for a long time."

"What about the choir boys?" I called out.

The Inquisitor scowled at me but turned back to Blanchet. "Tell me about these choir boys."

Blanchet swallowed furiously before he answered. "Messire de Rais would procure the very best boys from the elite choirs of France and Italy. He paid their parents fortunes if they would send their brilliant boys to Tiffauges. To some he offered grand estates. He was obsessed with creating the greatest choir that ever existed and it seems to me that he did that very thing. But there was none to listen to the choir but us servants and once in a great while the master also."

"Did these boys ever disappear?" the Inquisitor asked. Many of the choir boys had provided sworn statements already and so it was an opportunity perhaps to catch Blanchet in a lie.

"Some left," Blanchet said. "But there always seemed to be good reason. When I think of it now, it seems clear that some of the prettiest ones were taken and... slain. And yet as with the servant children, I did not think much of it until later. May God forgive me, if only I had noticed there were no servant children present."

"No children but one," the Inquisitor said. "Madame Martin's granddaughter."

"Well, they need her to get the others," Blanchet said. "They told me that she forms part of her grandmother's bait, along with the sweet treats and sweeter promises, and so Poitou and Henriet never go near her. Just leave her and La Meffraye to their business. The girl is old enough to be wise and imposing to very small children, and of course she is common as they are. And they trust her when she tells them what her grandmother says is true. She takes their hands and leads them through the castle gates and—"

He broke off, sobbing.

It was quite a remarkable act.

"Thank you for your cooperation, brother," the Inquisitor said, pleasantly. "And now we shall ask these questions again, this time seeking answers from your flesh as well as from your tongue."

∞

During the adjournment of the tribunal, Gilles de Rais asked for and was given permission to hear Mass. It was quite extraordinary that he was allowed such a thing but then he was still a powerful noble and had not yet been convicted of anything. Still, it made my skin crawl.

And while the ecclesiastical court was gathering evidence, the civil court met to consider the charges of murder and rebellion in a hall very near to ours. The Inquisition led the examination of the witness on behalf of both courts. And again, Gilles de Rais had declined the offer of counsel for his defence.

It reminded me that Joan of Arc had also decided to reject the offer of counsel in her trial, nine years earlier. It was an extravagant display of the arrogance that both she and Gilles shared. Perhaps it was not arrogance but ostentation. A kind of elaborate, theatrical gesture that was intended to show their contempt of the courts who deigned to try them. In the Marshal's case, it was not so surprising an attitude from one of the most celebrated and the richest men in France. And Joan had considered herself instructed by the agents of God, which is to say that God spoke to her almost directly, choosing her as the vessel for His divine will to be enacted upon the earth. It is difficult to imagine a greater arrogance than that, whether she was lying or mad.

We heard that the old woman, La Meffraye, had been captured attempting to flee, alone, toward Normandy and was then returned to Nantes. I doubted she was gifted with immortality but I intended to speak to her, also, just as soon as I had seen the torture of the servants. They were still looking for the granddaughter, but I doubt anyone was looking very hard. Children, even grown ones like the granddaughter, were subject to obeying the will of their elders and even La Meffraye was not looked upon with any real malice. There was a sense that the old woman was merely obeying her master's commands. Personally, I would still have the evil old witch hanged, and the granddaughter with her, but if they were mortals then it was not really my business.

The evidence was gathered not only from the accused's conspirators and accomplices but by the villagers and other victims. There were the sworn testimonies we had already taken in their scores but the Inquisitors wished to speak directly to a select few, who told their sad stories while the Inquisition scratched down their words.

I was present at the questioning of a distraught Perinne Rondeau of Machecoul.

"We came to Machecoul on account of my husband Clement was looking for work and we heard there was work there," she said, speaking quickly and wiping her nose with a filthy handkerchief after every sentence. "But my husband got sick, terrible sick, which caused us extreme unction and we thought sure he was going to die, thought it for a long time. And it was then when the Master Francis came to see us."

"Master Francis Prelati?" the Inquisitor asked.

"Just so, Milord," Perinne said. "And he came with a priest called Dom Eustache, who both of them asked to lodge in our room upstairs. Well, we had no choice, did we, on account of needing the income from letting it and on account of that we knew they both were in the service of the Marshal, and we can't be saying no to men such as them. It were strange, though, that they both slept in the same room together and also together with their pages, the two men and the two boys all together in the room. Master Francis and Dom Eustache went out often to dinner, back to the castle or elsewhere, as it suited them. It was one day when my husband was so very ill, my tears and crying at his illness was causing him such great distress that I took myself into the chamber upstairs. The pages let me in and they just lay on their pallets and I lay upon the bed, weeping to myself that I was soon to be a widow. When my lodgers returned, they were very irritated to find I had been allowed in and, showering me with the most filthy and vile insults, they did carry me, one by my feet and the other by my shoulders, to the staircase, telling me they was going to throw me down it from the top to the bottom. With this very thing in mind, Francis kicked me in the lower back with terrible force and I would have fallen had not the nurse caught me by my dress and arrested my fall. Together, me and the nurse fled until the men had fallen asleep."

"So, they assaulted you most terribly," the Inquisitor said. "You earlier indicated that you suspected the murder of a child?"

"Just so, Milord. It was soon after when I heard Francis say to Dom Eustache that he had found a beautiful page for him from around Dieppe, about whom Francis said he was extremely delighted. And so it was that a young, very beautiful child, saying he was from the Dieppe region and that he was of a good family, came to stay with Francis. And he stayed there for fifteen days, thereabouts. Then he weren't there any more. I was shocked and asked Francis what had become of the boy and he said that the boy had cheated him royally and that he had taken off with two crowns. I felt very strongly that he was lying, Milord."

"Is that all you have to say?"

"Only that Master Francis and Dom Eustache afterwards went to stay in a different house. I was right relieved they had gone, for no money is worth housing evil under your roof. But they went to stay in a small house in Machecoul, where a man named Perrot Cahu lived until they threw him out, stealing from him the keys to the house. That house, Milord, is far from all the other houses. An isolated place, on an outside street with a well at the entrance and in this small house was where Francis and Eustache lived from then on. And at times, the Lord Gilles de Rais was seen at night going into this place."

"Did you see him with your own eyes?"

"No, Milord, but the village seen him, if you catch my drift."

The Inquisitor called in Jean Labbe the Captain of Arms and requested that he accompany Perinne Rondeau back to the house of which she spoke and to investigate the place.

It was two days later when I heard that they had found physical remains. There were ashes removed from the house of Perrot Cahu, ashes with the bones of children in them, and the small shirt of a bloody child that stank so horribly that Madame Rondeau was violently sick at the sight of it.

The fates of Francois Prelati and Dominus Eustache Blanchet were surely sealed.

Taking supper at the inn, I drank heavily.

"He was lying throughout. They both were. Very carefully, very cleverly, admitting to only so much that they might hope to avoid the rope."

"The bloody vest of the child in their house surely puts paid to that," Stephen said.

"I will take your word for it and I pray that it does. But do you think that was true, what Blanchet said in his confession?" I asked. "That there were women at the prison bringing children to Gilles?"

Stephen chewed his mutton while pondering it. "Quite possibly. This makes you very concerned?"

"It makes me wonder how many other bloody things we missed. Other men bringing children to the Marshal and the servants. How many of his agents are there out there still? How many of them are revenants that I must slay?"

Stephen smirked. "I doubt he turned a gaggle of old women into revenants, Richard."

"No? How do we know? He might have a whole army of hunchback old nags and filthy little girls out there in the wastes as we speak."

Stephen sniggered and, after resisting, I laughed with him before sitting back and rubbing my eyes.

"You should get some rest, Richard. Tomorrow shall be extremely unpleasant."

In the morning we would hear the depositions of Gilles valets, accomplices and immortals, the servants Henriet Griart and Poitou.

"If I get through the day before murdering both of them it will be a miracle."

15

Evil Confessions
October 1440

THE INQUISITION WAS REMARKABLY professional. Even when confronted with men of pure evil, they applied what they considered to be the minimum agony required. As much as I have always enjoyed punishing the wicked and hurting bad people, I would not have done such a fine job. I would certainly have cranked that rack around until limbs were ripped from their sockets.

I was certain when they began their interrogations that the Marshal's two servants were revenants and so I felt like slitting their throats before they had even finished answering the first questions. But it was their statements which would serve to thoroughly convict Gilles de Rais and so I did my duty and resisted. Every urge, I fought down, as much as I shook to still myself.

The skinny young creature was lifted onto the rack and tied in place. He settled down and relaxed as if it was pleasant for him to do so.

When the Inquisitor began the questions, I held my fist over my mouth and listened.

"My name is Etienne Corrillaut but people call me Poitou. I was from Pouzauges. I reckon I'm about twenty-two by now, best as I can make it out. They brought me to Machecoul to be a page for my lord. I served as a page for many a year. Just doing my duty, as always, was good Poitou."

"What duties did you do with regards to murder?" the Inquisitor asked.

"Well, sire, it was me, Sillé, and Henriet what would find and lead children to Gilles de Rais, the accused person in this trial, sire, lead them to his room so we did. Many boys and girls on whom to practice his normal activities, as it were, sire."

"How many children did you personally find and escort to the rooms of your lord?"

"Oh, can't rightly say, sir."

"How many? Was it three? Four? Forty?"

"Oh, yes. Probably forty, sire."

The Inquisitor sighed. "Can you count?"

"Yes, most assuredly I can count. It was forty, sire, thereabouts. Up to forty, I would say."

Everyone in the room knew he was lying but it hardly mattered for the sake of the trial and the Inquisitor continued.

"What did Gilles de Rais do with these children?"

"Well, like I say, sir. He would tell them they was delightful to look at and so on and so forth and he would tell them they had nought to fear and he would say he was going to get them dressed in the finest clothes and take them to meet the King and all sorts. And then he would kill them."

"What method would he use?"

Poitou closed his eyes, a small smile on the corners of his mouth. "Sometimes he would throttle them with his own hand, especially if they was a noisy sort. Sometimes he'd have them suspended by the neck with ropes or cords, on a peg or small hook what he had in his rooms. Then he let them down ofttimes and would say again that he was only having fun with them. But then he would break their necks with a cudgel, slit their throats, or open their bellies, or just straight up remove their heads right away."

The Inquisitor took a sip of wine and a deep breath before continuing. "And did he practice his lascivious lusts upon them?"

"Oh yes, sire, but not usually until they was dead, sire. Or very nearly."

"What was your role in this? Yours and the other servants."

"Me, Henriet, and Sillé, would help hold them down, or string them up, and we'd gather up the blood in jars and cups and burn the bodies in the fire. Roger would join my lord in his debaucheries at times but he often just watched and drank wine. And..." he trailed off, looking left and right. He was hiding something but after what he had said, it was almost inconceivable that it could be anything worse."

"You will now give me specific details. You will provide the names of the victims and approximate times. As many as you can recall."

While Poitou began naming children he had taken, I stood and let myself out of the chamber. I found my hands were shaking. It was all I could do to stop myself from going back in, killing Poitou, then finding Gilles and all his other servants and cutting them into pieces.

But I knew that justice would be done. Each had confessed to mortal crimes. Each would soon face death and though it would be swifter and kinder than they deserved, at least it would be done. And the parents of the children would see proper justice being done under the law and I should not deprive them of that.

After two more hours, Stephen emerged, white as a linen tablecloth and shaking all over.

"Such evil," he muttered into his hot spiced wine. "How could they do it?"

"He is a revenant," I said.

"Are you truly certain?" Stephen asked.

"Did you not see his sickly pallor in there?"

"Some men have such a look," Stephen said. "He has been in prison for days. Surely, without blood he would be in a far worse state. Or likely dead."

"True," I admitted. "But I doubt it. I saw the way he moved that night, leaping further than a mortal man can. Either way, he is not long for the world. And I do not think I shall join you for the deposition of Henriet. It will be much the same as Poitou's, I expect, and enough to see him hanged."

"And so it will be just me in there with the Inquisitors and clerks of the court," Stephen said, running his hands over his face. "Listening to more of that. I cannot take it alone, Richard. At least if you are there, I will know you suffer with me, for a burden shared is a burden halved, is that not the case?"

"Suffer alone you must, for I have other business to attend to."

He peered at me. "What other business?"

"The old woman, La Meffraye. She is here and I will speak with her before she, too, is hanged. She is the one who took Ameline's brother. I will have from her what happened to the boy and then ride to the village. At least I can give Ameline that, if nothing else."

Stephen pursed his lips. "Well, enjoy your visit to your young lady, Richard." He planted his hands on the table and stood. "I am going to spend many hours recording accounts of the worst murders ever committed, given by the fiend himself. Good day."

∞

They let me into her cell. It was bitterly cold within, and dim with the only light coming from a slit of a window high above. It reeked of piss and mould and the stench made me angry just to be in its presence.

I held a lantern in my hand and stood over her as she sat on the stool they had provided for her.

"I know you," she said, giggling. "You're the one they was

afraid of."

"Are you a madwoman?" I asked her.

She shrugged. "Who's to say who's anything, my lord? Maybe I am mad and maybe it's you what is mad? Who's to say?"

"I will say," I said. "And you certainly sound mad to me. Now, tell me, woman. How were you recruited to undertake this work?"

She grinned up at me with her hideous, wrinkled face, and brushed her filthy grey hair away from her face. The rotten creature had a number of teeth missing and the ones that remained were either yellow or brown. "Recruited, sire?"

"How did you first come into the Baron's service?"

"Oh, I see now, sire. Yes, I see." She crossed her arms over her bosom. "Well, I don't rightly know. Long time ago now, so it was."

"Indeed? Was it before he was calling himself Gilles de Rais?"

She glanced sharply up at me. "What you mean when you say that?"

"Only that the Baron is far older than he appears and has likely posed in many guises this last century or two. Who was he posing as before?"

She looked away. "Don't know what you mean, sire."

"Well then, let me tell you what I mean. It is my sworn duty to slay all men who are like your master the Baron de Rais. All who live on, ageless, staying youthful by drinking blood. All men like him, and all women, also."

The old woman gaped at me. "Right then, well you best be off doing that then." She pointed at the open door behind me. "Go on."

I smiled. "I shall. Once I determine if you are likewise one of them or not."

She gasped. "Me, sire? But I ain't like them, sire. Don't tar me with that brush. I am a humble and obedient servant, so help me. Always have been."

"If you do not convince me thoroughly, I am afraid I shall have to gut you here and now."

"All I ever done is follow the commands of my lord. Just a girl, I was, when he first sent me off for him."

"Oh? When was this? What year?"

"Don't know. What year is it now? I was a girl and he was going by the name Jean de Craon. He had these folk pretending to be his family, but they weren't truly. They come and go, some living and others dying. Later on, he sent me to find little boys. Handsome little boys who weren't afraid, is what he wanted. I brought a few but he never seemed happy until there was this one little lad I brought and my lord said he was the one. Charming little fellow, he was. Bright and full of beans and my lord gave him an education. Called him Gilles. Called him his grandson and showed him off while he grew. My lord told folk young Gilles had gone away and he himself hid in his castle, dismissed servants and friends until one day my lord died, almost unnoticed. And this boy Gilles inherited everything. But when he came back home to claim it..."

She broke off, covering her mouth and looking down.

"Go on."

"When the boy Gilles come back I saw at once it was in fact my lord Jean de Craon. Somehow, it was him, unaged and same as he ever was but pretending to be named Gilles. And he sent me to work, luring in the boys and sometimes the girls. I was told that the children could be boys or girls but that for preference they should have fair hair and be clean-limbed. The Sire de Rais liked best for children to be between eight and twelve years old but there were a few that was younger and some that were older. Youngest one I found was about seven, and his brother was fifteen, he came along with me, too. And that's all there is to it. I ain't one of them. Not me, my lord. I'm a loyal servant, that's what I am and nothing more, so help me."

"What of your own family?"

"What family?"

"Have you not had children of your own?"

"Oh. A few. They ain't got nothing to do with it, you leave them out of it, do you hear?"

"So they are yet living?"

She wrinkled her nose. "I ain't offered one of my own up to him, for God's sake. How could you say such a thing, sire?"

"No, quite right, that would be monstrous. But you were complicit in scores of murders. Hundreds, perhaps. And so you will soon die by hanging on the orders of the court."

She screwed up her face. "Only following what my lord ordered me to do. All I am is a humble servant. Most humble."

"Tell me, do you remember a child named Jamet Mousillon? The son of a physician?"

She wrinkled her nose. "Why you want to know about him? Why is he special?"

"What happened to him? I am sure he was killed eventually but how did you take him?"

"So many boys. Can't recall them all."

"No? And yet I recall that you worked often with your granddaughter. A girl old enough to be charged with the same crimes as you and yet so far she has evaded justice. An oversight that I can easily put right."

"No!" She scurried forward. "No, sire. Not her. You stay away from her. My family must be safe. My dear girls, my dear boys. You'll not go near her if you know what's good for you. Hear me, do you?"

"I am not sure I do. Why should I not seek justice? Perhaps it was your granddaughter who enticed away young Jamet from his village?"

Her face drained of colour. "No, no. It was me. It was all my doing, I swear it."

"Tell it, then. How did you get a learned young boy to obey you? What magic did you employ?"

"No magic. It was a simple enough thing. Simple as any. He was on his lonesome, tossing stones into the pond. The little ones just want the attention of a kindly person. I asked him all about himself, usual questions, and they love to tell it all. All about themselves and what's on their minds and the battles they been fighting with one child or another or with their mother or father. Don't recall what he said in this instance. I asked him if he would like some sugar cakes and he said yes and off we went."

"Why on earth would he follow you all the way back to the castle?"

"Don't know why they do it, truth be told? Ain't got no fear in them. Even when they been told to watch out for me, to watch out for La Meffraye, they just come along. Hop straight into my hand like a little bird what never seen man before. Innocent little lambs they are with no notion of danger. Can't imagine the evil, sire. Ain't in them. Then I gives him by the hand to Poitou and he leads the lad away into my lord's chambers. And that be that."

"Dear God Almighty. Your heartlessness is overwhelming. At least there is some comfort in knowing that you will hang for the evil that is in you."

She let out a juddering sigh. "As long as my family goes on, I can die satisfied I did my duty."

I was appalled by her hypocrisy at the time but later I realised she was behaving naturally. We all chose our own offspring, our own family, over the rest of the world. If we do not do so, in fact, it is we who are acting against nature. And to act against nature is to sin.

Overcome by her witless evil, I suddenly wanted to be done with it. All the endless questioning and feet dragging. The absurd denials by Gilles de Rais, or whatever his true name was, were simply drawing out the farcical trial. All the Dominicans from the Inquisition, all the bishops and the lawyers, all poking away to uncover a truth they would never find or not comprehend if they did. And, I was realising, I would never know it myself. None of his followers knew enough to fill in the gaps.

Returning to the chamber, I found Stephen sitting on a stone bench with his head in his hands.

"Is the Inquisition done with Henriet Griart?"

Speaking from within the shield of his own hands, Stephen groaned. "I am done with being a lawyer."

"Good," I said, sitting beside him and clapping a hand on his back. "It is a calling for scoundrels and knaves. Though I must say, you seemed quite suited to it."

He laughed a little and sat up. "The things they did, Richard. I shall have to live now for the rest of my life knowing that men are capable of such things. And if men can act in such a way, what then can it be like in the bottom level of Hell?"

"You will never know. But those men will. And their master, too. Listen, Stephen. Get me into his quarters. Tonight."

"Who? De Rais? You mean to kill him? After all this?"

"No, no," I said, though I half expected that I would. "Soon, after all these statements are read to the court, he will be sentenced and executed. And I will never know where he came from. What my brother told him."

And I will never know about her. Was she one of us? Was she a military genius who outwitted me on the battlefields of Orléans and Patay? Or was she just another poor victim of this monster?

"I shall have to use every favour I have yet to call in," Stephen said. "He is well guarded and I may be rebuffed."

"You must overcome their doubts. Tell them that you are prosecuting the crimes on behalf of the common people, who are too weak to do it themselves."

He glanced at me with a dark look in his eye. "You continue to sneer at the common people as if you were not one of them yourself."

"What do you mean by such a remark?"

"Nothing, sir. I am tired, that is all."

"You say I am a commoner myself?" I pondered it for a

moment. "I take it you say so because my natural father Earl de Ferrers was in fact a bastard son of Priskos? No, you are right, that is a fair observation. And yet my mother was nobly born, to a proper English lineage. And one might say, considering that Priskos spawned such men as Alexander and Caesar, that my blood is as noble as it comes."

"All I mean, Richard, is that your blood might be noble but you are one no longer. A nobleman lives as one, holding land for his lord, and is recognised as one by commoner and by his peers and his king. But you spend all your time amongst commoners, all men see you as one, and your king does not know you. As far as the law is concerned, you are a commoner."

"I do not know about that," I said. "But I suppose you are right enough." Even as I said it, I knew it was not the whole truth. The law applies to all men but it was never written with a man such as me in mind. Perhaps I was a lord no longer but I could not see myself as a commoner either. I was a knight in my heart but an immortal in my blood and what that made me as a whole, I did not know. "But I must speak with Gilles de Rais tonight. You can make it happen, I know you can."

"If we are discovered, it could end badly."

"Stephen, if it goes badly, I shall simply have to kill them all and we will have to escape before they catch us."

He sighed. "Hardly the virtuous path."

"We have done such sinful and illegal things before, have we not? At the least, I know I have done and will gladly do so again, if need be. Come, now. Take me to Gilles de Rais."

Gilles de Rais had been in command of the forces that

238

crushed us at the climax of the Loire campaign eleven years earlier and on my way to speak to him, face to face, I could not get that final battle from my mind.

240

1 6

The Battle of Patay

June 1429

AFTER WE ABANDONED THE SIEGE of Orléans on 8 May 1429, our armies withdrew to our nearby garrisons all along the Loire. We were split into smaller groups and companies and distributed fairly in this fortress or that. I was commanded to join the garrison at Meung-sur-Loire, not much more than ten miles away from Orléans, downriver to the southwest.

It had been an enormous setback, there was no doubt about that. But equally, it was not an unrecoverable military disaster. We still had thousands of superbly equipped and supplied veteran soldiers holding well-fortified positions in towns that were large enough to support us on both sides of Orléans up and down the river.

Still, there was something indefinable in the air. A vague sense of disquiet over and above that which might be expected from such a setback.

"Bunch of whiners," Walt said about our fellow garrison troops, who grumbled about being defeated weeks before.

"Ain't used to defeat, are we," Rob said. "They'll get over it and then we'll charge back in and finish them off. Right, Richard?"

I did not answer, because I was as disquieted as anyone. Though, I did not make my feelings known and as much as I could, I kept my concerns to myself and instead focused my attention on the defences and getting to know the men that I found myself garrisoned with.

They were good men. About five hundred had been in the forts around Orléans and the other eight hundred had been established there before our evacuation. Our defences at Meung-sur-Loire consisted of three components. The walled town, the fortification guarding the bridge over the Loire, and a large walled castle just outside of the town. The castle was small but well-made and served as the headquarters for our commander the Earl of Shrewsbury John Talbot. I did my best to keep out of his way.

We bedded in and waited for our reinforcements to arrive. Word had been sent that Sir John Fastolf was on his way from Paris with a reinforcing army of several thousand, headed for the Loire River valley.

Once they arrived, we might actually attack the French again or perhaps we would continue to wait for them to come and attack us. A surprising number of our soldiers did not believe that the French would follow up on their victory, for they had conducted only defensive campaigns for decades and as the days turned to weeks, it seemed ever more likely that they were right. The French forces held at Orléans, as if they had no idea what to do next.

As the atmosphere of indecision settled over us, I increasingly wondered why I was there at all. I was doing nothing at all for the English cause in France, and I was certainly not acting to further the aims of the Order.

"We can't leave, Richard," Rob said beside me from the top of the walls of the town, where I had raised the question with my men. "Can't leave our friends to their fate."

"Can't we?" Walt asked. "What good we doing sitting here on our arses?"

It had been a month since fleeing Orléans and we wondered if we would pass the whole summer without fighting again. Many soldiers are happy with avoiding battle. But not me and not my men.

"You are right," I admitted. "I should have made myself a lord. Going about in war as a commoner is no use at all. It seems that no lord these days cares one whit whether a man has ability if he is not a gentleman of some description. It was foolish of me to think that my inherent nobility, and my knightly qualities, would shine through and overcome the limitations of my apparent station. If I was a lord in this moment then I could do something about all of this but instead my presence simply angers them."

"When you made us knights," Rob said, "we knew we would rarely be recognised as such. But you told us that we would be knights in our hearts and so we have been from that day to this. And you have fought, as we have, for free companies and captains, from Athens to Avila, and never were we regarded by our companions as knights or nobles but we knew in our hearts that we must act with knightly virtue in all things. And so we did, come what may."

"Yes, yes," I said. "And so we will continue to do. But this is different. Our companions are Englishmen, fighting for the King of England. And even if he is a useless boy and his lords are witless cowards, they are the lords of England. I had expected that they would respond to my suggestions more favourably rather than to dismiss me as a useless commoner."

"Talbot hates your guts, alright," Walt said, grinning.

"Fastolf and all," Rob added. "When he gets back here, you'll be getting it in both ears."

"I do already from you two damned jesters."

Walt shook his head. "Perhaps if, instead of making yourself a lord, you should have pretended to be an obedient soldier, Richard."

"Aye," Rob said. "That's what makes the lords angry. Choose one or the other. You can't be both."

"Yes, yes, very amusing, I am sure."

"True though, ain't it," Walt said.

In the distance, a group of horsemen rode hard toward the town. Dust kicked up behind them and even from so far away I could see that their horses were struggling and the men were agitated.

"That our men?" Walt asked, squinting.

Rob nodded. "They were watching Orléans. Look at the state of them. Must have been galloping all the way."

"Only one reason to ride like that," Walt observed.

"Yes," I said. "The French are coming."

The French army came up quickly and in great numbers. We had been expecting a siege of the town and castle but instead they threw all their numbers at the fortified bridge over the Loire and took it by storm inside of a single day.

Joan of Arc controlled a force that included captains Jean d'Orléans, Gilles de Rais, Jean Poton de Xaintrailles, and La Hire. The French had five thousand soldiers. Bypassing the city and the castle, they staged a frontal assault on the bridge fortifications, conquered it in one day, and installed a garrison. Immediately they had cut off our ability to move south of the Loire.

Still, we expected that they would invest Meung-sur-Loire but instead they marched on without attacking town or castle and turned to march to Beaugency just five miles away downriver and put it under siege.

At the same time, another French army assaulted and defeated our garrison at Jargeau on the other side of Orléans which was commanded by Suffolk, William de la Pole. Their defences were good and there were seven hundred men under his command. Somehow, the French simply overwhelmed them and there was another fortress lost. We suffered heavy losses and Suffolk was captured.

Unlike Meung-sur-Loire, the main stronghold at Beaugency was inside the city walls, forming an imposing rectangular citadel. By the time the French had assaulted the walls a couple of times, our soldiers abandoned the town and retreated into the castle. The French brought up their cannons and bombarded the castle with artillery fire. That evening, with the cannons still firing at the walls and towers of the castle, the French received more reinforcements from the east.

Hearing news of an English relief force approaching from Paris under Sir John Fastolf, d'Alençon negotiated the English surrender and granted them safe conduct out of Beaugency.

Our long-awaited reinforcement army under Sir John Fastolf, which had set off from Paris following the defeat at Orléans, now joined forces with survivors of the besieging army under Lord Talbot and Lord Scales at Meung-sur-Loire.

"We must launch an assault on the French now, my lords. We must."

"Why do you insist on speaking when we care nothing for your opinions?"

"If we do not stop this wave of assaults now then we will not do so at all. They will roll over us all the way to Paris."

"Do not be absurd, man," Fastolf snapped. "We cannot risk a pitched battle against a foe who so outnumbers us."

"Why not?" I said. "Overall numbers matter only in the minds of the soldiers. What is important is how many soldiers we can bring to bear at any one time."

"We must retreat back to Paris," Fastolf said.

"No, we cannot abandon the remaining garrisons to their fate," Talbot argued. I thought that he was coming around to my way of thinking but that was too much to hope. "We must find another town to take and hold. If we can encourage the French to besiege us, we can split their forces and assault them in turn, perhaps in spring next year."

"That is madness," I said. "We would then be crushed in turn."

"You are not part of this conference and you will now leave."

There was nothing left to do but follow Fastolf's plan to retreat towards Paris.

Our forces were in constant contact and so when we marched away northward, the French set off immediately after us.

We were in the lead and had half a day on them, so it should have been a simple thing to outmarch the enemy. We had done so many times before. Yet again, though, it was down to a matter of will. Ours was perhaps not broken but it was subdued. Even though we knew the enemy was after us, it seemed that the men trudged in weary defeat rather than raced away for the sake of their lives. We had not gone fifteen miles when they caught up with us near to the village of Patay.

That little village was one I knew well enough, for it was just a day's ride north from Orléans and our patrols had gone around it and through it a dozen times.

"That city is cursed," Walt said, spitting, as the enemy horsemen massed through trees and hedgerows to the south. "Why can we not win when we are near it?"

"Not the city, is it," Rob said, stringing his bow. "It's the witch."

"Can it be true?" Walt asked. "Is she using magic?"

I thought she probably was.

"No," I said. "Her presence has put the wind up them, that is all. It will take one sharp defeat for the French to return to their craven ways, mark my words."

"Form up," came the orders relayed from Fastolf.

In this battle, we employed the same methods we used in the victories at Crécy in 1346 and Agincourt in 1415, deploying an army composed predominantly of longbowmen behind a barrier of sharpened stakes driven into the ground to obstruct any attack by cavalry.

This time, however, it would not go so well.

"The French are coming. They be right on our heels, sir." Rob said. "We won't make it to a better position."

"Where is Talbot?" I asked the fleeing archers around me. "Where are the lords?"

"Ahead," they said. "Far up ahead. Not here."

"Got to do something, sir," Walt said. "Look, there. Riders gathering."

"Listen to me," I shouted. "Pass the word. Fill the trees by the road and prepare to ambush the enemy as they pass. They will not charge us in the trees. Pass the word."

Wonderful men, they were. Proper soldiers. The senior men chivvied the new lads and together they took positions along three hundred yards at the edge of the woodland and made ready for the mounted men-at-arms to approach along the road below. They were tense. We all were. But we had plenty of arrows and stood a good chance of driving the enemy vanguard away with heavy casualties and by then our own soldiers would hopefully return and deter the rest of the French army.

Talbot and his knights rode back toward us. They were just a score but dozens more came behind him.

"Thank God," Rob muttered.

"About bloody time," Walt said.

When Talbot approached, he began issuing commands all along the line and our archers began trudging down the hill toward the road.

"What in the hell are you doing?" I shouted, riding toward him.

"We must block the road," Talbot called, irritated by my question and yet answering all the same and indicating the position with his sword. "Archers to redeploy. Five hundred of them will hold the road with the remaining men to shoot from the flank."

"There is no time," I said. "The French are there. You can see them, my lord, with your own eyes."

"A handful of scouts, nothing more. There is time." He turned from me and took position on the road, as did his knights and the other mounted men until there were perhaps three hundred of them.

It was then that I realised just how mad I had been in making war as a commoner, without any significant official position. It was true that every decade it became more difficult to buy my way into the nobility and yet I could have done it, had Stephen and Eva prepared my lineages properly beforehand. And yet in my arrogance I had thought my natural leadership qualities would overcome all social distinction during battle. Men would follow me, that had proved true enough, but lords would not step aside for me. How could I have been so utterly foolish? The coming disaster was Talbot's making but it was mine also. Mine even more so, for I should have known better.

"Where's the rest of the bloody army?" Walt cried. "What are they doing?"

"They are coming back, there, do you see? Banners and pennants above the hedgerow, coming this way."

"Make ready!" the cry went up all along the line and my heart sank.

French men-at-arms appeared in their dozens and formed up, until they were hundreds.

Joan the Maiden was at the rear, her great white banner with the fleur-de-lys and the angels held aloft like a beacon, drawing in ever more French warriors, desperate to fight for the Maiden of Orléans and so for God. I understood then why the French were so revitalised. What it was that had possessed them. It was not simply courage and a new belief that they could win against us, finally. Joan had filled the French with the zeal of a holy war and they were become weapons of God to drive out the heretical English invader once and for all. Our presence upon French soil was sacrilege that would be cleansed only with our blood.

 Our archers were halfway down the hill and spread out in no formation at all and almost none had planted their stakes in the ground to deter attack.

It took just a few moments for the hundreds of French to become a thousand and then so many that I lost count. Among them, I recalled later when it had meaning for me, was the black and gold banner of Gilles de Rais. Indeed, it was he who was commanding the forces of the vanguard and urging them on with great passion.

I could see what was going to happen. We all could.

"Shoot!" I called to the archers. "Get arrows into them. Shoot, now."

It was a mad hope perhaps but I thought we could scare them away by showing we were waiting in the woods, coming out of the trees to shoot at them. But the French knights saw English archers scattered and unprepared and nothing was going to turn them from such a thing. It was the kind of thing a mounted soldier lived for. Something dreamed about but hardly realised.

They came at us in a great mass of horse and steel, with lances and axes and swords. Our archers shot what arrows they could but they were so many that they ran right over the scattered archers, cutting them down with such ease. I saw Old Simon amongst them, raging even as they hacked him to pieces. Around me, the archers cried out in anger at the sight of their brothers down on the road being so destroyed but still they turned and filed away through the trees.

"Stop, wait. Keep shooting!" I shouted. Walt and Rob attempted to stop them but they knew the battle was lost, even before I did.

"Fastolf has come," Rob said, pointing with his bow down to the road. "A counter charge could hold them."

When Fastolf and his mass of knights instead turned and fled, it was as though I saw England dying. Where were the great men of the past who would have ridden to their deaths? For glory, even if nothing else?

"All is lost, Richard," Rob said.

"There must be something..." I muttered.

"It's over, sir," Walt cried. "It's over."

Before I pulled back through the trees with the archers, I saw Talbot and his knights riding hard, northward. Away from the battle. Away from the dying archers Talbot had sent to their deaths with his idiotic command. Talbot rode on by the rest of our army, who were spread out along the road coming to relieve archers who had already fallen, and Fastolf rode with him, escaping with their lives but leaving their honour trampled in the dirt.

The French vanguard slaughtered our archers and continued on until they smashed into our main force who were not deployed. It was not two armies fighting but knights against men. It was not battle but murder and Englishmen died in their thousands as we fled from the slaughter and were picked off one by one.

Out of our army of five thousand, we lost more than two thousand that day. Most of them were our archers. The French lost almost no one.

Fastolf escaped all the way back to Paris but Talbot was captured. Talbot actually had the gall to accuse Fastolf of deserting his comrades in the face of the enemy, a charge which he pursued vigorously once he had negotiated his release from French captivity. Fastolf hotly denied the charge and was eventually cleared of the charge by a special chapter of the Order of the Garter but everyone knew the truth. Every soldier of England. His name will forever be tainted, as rightly it should. Talbot, though deserves as much blame as anyone. But so do I. It was in my power to make myself a lord and so lead an army to victory but instead I was playing at being a soldier and it cost those brave men their lives and ultimately it cost England the throne of France.

The destruction of our army and the loss of veteran commanders had immediate and terrible consequences for our strategic and political position in France. It was a loss from which we would never recover. We were disorganised and frightened and over the following weeks the French swiftly regained swathes of territory to the south, east and north of Paris, filled with an energy that they had not possessed for a hundred years.

The French marched to Reims and there the Dauphin was crowned as King Charles VII of France on 17 July.

We knew the country so well and had been routiers and bandits for long that we slipped through the worst of it and smashed through the rest, until we made it back to Paris. We brought thirty-four archers with us, as well as a few pages and servants. It was a measly number and half of what we started with but those men were forever grateful to me for getting them home. So grateful that they stuck with us when we set out to fight the enemy once more. This time, I was determined to defeat the one who was responsible for the disaster.

I swore that I would find and kill Joan the Maiden.

17

Gilles' Confession

October 1440

STEPHEN ARRANGED IT SO THAT I was let into Gilles' chambers in the dark of the night. We were able to lean on enough people to gain access but it was far from officially sanctioned and Stephen kept watch from the other side of the chamber door while I went in. He seemed convinced that we would be discovered and rousted out at any moment.

"Are you going to kill him?" Stephen had asked a dozen times on the way to his quarters.

"No, no, certainly not," I said. "Most probably."

Stephen grabbed my arm. "We shall have to flee immediately if you do."

"I will restrain myself." After I spoke, I pulled away my arm away.

"Why do this at all, then? Merely to satisfy your curiosity? You risk spoiling the entire trial."

What could I say? That I wished to face the man who had defeated us on the battlefield? That I also needed to understand what had turned him into the monster that he was and whether such a degeneration was something that might lie in store for me or for my men?

"I simply must, that is all. I must."

When I closed the door behind me and stepped within, I was still not certain if I would do the deed. A murdered Gilles would leave the bereaved families without the sense that justice had been done. There would be many who would say he had been innocent of the charges and where would that leave the people? I would have to kill Poitou and Henriet, also, although I was dearly looking forward to that.

But I was so curious. I wanted to speak to him and find out why. To find out what he knew of William.

Perhaps these were excuses I told myself while yet knowing deep down that I was there to cut out his heart and feed it to him.

He stood across the other side of the room, watching me enter. An imposing figure in his own hall and in the courtroom, seeing him standing close made his stature and bearing even more impressive. Broad at the shoulder, tall, and slim, he looked like a man of immense strength and also gracefulness. Dressed in black velvet with silver embroidery, he looked like a starry night or a pot of black ink spilled across a desk reflecting candlelight. His hair was as black as the midnight outside the window.

"So," he said, holding his palms out by his side. "You have come at last." His voice was level and self-assured.

"How do you know me?" I asked him.

He raised one eyebrow and peered at my face. "Do you not know me, sir?" he replied. "You do not recognise me?"

"Certainly, I do. But I do not know from where. Or from when. Was it long ago?"

His shoulders slumped. "Long enough. As for where, why, it was here."

"Nantes?"

He seemed disappointed. "I suppose you have lived so long and done so much that it was an event of little significance to you. But it was near Tiffauges, a little less than a hundred years ago. Even then, I was the lord of Tiffauges, having taken it from another. But the castle was smaller then, and the lands about a little different. There is a hill, now bare and wind blasted and cropped close by the sheep but once the place was covered by a woodland. It was there where you ambushed me and my men. I called myself Charles de Coussey. You were looking for a knight who fought under a black banner. One of us."

"By God, I think I do recall it. I lost most of my company." That was the battle where Rob had been almost killed before I turned him and the other survivors into immortals.

"I very nearly defeated you," he said, smiling. "Though, you killed my horse and put your heel through my face. I had never known strength like yours and it terrified me, certain that all my efforts were to be undone. But I played the mortal and told you what you wanted to know about and you ransomed me back to my men, thank God. I knew at once who you were. You are my lord's evil brother, who he had warned me about so many years before."

"Your lord? Your lord is William," I said. "He told you that I was evil?" I scoffed at the audacity of it. "And William turned you into an immortal and he commanded you to become powerful and rich and to wait for his return."

"Just so," he said. "I was nothing when he found me, nothing. Not even a knight. My father was a carpenter, though I always liked to fight and I knew I would be a soldier one day. And then my lord found me and raised me up."

"Well, I must say that you have done well to raise yourself up. Another generation or two and you might have made yourself into a duke and one day even a king."

His lip trembled. "It was a long road from my beginnings to here."

"My brother chose you well, that much is clear. You have done remarkably well and to have done it alone, without others like you to help you. But then you went mad. You began murdering children, and delighting in their deaths, and practising perversions upon them."

He took a shaky breath. "Yes."

"Why?" I asked him. "Why have you done this?"

"You ask why?" he said. "My lord promised to return but it has been two hundred years! He has abandoned us, sir. It is clear that he meant never to return. And so what was I to do with my wealth? With my power? I was ready ten years ago, twenty. But now I know that it will never be. All that effort wasted. All the deaths, for nothing."

"But why the children, man?"

He shrugged. "Surely, you know the power in the blood of a child? It is powerful and pure. It gives us great strength, greater than a grown man can give. You have felt it."

"I have not felt it, nor will I ever."

"You pretend to some great morality? You, who are the incarnation of evil, like my master, your brother? Surely, you know that you are no different to me. How many have you murdered in your life? Hundreds? Thousands? There is no greater killer in all the days since Adam was thrown from the Garden than you, sir, and you look down on me for taking the lives of a few worthless peasant children?"

"Your evil will soon be ended. The lords of this land have finally done their duty to end you, and so they will."

He tilted his head, a small frown on his face. "The lords of this land are doing their duty? But, what on earth do you mean, sir?"

I scoffed. "The Bishop of Nantes has pushed for this investigation. And the Duke of Brittany also. The people could do nothing and that was what you counted on in order to carry out such an evil campaign of horror but your betters have done their duty."

Gilles' smile grew until he laughed. "You are more ancient and more powerful than I will ever be and yet you have a strange innocence about you. A guilelessness like that of a child... no, not quite. Not in all things. Only where lords and princes are concerned. It is a failing one sees in men cursed by noble birth such as yourself where you believe that the nobility are at their heart good and decent and virtuous yet the common man is base and petty and sinful. Well, let me tell you that I have been both commoner and noble and I see that there is no difference between the two."

"Utter nonsense," I said. "You are quite mad."

"Why, then, has our Duke acted to stage this trial now, sir? Why has his cousin the Bishop of Nantes acted on his behalf now?"

"Because I gathered the necessary evidence," I said, feeling uncertain.

"Indeed? And this could not have been done in the years gone by?"

"Why then?" I said, sharply.

"I am the vassal of Duke Jean of Brittany. And if I should be convicted of a capital crime, why, all my earthly property will become his. All of my castles, manors, my mills, villages, my libraries, and all my possessions. You should have no doubt that his first cousin and dear friend the Bishop will receive a considerable fraction of the total."

"You ascribe base motivations to those who are doing no more than their duty," I said. "You speak as though you are an innocent man being persecuted instead of a monster being dealt justice. I had hoped that there would be some secret to be revealed but now I see that you are nothing. For all your achievements, for all the wealth and power you hoarded, you are an empty vessel and when you are gone nothing will be different except that the children of these lands will be safe, finally."

He snorted. "You are nothing like your brother. He was wise beyond measure and learned in the arts and poetry and history and in the faith. A demon in human form and evil to his core, yes, but he was wise as God Himself. Yet you know nothing at all. You think these children will be safe, now, when I am gone? What world is it that you are from, sir? Do you believe that we live in Heaven already or do you understand that the earth we walk upon is already Hell itself?"

"You speak so lightly of Hell but soon you will go there. Perhaps you will meet that poor girl you sent there by your actions, the poor mad girl Joan of Lorraine, who you used for your earthly gain only to abandon and then see sent to the eternal flames when she burned at the stake."

He whipped around, eyes bulging, and he roared in my face. "Do not speak of her!"

Every inch of him shook as he stood with his fists raised. He was undoubtedly strong after so many years drinking vast amounts of blood every day and perhaps he was even stronger than I was. Still, he resisted attacking me and I resisted striking him.

Letting out a growl, he turned back and stalked away with his fists clenched at his sides.

"I will speak of what I like," I said, though I said it softly. "And I may even have you tortured so that you would speak the truth to me about her."

That brought him about again with fear in his eyes. Fear of the pain? Or of something else? The pain was enough, God knows.

"I will not have her good name sullied by doubters such as you."

"Her good name?" I said, incredulous. "She was burned as a heretic, sir, and she has no good name."

It seemed for a long moment that he was going to assault me after all but something passed behind his eyes and a forced casualness descended over him. "Even you must know her trial was a nonsense. An assassination by legal means."

"Must I? What about it was a nonsense?"

"Everything about it, from start to finish. It was theatre, played to convince the masses that her brilliance was not only over but that it had always been false. I am astonished that you lack the wit to see that."

"Why do you not convince me?"

He shrugged, suddenly affecting a lack of interest and turning away. "I have no need to convince you. Believe what you will, it is no concern of mine. Let us speak of it no longer."

"I know all about what happened," I said. Although I was guessing, I could not imagine it any other way. "What truly happened with you and Joan."

"Oh?" he said, warily, half turning and pausing where he stood.

"You discovered her, did you not? Knowing of the prophecy about a maiden from Lorraine who would save the kingdom of France, you found a girl who would act the part. You engineered the theatrics of her appearance. And then, when you were done with her, you cast her aside and she burned for it."

He turned slowly and gazed at me, his eyes narrowing

twinkling dark in reflected lamplight. Then he snorted. "Yes, yes," he said. "That is it. How insightful you are."

His manner was profoundly irritating. Childish, almost. It was enough to make me want to throttle him. "Tell me the truth, then."

He wafted a hand in the air. "The truth? You would not believe it."

"Do you not understand that you will face the Inquisition, Gilles? Whatever you are doing with your attempts at delay, they have failed. The King is not coming to save you. We have had word from the King's agents. You are abandoned. There will be no reprieve. All that remains is to have you put to the Question and there we will get the truth of your crimes from you."

His face took on the aspect of true despair, then. It seemed he had been hoping that the King would come.

"So be it," he managed to say.

"I will ensure they ask you about Joan of Lorraine," I said. "Everything about the Maiden. Where you found her, how you educated and trained her. It will be entered into the court documents and all France will know she was a fraud."

He sagged further and collapsed down into a chair by the window, hanging his head. "That is not it at all."

"Well, we will see," I replied. "I for one will delight in hearing your manipulations. You say that her trial was theatre to convince the masses that she had always been false but there are many in France who still believe in her. In her divine mission. One might say it yet moves the hearts of the common soldiery so that they fight with her inspiration stirring their hearts. But the Inquisition will pull the truth from your flesh and you will tell how you turned a young girl into a blood drinking demon and manipulated her into doing your bidding. Into deceiving even the King. Do you think France will still be inspired by her after the masses hear your words? Do you think the King will remember you well? Yes, I shall enjoy the sight of your tortures very much indeed, sir."

He gaped at me as I spoke and when he did not respond, I turned and strode away from him to lift the latch and so leave him to his fate.

"Wait!" he cried. "Wait. I will confess."

I turned from the door. "Come again?"

His face was white. "Call the Inquisitor. Call him now. I will confess my crimes now, this very night. The illusion has gone on as long as it needs to. I will tell it all."

"All?" I asked. "You will tell them that you are over two hundred years old and a drinker of blood? You will tell them of William?"

"Oh?" he said, a sly look creeping onto his face. "The whole truth concerns you, does it, Richard? You will be undone if I do, is that it? Perhaps I will tell them everything, not only about my own crimes but about yours as well."

"Feel free to do so. It will serve only to condemn you to die as a madman as well as a murderer."

He sagged again. "Yes, yes. What you say is true. And so I mean only that I will confess my crimes with the poor children. Then they will hang me." His voice shook as he spoke. "They will hang me and then, praise God, it will be done."

"You will hang," I said. "And you will burn."

He nodded, though he hid his face with his hands as he did so.

"Stephen," I said through the door. "Can you hear this?"

From the other side of the oak timbers, he replied without delay. "I will bring the Inquisitor at once," Stephen said.

While we waited, I observed Gilles de Rais, slumped in his chair. He seemed defeated but whether it was an act, a play performed only for me, I could not say. I recalled then the grand play he had put on in Orléans, an event so lavish that it had almost ruined the richest man in the kingdom. He had been playing the parts of so many men for so many years that surely deceit came easily to him. It certainly came increasingly easily to me and I had suffered and continued to suffer the consequences of it. All I could hold on to was that I was, by birth and by heart, an English knight. With that core knowledge of who I was, I could weather the storms of self-doubt and look to sustain the moral framework that such knowledge provided.

But Gilles was nobody. The son of a carpenter, he had said, who had likely gone off to war and done well. Perhaps he was destined to be a man-at-arms, for a lord or as a mercenary or as a roadside robber. But then he had become immortal, required to drink blood, and had been given a quest by a powerful immortal to grow rich and powerful and he had done it. To get there, however, he had been one man after another. Whatever his birth name had been, he had become Charles de Coussey, a routier knight. Later, he had made himself into a noble, and become Jean de Craon, a famed brute but a lordly one. And finally, he had become Gilles de Rais, a famed soldier, companion of Joan the

Maiden, become a Marshal of France. Who was he, really? Was he any of them? Which one of those men was sitting before me in that luxurious prison in Nantes? Did he even know himself?

"You need blood," I said, drawing his attention. "You need blood every day or two. Every three at the most, or else you will grow sick and lose your wits."

He eyed me warily. "Yes. But I am strong. From all the blood I have taken."

"Someone has been feeding you blood," I said.

He scoffed. "No."

"Who is helping you?" I asked, considering that his vast wealth would open many doors and perhaps even veins. "You have bought off servants, even here?" He clamped his mouth shut and turned away. "I suppose it hardly matters. Of course you have paid men to care for you. You have spent many lifetimes accumulating riches but you have never been shy about spending it to achieve your aims. You made and spent a fortune as if it were nothing to you. Are you being honest about your low birth? Or are you a nobleman after all?"

"I have no need to convince you of anything further," he said, and yet he continued. "I was born as low as can be. My father was not even competent as a carpenter. He could barely construct a coherent sentence, let alone build well or make wealth. If he had seen me as I was to become, he would have bowed and scraped low, like the miserable fool he was. I am to him as an angel might be to a mortal. The worlds I have seen would be so far beyond his comprehension that he would be forever blind to them and yet look what I became. It was difficult, at first, painful even. Learning to read and to write but there was some indefinable magic to it all that drove me on, some deep fascinating at the wisdom that might be contained in those black scribblings upon the page. In time, I found such a great love of literature in Latin and in Greek. By God, how I have loved the Lives of the Caesars by Suetonius. Do you know it, sir?"

It sounded familiar, but I could not bring myself to admit my ignorance to such a monster. "I cannot say that literature has touched me as deeply as it has you."

"Ah, such a magnificent work. Do you know, he describes the third emperor, who was Tiberius, as a man who enjoyed the secret practice of abominable lewdness? At his secluded palace, he entertained companies of young girls and catamites and assembled from all across his lands inventors of unnatural copulations, who defiled one another in his presence to inflame his ardour. He had several special chambers set round with pictures and statues in the most lascivious attitudes, contrived recesses in his groves for the gratification of lust, where young persons of both sexes prostituted themselves in caves and hollow rocks, in the disguise of little Pans and Nymphs before he himself—"

"Enough of your damned perversions!" I snapped. "Your professed love of literature is revealed as nothing more than your love of depravity. Not finding enough of it in Christian lands, you found it in the wicked texts of pagan kings and sought to fulfil it in life. It is all very clear, sir. Now, hold your damned tongue until the lords of the court come to hear your confession."

Gilles curled his lip in disgust and could not control himself enough to cease his crowing. "The subject may be depraved but the quality of the literature is itself inspiring. You would not understand. My lord said your soul was a small and shrivelled thing and I see that it is so."

"My soul is not perfect but yours has led you into a miserable existence, scurrying from murder to murder in the dark."

"Are you certain that you do not speak of yourself, sir?" His lip curled as he regarded me. "I made myself the most celebrated man in France. I wrote poetry and plays. I won the war for France, did I not?"

"And yet here you are. Soon to be hanged. A wasted life, is it not? You failed my brother."

His eyes flashed. "He failed me!"

"How so?"

Gilles almost wailed as he spoke. "He has abandoned us."

Us, he said.

"Who has William abandoned other than you? Certainly you do not speak of your vile servants in such terms."

Gilles covered his eyes with his hands and when he looked up and spoke, he seemed calm once more. "He has abandoned Christendom. A betrayal. Such a betrayal. And where does his betrayal leave me? What now am I?"

"A murderer of children?"

He grimaced. "Am I? Is that what I am? That is how the world will remember Gilles de Rais, no doubt. But that does not undo all that I have become."

"Some deeds are so evil that they define a life."

"I suppose that is true. I did try to stop it. I hope that I am allowed to beg you this much. That you believe I did try to stop it. But I was weak. I was powerless."

"There can be no excuses for this evil."

"I remain a good Christian. A perfect Christian, from my youth until this moment."

"You make a mockery of your words. You are a heretic."

"Never! Never that, never. I love Christ. He will forgive me. I will enter Heaven."

"If you make it to Heaven, I will slay you there, also."

He smiled. "What makes you believe you will go to Heaven? Do you attend Mass? Do you confess your sins? Do you believe in your heart that only Jesus Christ can bring you salvation?"

"I will not be questioned on my faith by you, demon."

"You and your traitorous brother are the cause of this evil, not me. I am a victim of it."

There was more truth in that than I cared to consider. "After you, William will die also. Have no fear of that."

"I pray that you each slay the other."

"What else has he done to you? Other than to abandon you after promising to return. You say he has turned against Christendom. How can you know this, if you have not heard from him?"

He opened his mouth, whether to answer or to deflect I do not know, as the door behind me was thrown open and the Chief Inquisitor strode in with the other chiefs of both courts trailing behind him in a swirling mass of robes and finery.

"What is this about a confession?"

"Praise God!" Gilles cried, and fell to his knees, clasping his hands together. "Please, Inquisitor, I beg you. Hear my honest and true and freely given confession and after, have me executed so that my torment is finally ended!"

∞

Present for the confession along with the Inquisitor was the Bishop of Saint-Brieuc representing the ecclesiastical court, and Master Pierre de L'Hopital from the civic court, Captain Jean Labbe on behalf of the Duke, and Stephen, the prosecutor. The Inquisition's scribes wrote down what was said and servants attended to their masters.

I was present, as a squire in service of the ecclesiastical court, and none of those great lords attempted to be rid of me, for they were rightly afraid of Gilles de Rais, a big and powerful soldier as well as likely heretic and murderer, and needed a brute like me to make them feel secure.

He was seated in a chair by the narrow window, facing us. We stood or sat or leaned in a great arc around him, from one side of the room to another. The Inquisitor sat at the centre, upright and leaned forward on a rather high stool.

"So, then," the Inquisitor said. "On the subject of the abduction and death of many children, and the libidinous, sodomitic, and unnatural vice, the cruel and horrible manner of the killings, and also the invocations of demons, oblations, immolations or sacrifices, the promises made or the obligations

270

contracted with the demons by you, you wish to make a statement of confession?"

"Yes," the Marshal said without hesitation. "Yes, to all."

The Inquisitor sighed and looked down his nose. "You shall have to do better than that, my lord."

He nodded frantically. "I will say anything that I am required to say to swiftly end this ordeal. An ordeal I richly deserve, of course, my lords. And so I must say that I freely, voluntarily, and grievously confess to committing each and every crime for which I am charged by both courts. I have committed and maliciously perpetrated on numerous children the crimes, the sins, and offences of... of homicide and... sodomy. I confess also that I have committed the invocations of demons, what was it? Oblations and immolations. That I made promises and obligations, as stated, to demons. And done all the other things to which I am charged."

"Very good. We will require more. We must have details. We must have reasons."

"Reasons, my lord?"

"Your motivations, no matter how perverse, for committing these crimes."

"Yes, yes, of course. How would you like me to say it?"

"In your own words, tell me, when did you begin committing these crimes?"

"In the Champtoce Castle, during the time when my grandfather was alive. I do not know what year. I suppose it really started when my grandfather died and Gilles de Rais took over. When I inherited."

"Who persuaded you to commit these crimes?"

"Persuaded me? No one persuaded me. I committed them according to my imagination and my ideas, without anyone's counsel and following my own feelings, sir."

"But, for what purpose?"

For the purpose of blood, I thought. For his need to drink. But of course it was far more than that.

"Solely for my pleasure and my carnal delight. And not with any other intention or to any other end." As he said this, he glanced briefly at me and then looked quickly away.

"I struggle to understand," the Inquisitor said, shaking his head. "I find it very surprising that a man could commit crimes such as this for no reason. To what ends have you had the children killed and committed on them the sins we have heard about and had their cadavers burned?"

"I confess that I took pleasure in the hurting and the killing of them. Some I killed by removing their heads from their bodies, others by striking with clubs on their heads or necks. Others I throttled by hand or by ropes and cords, suspending them from hooks and pegs on my walls. It gave me joy to watch their anguish and confusion as they died. I delighted in destroying innocence, I suppose. It was satisfying to me to eradicate their innocence in every way that I could imagine. I am the opposite of innocence, you see. It is the antithesis to what I have become. It is something so far removed from what I have made myself that I sought to destroy it from the face of the earth. And my perversions knew no bounds. Even in death, I enjoyed defiling their corpses further. After so many killed, it slowly became tedious to me and I had to become ever more creative in my activities in order to maintain the joy. Even then, it grew ever more mundane until I found myself filled with misery but unable to stop." He broke off, his voice shaking.

"Please, continue to explain your crimes."

"Alas, my lord, you torment yourself and me along with you!"

The Inquisitor looked down his nose and replied calmly. "I do not torment myself in the least but I am very surprised at what you have told me and simply cannot be satisfied with it. I desire and would like to know the absolute truth from you for the reasons I have already told you."

Gilles glanced at me again. "Truly, there was no other cause, no other end nor intention, if not what I have told you. I have admitted to enough to kill ten thousand men. Let it be done but once to me."

"Well, my lord, we shall certainly see it done but it must be done in the proper, legal fashion. And so I will have you speak of your dealings with the invocation of demons and the oblation of the blood of the said small children and the places where you performed these acts."

"In order to solicit from the demon's evil, I had a note drafted in my own blood promising to give the devil, when he appeared, whatever he required excepting my life and my soul. My soul is still mine and God's and has always remained so. I must be sure that you understand that. I must be sure."

"I hear you and your assertion is so recorded. Continue."

Gilles took a slow breath and nodded. "Prelati summoned them many times and told me he saw them and spoke to them but I never did see them, not once, sadly. I gave him whatever he needed, whether it be blood or limbs or gold."

"Why did you wish to summon a demon or many demons? For what purpose?"

"To have powerful creatures to do my bidding. Prelati assured me that a demon would help in the transmutation."

"You wanted the demons to help to create gold?"

"Yes, indeed. I found myself in financial difficulties due to large expenses and I wished to recover it, and to make more. To make a fortune. To make myself richer than any king. Alas, alas, it did not work."

"We have heard from Prelati, who stated that you provided him the blood, the hands, eyes, and the hearts of children. You did this in the hopes of creating gold?"

"It is true, yes."

The Inquisitor sighed and rubbed his eyes. "We shall end this now. I suggest that you repeat what you have spoken here during the next session of the court and the Bishop will move to pass sentence."

"I will," Gilles de Rais said. "Praise God."

We filed out and before I left I looked back at him. He seemed relieved and that was understandable, assuming he was seeking the relief of death. But I thought I sensed something else. Just a hint of triumph, quickly suppressed. At the time, I convinced myself that I was imagining things. I would soon discover it was triumph indeed and everything was going according to his plan.

But the overwhelming thoughts on my mind after I left was how impassioned Gilles had been when he spoke of Joan.

Do not speak of her! he had said, raging at me. Even you must know her trial was a nonsense. Everything about it, from start to finish. It was theatre, played to convince the masses that her brilliance was not only over but that it had always been false.

It was plain to see that it had affected him profoundly. Perhaps her death was what had finally driven him into madness.

I wondered also whether he knew how close I had come to capturing her myself.

18

The Trial of Joan

March 1431

AFTER THE DAUPHIN WAS CROWNED and became the King, Joan had urged the new king to storm Paris, as she had foretold.

We fought off the assault and Joan was wounded in the leg by a crossbow bolt. King Charles ordered the retreat from Paris and sought to find a diplomatic solution with the Burgundians that would allow him to be rid of the English and at the same time he quietly excluded Joan. Her manic pleas for endless assaults and grand pronouncements ceased being helpful and began to be a hindrance. In the hope that she would take the hint and go away, he made her and her family into nobility. They were awarded an annual sum from the crown and were allowed all the other legal benefits of being above the station of commoners. Such a thing was not unheard of but usually was granted only to a fabulously wealthy and successful soldier or courtier after a lifetime of service and most people, lords especially, saw the ennobling as the farce that it was.

As the King withdrew active support, so too did other lords and knights until the number of men around her dwindled. Of the great men, only Gilles de Rais remained at her side. And he did so almost to the end.

But Joan did not take the hint and she would not give up her struggle. She would not be sidelined by anyone, not even the King of France, and so she continued to throw herself into any conflict that she could find in the hope that her strength of will would carry the day.

In May 1430, a year after her triumphs at Orléans, she led a force that attempted to attack the Burgundian camp at Margny north of Compiègne.

But I was hunting her.

Together with a handful of loyal archers we had tracked her from Saint-Pierre-le-Moûtier to La-Charité-sur-Loire to Compiègne but she was always too well protected. Once, we saw her at a distance and Rob had begged to be allowed to shoot her with an arrow but I had denied him.

"It must be over two hundred yards, Rob," I said. "It would serve only to alert them to our presence and we would be killed."

"I can hit her in the crown, I swear it."

"And you could hit her in the eye if only she was looking up," Walt said. "And shoot it up her arse if only she was bending over."

But with every failed attack that Joan led, her protectors dwindled in number and we got closer and closer to springing an ambush on her so that I could cut her damned throat.

When the French army withdrew into the fortifications of Compiègne after six thousand additional Burgundian soldiers arrived, Joan stayed with the rear guard of the army. We stayed close, moving parallel to Joan's position at the rear, keeping our distance. But when the Burgundians caught up with the French, they began skirmishing as they moved. Darting attacks by mounted men attacked stragglers and picked them off, which drew more French soldiers back to protect their comrades. And so the Burgundian vanguard crept up and slowly consumed the French rearguard, nibbling away at it until their flanks started to envelop them like a snake swallowing a rat. Joan's banner was visible as she attempted to rally her soldiers.

"This is our chance," I said, kicking my heels back and started out toward them. "We have to get through the lot of them and take her."

"They'll take us for Frenchmen," Walt pointed out, using his spurs to catch up with me.

"What's the Burgundian cry, now?" Rob asked, coming up behind with the archers.

"We will cry for Duke Philip," I said.

And that is what we did, crying his name as we pushed our horses boldly through the flanks of Burgundian forces and they cheered us on. Many even followed us in as we clashed with desperate Frenchmen and cut them down or drove them away.

The Maiden's white banner fluttered above the mass of men

so closely that I could have thrown a stone and hit it but there were many fighting to protect her. I did not know whether I would have the courage to cut her down or if I would have to take her prisoner but I was saved from making the decision.

From the opposite flank came a massive charge by two hundred Burgundian men-at-arms, crying out for their lord and for their duke and the hooves thundered and trumpets blasted and the fear of it overwhelmed the French, who dropped their weapons and fled as the assault crashed into them. It was slaughter and they abandoned their beloved Maiden to her fate.

Many ran toward the rest of their army but even more ran directly opposite to the attack, which meant they were driven into us. We cut them down and pushed on through the press of desperate men and I shouted and cursed but it did no good.

Amongst so many men and horses, she appeared to be very small to my eyes. She wore a helm with no visor but I could not get a good look at her face. At a glance, it appeared snub-nosed and quite unattractive. Her armour was excellent, and her horse was one I would have killed to have under me but she did not use his size and strength in an attempt to break free of her encirclement. Perhaps it was my imagination but she seemed stunned by being abandoned and surely believed that it was all over. Still, she refused to lower the great banner and her squire, the only loyal man remaining, did not lower his sword. The Burgundians shouted at her to dismount and to give herself up but she sat and stared back at them.

"I could shoot her now, Richard?" Rob suggested from the saddle, his bow in hand with an arrow nocked. Even from horseback, I expected he could hit the target.

I sighed. "A thousand Burgundians would tear us to pieces for denying them their prize. Leave it, Rob. It is done."

The Maiden of Orléans was pulled from her horse by a Burgundian archer who rushed forward to do the deed and she fell hard. This brought others crowding in close about her so that when she regained her feet, covered in mud, she found herself surrounded by half a hundred soldiers with no ally but her squire at her side. Even then, she was too proud to give herself up until a nobleman from Luxembourg volunteered to be her captor. This she agreed to and she was seized. Her famous banner was grabbed and torn and trampled as men tried to take a piece for themselves.

It was done but I could not entirely rid my thoughts of her.

Joan was imprisoned by the Burgundians at Beaurevoir Castle, north beyond Paris and I made sure to follow closely what happened to her by employing Stephen and Eva's agents. The girl made several escape attempts, one of them being her leap from seventy feet up. When she recovered the use of her legs after a few days, she was moved further north to the Burgundian town of Arras.

Throughout her imprisonment, the lords of England negotiated with the Burgundians to transfer Joan into our custody. Eventually, we bought her for ten thousand livres, which was a vast sum.

Immediately, she was transported to Rouen, our soundest stronghold on the continent and I took my men there. Lucky that I did, for the French launched a number of small campaigns against us there in the hopes of rescuing her. One campaign occurred during the winter of 1430-1431, another in March 1431, and one in late May shortly before her execution. Of course, each time we beat them back. We were not so far gone as all that.

The French were outraged that we had their beloved Maiden of Orléans. King Charles VII threatened to exact vengeance upon Burgundian troops in his captivity and also he threatened a terrible fate for the English and women of England in retaliation for our treatment of her. Many believed that the French meant to invade England but I doubted such a thing was even possible for a kingdom still so divided and in turmoil as that of France. Still, they were angry to say the least.

The English celebrated the coronation of Henry VI as King of France at Notre-Dame cathedral in Paris on 16 December 1431, the boy king's tenth birthday. Charles VII however continued to act as if he was the legitimate king and it was difficult to argue. Indeed, his diplomacy was far greater than ours. Before we could rebuild our military leadership and replace our veteran archers, we lost our alliance with Burgundy when the Treaty of Arras was signed in 1435. The Duke of Bedford died the same year and Henry VI became the youngest king of England to rule without a regent.

But back in January 1431, in Rouen, Joan was put on trial. The tribunal was composed entirely of pro-English and Burgundian clerics and overseen by the Duke of Bedford and the Earl of Warwick. They meant to not only destroy her but also to humiliate her and through her, all France.

"It is we who shall be humiliated," Stephen grumbled after it started. We sat drinking in our rooms in Rouen one night after the trial had begun.

"You believe she will be acquitted?"

"Ha! No, indeed. Far from it. These bastards are going to convict her no matter what. The law be damned."

"What law?"

He waved his hand. "Ecclesiastical law, English law. Bishop Cauchon lacks jurisdiction over the case but he oversees it anyway purely because of his open support of us. And the English crown is paying for the entire thing, all expenses, so what does that mean for a fair outcome? The Inquisition has very clear rules regarding the standard of evidence allowed for the trial but this has been utterly disregarded and the evidence so far submitted is absurdly weak."

"Oh?"

"Look, the testimony gathered by the notary does not even technically allow the court to initiate the trial but they have gone and done it anyway." He took a great gulp of his wine and wiped his lips before ploughing on. "And then they violate the rules again by denying the girl the right to a legal adviser."

"That girl is an enemy of England, Stephen."

"The rule of law should be followed nevertheless. The law must be applied equally to all or else it becomes a worthless thing. If she truly is a heretic, she should burn. Of course she should. But every member of the tribunal is bought and paid for by the English, one way or another."

"The Inquisition are supporting it," I pointed out.

Stephen laughed. "The Vice-Inquisitor objected to the trial from the outset and yet his life was threatened."

"Rumours, that is all."

"It is true for him and for other clergy at the trial. I spoke personally to that Dominican Isambart de la Pierre, and he swore to God that Englishmen had threatened the lives of his family, Richard!"

"If true, that is rather heavy-handed, I admit." I pointed over my cup at him. "If true, that is."

"The standards for heresy trials are very clear. They must be judged by an impartial or balanced group of clerics. It is heresy, Richard. It hardly gets more serious than this and yet the rules are being discarded in order to achieve the desired outcome. The law is what protects the common man from the rampant predations of their lords. Disregarding it demeans us to ourselves and also to our enemies. Were we not better than this, once? Do you think the third Edward would have allowed this? Or the fifth Henry?"

"They would not have lost the damned war in the first place," I said, growling as I thought of it. "And yet you are right."

"I am."

"You know so much about the law, Stephen. Perhaps you should use your coming time away from London to train as a lawyer. You have mentioned wanting to do so in years gone by, I believe."

"Bah, I have so much else to do from afar. I would not like to leave it all to Eva in my absence, there is too much business to attend to on behalf of the Order."

"And yet you have such a passion for it. The Order's finances are strong enough, thanks to you, that we can do without you for a while. Why not take a decade or two? Perhaps if you had already made yourself into a powerful lawyer, you could have had an influence on this trial. Perhaps you could have persuaded them to follow the rules a little more."

He took a long while to answer but, in the end, waved it away. "They will have her destroyed no matter what. I could do nothing to change her fate."

I shrugged. "Especially as she is a heretic."

"So sure, are you?"

"She is either a heretic or God Himself is a Frenchman. And that is too terrible a notion to entertain."

Even Joan herself complained on her first day being questioned that the tribunal were all enemies and she requested that ecclesiastics of the French side be invited to provide the balance required in law. This request was simply denied.

The Maiden of Orléans continued to do very well for herself when questioned in the public court. I could not bring myself to attend for most of it and the couple of times I did, I stood at the rear of the hall. When she spoke, however, she did not sound like an illiterate commoner from Lorraine. That is, she had the rough accent of such a girl. But she spoke with such forceful confidence that it seemed she was filled with the righteousness of one of noble birth. And not so much a princess as she seemed a prince, arrogant and dismissive when questioned and openly contemptuous of the intelligence displayed by the members of the tribunal who launched questions at her unceasingly.

Somehow, without the presence of legal or ecclesiastical advice, this young girl was able to evade the theological pitfalls the tribunal had set up to entrap her.

One day when I was there, a bishop launched one of those traps.

"Tell me, do you know if you are in God's grace?"

Stephen, at my side, winced.

"What is it?" I whispered, while Joan hesitated in answering.

"If she says that she is then she is admitting that she knows God's will."

I shrugged. "And?"

Stephen sighed. "If she says yes, she is admitting to heresy, Richard!"

A single question with the power to convict her before all the lords of the Church. After so much of her grandstanding and insisting on her closeness to God's angels, it seemed impossible that she would avoid falling for it.

Finally, she spoke up in a clear voice that echoed like the ringing of a bell. "If I am not, may God put me there," she said. "And if I am, may God so keep me."

The lords of the church sitting behind their benches were struck dumb at her answer and the public muttered and sighed.

Stephen let out a surprised exclamation. "Well, I never."

"That was a fine thing to say," I said.

"It was brilliant, Richard," he replied, shaking his head in wonder. "Quite brilliant."

On and on the trial went, with repeated days where she was questioned for hours and in between was kept in awful conditions in prison under the guard of English soldiers. The Inquisition's rules dictated that she should have been kept in an ecclesiastical prison with nuns watching over her but again this was simply ignored. She appealed to the Pope but her appeals were not passed on. Over the weeks, she grew thinner and paler. Never an attractive girl, she became quite unpleasant to look upon. All this was of course another attempt at breaking her will. It grew hard for me to maintain my anger at her.

When she was stupefied by the physical and mental exertions, they cornered her and forced her to sign a document on pain of execution if she did not. The girl was illiterate and knew not what she had signed and even then the admission of guilt which she signed was substituted for another before it was submitted to the court.

But even conviction for heresy was not a capital offence. She was condemned to live her life in prison and all expected her to be transferred to a convent for the rest of her days. It seemed done and dusted and few English or Normans complained about the sentence. It seemed fair to me and to everyone I spoke to.

And yet the lords could not abide her getting away with her life and so she was set up in such a way as to condemn herself.

Ever since setting out from Lorraine on her God-given quest, Joan had dressed a page and also in armour, although this was allowed under Church doctrine where cross-dressing was permitted if it was to protect the wearer from rape.

Joan had agreed in her signed abjuration document to from that day on to forever wear feminine clothing. A few days after her abjuration she resumed male attire as a defence against molestation and because her dress had been taken by the guards and she was left with nothing else to wear.

The lords of the court were conveniently marched in at that

very moment to catch her in the act of wearing a man's clothing. And thus she had gone back on her abjuration agreement and so she was now legally a lapsed heretic.

This verdict meant death.

I heard in the taverns and inns after it happened exactly how it had occurred. It made me miserable to hear it but the place was awash with the tale. Joan was brought out into the marketplace in Rouen. They had put her in a pretty, long white dress. She was far from her former, fierce self and came on with her head bowed and her body shaking. In the square was a great stake standing up, twice the height of a man, with bundle after bundle of branches and logs all around it, drenched in oil. It was to that stake that she was bound with chains and they came forward with a torch and set the mass of it ablaze. The oil went up quick, catching the dry sticks and burning white hot.

"An English soldier gave her two sticks tied together in the shape of a crucifix," one old man said to me, showing me the size of it with his hands. "Little one, about so high. She placed it against her bosom."

"Shut up, did she," another man said. "I never saw that."

"She bloody well did and I'll knock out the teeth of any man who says otherwise."

Most agreed that the girl said nothing the entire time. The girl who had said so much, who had spoken with such certainty that an entire nation had been moved to action, moved to victory, hung her head and said nothing when she was burned. Nothing, that is, until the flames took her and blackened her feet and legs and blistered her skin in boiling agony, when she cried out the holy name of Jesus Christ in a plaintive, terrible cry.

The fire was enormous and burned high and hot and turned the girl's body to ashes, even the bones. All swore, though none knew how they knew, that the only part to survive was her heart. But they swept up her ashes and threw them into the Seine, and then they tossed her heart in after.

And although I saw none of it, I could see it all in my mind's eye as if I had been witness to the terrible event.

"You feel guilty," Stephen pronounced.

"Nonsense," I replied. "It was nothing to do with me. Anyway, what happened? She had told them what they wanted to hear. She was bound for a convent, perhaps one day they would have freed her and sent her home. What occurred to cause her to destroy herself?"

"After she signed the paper of abjuration, she lay in her cell for two days, wearing ordinary women's dress. But someone meant to do her in, I must suppose. Someone wanted her to fall. To burn. So they took away her dress and in its place brought the clothing of a boy and laid it before her. It was the very same clothing that she had been forced to give up before. For a time, she refused to don that clothing, knowing what it would mean. But she was naked. Naked before her guards, the English guards, who leered at her and told her what they meant to do to her body. She was yet in chains and confined to that cell and had no one to turn to for protection. And so she put them on."

"That was enough to convict her?"

"It was theatre, of a sort. A pantomime. The next morning, after she dressed in the forbidden clothing, a procession of judges burst in on her while she lay in bed. They crowded around her and demanded to know why she had sinned once more. Why she had relapsed into heresy. She did her best to explain that she had worn the clothes only to protect her modesty, they railed at her and named her a witch and a prostitute and a heretic and they were overjoyed to condemn her. Joan would be burnt after all."

"She would have known that they would have killed her. Why did she choose to wear the clothes? Surely, better to be shamed and abused than burned on the pyre?"

"Is it? Would you allow your body to be so violated? Think of it. Think how she guarded her maidenhead. Her virginity was in part the source of her holy power. Perhaps she knew they meant to destroy her by any means necessary and so she decided to embrace it. Would you live life as a slave, Richard?"

"Not if there was no hope of escape."

"Why did you not attend the execution?"

"Why would I wish to witness such a thing?"

"She has been your enemy. She was the instrument of your losses in the war."

"Our losses, Stephen. England's losses. But was she the cause of it all? Or was she a victim? There must have been a man telling her what to say and how to act. More than one, perhaps. How could a mere girl do such things as she did? How old was she at the end? She had not yet twenty years. Perhaps it was this man who inveigled to have her so executed, in order to stay her tongue for eternity lest it might reveal his hand."

"What man?"

"What man indeed? The new King of France or one of his

courtiers?"

"Do you not think she may have been one of William's? That business with her wounds, and the leap from the tower."

"Yes, it is of course possible, but it is not enough in itself. These things are perhaps within the limits of mortal endurance, just about, if that mortal is filled with passion."

"Or perhaps God truly did send angels to speak with her."

"I refuse to believe that God favours the French," I said but I did wonder whether it was true. "Anyhow, it matters not at all. Not any longer. The heretic has burned and that is the end of it."

"It is," Stephen said, his face grey and drawn as he looked up at me. "You know, Richard. I do believe I may take up your suggestion. To become a lawyer. It would be a good thing for the Order to have me educated in such matters and perhaps... perhaps one day I might even see some justice done thanks to my hand. Justice done for the common people against the exploitations of the powerful lords."

I thumped him on the shoulder. "A noble intention, sir. I wish you well in it."

Whether she had been an immortal, or the victim of a clever lord's manipulations, or inspired genius or even, heaven forfend, a genuine messenger from God, she had not deserved her suffering and her awful death. And I felt guilty for my part in all of it, as small as it was.

At least, that is what I thought and felt for many years, until shortly after the execution of Gilles de Rais when I would finally discover the terrible truth.

292

19

The Execution of Gilles de Rais October 1440

IN THE ECCLESIASTICAL COURT IN NANTES on Saturday October 22nd 1440, I watched the prisoner Gilles de Rais admit before the assembled bishops, vicars of the Inquisition, and members of the public, that he was guilty of every crime that he was accused of.

He wept as he spoke, though he spoke at length and detailed his actions, drawing gasps and exclamations from his audience.

At one point, as Gilles described his processes of dismembering, the Bishop of Nantes stood and covered the golden crucifix behind him with a white cloth, lest it be tainted with the evil before it.

He also named his accomplices, pointing them out in their iron cage, and condemning them utterly, though not all would suffer the same fate. During his confession, he also reaffirmed with passion his assertion that he never promised his soul to the demon he wished to summon with Prelati.

Finally, it came to the long-awaited pronouncement of guilt and the sentencing from the ecclesiastical court.

"We decree and declare that you, the aforesaid Gilles de Rais, present before us in trial, are found guilty of perfidious apostasy as well as of the dreadful invocation of demons, which you maliciously perpetrated, and that for this you have incurred the sentence of excommunication and other lawful punishments, in order to punish and salutarily correct you and in order that you are punished and corrected as the law demands and canonical sanctions decree."

"My soul remains mine and my soul remains God's!" Gilles cried, shaking with passion, with tears streaming down his cheeks. "I am a sinner, I confess it, I am the worst sinner who ever was and I beg God for His forgiveness before I die. I humbly implore the mercy and pardon of My Creator and most blessed Redeemer, as well as that of the parents and friends of the children so cruelly massacred, as well as that of everyone whom I could have injured in regard to which I am guilty, whether they are here present or elsewhere. And I ask all of Christ's faithful and worshippers for the assistance of your devout prayers."

At this theatrical confession, the Bishop was almost weeping himself, for such great sin allowed for equally great forgiveness and so was delightful to a true Christian.

It was a convincing spectacle, though Stephen and I exchanged a look. I admit that even I was halfway convinced of his contrition.

"You will have opportunity to undo the sentence of excommunication," the Bishop said. "It is clear that, despite your crimes, you remain a true Christian in your heart and I confirm that you will be allowed to make your final, secret confession. And you will have the opportunity to be absolved of your sins, and you will have imposed on you for all your sins a salutary penance in proportion to your faults, as much for those you have judicially confessed as for those you will confess at the tribunal of your conscience."

"Oh, God bless you," Gilles cried, falling to his knees. "Praise God!"

Afterwards, the accused was brought to the civil court, where his previous confession was read aloud and he confirmed it was true and then he was condemned for the murders and rebellion that he had admitted to. And then he was sentenced.

"We declare that you are to be immediately taken from this place to be hanged and then burned," the President of the court said. "But, in conjunction with a request from the ecclesiastical court, you will be given time to make holy confession and then to beg God's mercy and prepare to die soundly with numerous regrets for having committed the said crimes. The clerical servants Prelati and Blanchet are sentenced to spend the remainder of their natural lives in prison, on account that neither are found guilty of committing murder by their own hands and were found to be orthodox in their faith. The servants Henriet Griart and

Poitou are sentenced to be hanged and then to be burned."

"Thank you, my lord!" Gilles cried. "May I beg that my servants, Henriet and Poitou, be executed immediately after I am so killed? And might it be that I, who am the principal cause of the misdeeds of my servants, might be able to comfort them, speak to them of their salvation at the hour of execution, and exhort them by example to die fittingly. I fear, if it were otherwise, and my servants not see me die, that they shall fall into despair, imagining that they were dying while I, who am the cause of their misdeeds, go unpunished. I hope, on the contrary, with the grace of Our Lord, that I who made them commit the misdeeds for which they are dying would be the cause of their salvation."

The President of the court was clearly deeply moved by Gilles' profound contrition and accorded him this favour.

"Praise God," Gilles said, crossing himself and gazing adoringly at the President.

"What do you make of it?" I asked Stephen, when the court was adjourned.

"Do you mean is he mad or is he truly seeking salvation?" Stephen asked.

"I mean, what the Hell is the sneaky bastard up to, Stephen?"

"Up to?" Stephen asked. "What can he be up to? He is about to be hanged and burned to ashes. What can he do?"

"I do not know," I admitted. "But I know that I do not like it. He has obviously been drinking blood in his captivity. And so have the servants, who are revenants and require it every day."

"So you say," Stephen said. "And yet you have been unable to discover who has been paid off."

"It could be the whole bloody episcopal staff, for all I know."

"You are allowing your apprehensions to get the best of you. He is in irons. He will make his last confession and then he will burn, along with the revenants. So what does it matter?"

"Yes, yes," I snapped, irritated by his damned reasoning. "Let us go and watch them burn."

"The crowds already gather," Stephen said. "But we can witness it from the balcony in the palace. Come. I am going to enjoy this greatly."

"As shall I."

By the time we reached the chamber on the fourth floor of the Bishop's palace, the square was packed with people standing shoulder to shoulder and nose to neck. None of them had ever seen anything like it in all their lives and every road approaching the square was likewise filled, as were the bridges across the river. The entire city had come to a standstill and the Bishop and the Duke's soldiers struggled to keep them back from the scaffold and the stakes with their mounds of logs and kindling already prepared. A noise welled up as the condemned were led out from a doorway into the hall on the far side, and the soldiers fought to push back at the surge of the crowd.

As Gilles stood before the dangling noose, he raised his hands and called for silence. We were very far distant and far above him but his voice was loud and it echoed from the four sides of the square.

"Pray to God for me, good people," he said. They fell quiet, perhaps astonished at his brazenness or his piety. "I confess once more, this time before you, to all the crimes to which I was charged and found guilty. Before you, I beg my two servants to in their hearts seek the salvation of their souls and I urge them to be strong and virtuous in the face of diabolical temptations, and to have profound regret and contrition of their misdeeds, as do I. And also to have confidence in the grace of God and to believe that there is no sin a man might commit so great that God in His goodness and kindness would not forgive, so long as the sinner felt profound regret and great contrition of heart and I ask Him for mercy. Dear God, have mercy."

Poitou and Henriet appeared distraught but hopeful and they thanked their master for his words.

Gilles then fell to his knees, folded his hands together and begged God's mercy again. "My friends, who have come here to see a sinner, you should know that as a Christian, I am your brother. Those amongst you whose children I have killed, for the love of Our Lord's suffering, please be willing to pray to God for me and to forgive me freely, in the same way that you yourselves intend God to forgive and have mercy on yourselves."

"What a disgusting display," I said.

"Nothing he says is inconsistent with orthodoxy," Stephen said.

"I know that I am uneducated in these things but surely you see that it is monstrous, Stephen. He compares himself with them."

Gilles raised his voice. "Let me be killed first," he cried. "And my men to follow. Please, good fellows of Nantes, build the fires and prepare the noose."

"Finally," I muttered.

The fires were started in the base of the three bundles and the flames grew. I wished that the living, conscious Gilles would be placed in the fire so that his agony would be prolonged and terrible but he would hang first.

"Now we will see," Rob said.

"Prepare your coin, sir," Walt replied.

"Coin?" I asked, turning to them. "What coin?"

"Ah," Rob said. "It is nothing, Richard."

Walt suddenly studied the clouds above, pretending not to hear me.

"What are you up to?"

Rob sighed. "Walt does not believe that the noose will kill him. But I say that it will throttle the life from an immortal and the revenants, just as it would a mortal man. How can it not?"

I stared at them both. "And you are betting coin on the outcome?"

Walt looked at me, then. "Do you wish to place a bet, Richard?"

"I wish that the noose does nothing and that the man dies in the fire in the full possession of his wits. I wish that his immortal strength prolongs his suffering in the flames. I would cook him slowly, if I was down there. I would feed him my own blood to keep him in agony for hours or days so that he begs me to end his life."

"So," Walt said, "how many ecus do you want to put in?"

"There he goes," Stephen said.

A heavy silence filled the air. Down in the square, Gilles stepped up to the noose and up onto a short stool. The noose was placed over his head and tightened around his neck. A shouted order was given and the stool pulled away.

Gilles dropped and his feet kicked and his body thrashed. It did not take long until he was motionless and he was lifted by the executioners, the noose removed and he was carried to the fire. His body was placed upon the burning logs at the base of the fire and his hair was singed and his clothes caught fire. His skin reddened and shone.

Then they pulled him out.

I grasped Stephen's arm. "What are they doing?"

The executioners patted the fire from his clothes and lifted him onto a handcart and pushed him through the lines of soldiers back toward the hall on the other side of the square to us.

"What in the name of God is going on?" I asked again.

Stephen turned to me, his eyes wide. "I do not know."

"Where is the Bishop?" I asked the men behind me. "Where is the bloody Bishop?" I grabbed a priest by his robes and glared at him.

"He is viewing it from his chambers, sir," one of the other priests said.

We raced through the corridor and threw open the Bishop's door with his guards trailing after us, shouting warnings even as Walt and Rob held them back.

"What is going on?" I shouted at the Bishop, who turned from his window with fear and outrage in his eyes. "Why was he not burned?"

"Who are you to speak to me in such a way?"

I grasped him by the neck and lifted him from his feet,

pushing him against the wall. "Where are they bloody-well taking him, you God damned fat fool?"

The Bishop's eyes flicked over my shoulder, searching for rescue. I slapped his face and shook him.

"He... he... he begged to avoid being turned to ashes. He begged for his body to be allowed to be buried. His request was granted. What does it matter if he is dead all the same? He died in a state of—"

"You fools!" I said, and threw him down to my feet. "He is escaping. All he needs is human blood and he will be returned to full health. Where did they take him? Who took him?"

The Bishop shook his head. "He was to be taken by certain ladies of high rank and prepared for burial. I know not where."

I turned to Stephen. Behind him, Walt and Rob held five of the palace guards prisoner with their own weapons.

"We must cross the square to the hall," I said. "But we cannot go through that crowd."

"I know a route," Stephen said. "Through the palace, crossing by the cathedral and then on to the hall."

"Lead the way!"

We raced through the palace after Stephen, clattering down stairways and pushing priests and servants aside. We were faster than mortals and left the trailing guards behind but once we left the palace, the crowds were so great that we had to force our way through men and woman and children. As we crossed a street, I saw over the heads of the crowd into the square. Two great plumes of raging red fire and filthy smoke lit up the blackened corpses of Poitou and Henriet Griart.

By the time we made it to the hall, the body of Gilles de Rais had disappeared.

"He was taken for burial by high-born women," many told us.

"What does that mean?" I cried. "Where did they take him? Where?"

No one knew.

We raced from the city and watched the roads south and north and chased down every possible wagon and company that it might be but none were Gilles, nor these supposed high-born women.

"It is my fault," I said to Stephen as we looked down yet another empty road as night approached. "The entire time, he has been getting help from people in Nantes. Someone was bringing him blood, even to the servants, but I did not care about that. I thought it mattered not and yet he somehow retained servants, guards, these damned women. I thought we had him. I am a fool. Such a fool."

I had lost him.

He was gone.

20

A Bloody Messenger

October 1440

WE SLIPPED BACK INTO THE CITY before nightfall, hoping to avoid the Bishop's palace and any guards who we knew would certainly still be looking to arrest us.

"Where would he go?" I asked Stephen in the darkness, riding toward the centre of Nantes. "Surely, not to Tiffauges. He knows that we would look for him there."

"He has a dozen castles to choose from and surely it must be at least one of them. Where else can he go?"

As a mounted group, we seemed too conspicuous and so we dismounted, pulled our hoods up or hats down, and moved on through the crowds hurrying home. Many who had attended the executions were steaming drunk and rowdy, while others stumbled away from the city or to their rooms as if they were yet stunned by what they had witnessed. The hum and hiss of voices echoed through the streets. I felt for them because in their ignorance they believed that their tormentor was dead and that justice had been done.

"It would take days to travel to each of his castles," I said to Stephen. "Weeks to search them. Months, perhaps. He escapes, Stephen. Now, as we speak, he escapes and if we do not catch him now, he will be in the wind. Who knows what evil he will do in the years to come?"

"Do not despair," Stephen said. "We will find him."

I turned on him. "How?"

He looked away, for he had no answer. We stopped and looked at the crowds filing by us. A woman wept, her husband's arm about her shoulders. A group of young men argued and jostled each other as they passed us, agitated and spoiling for a fight.

"What do you reckon they would do if we told them?" Rob asked.

"They would not believe it," Stephen said. "Even if they could be made to understand it."

"Shame them two servants got burned up, ain't it," Walt said. "Might be they knew where their master might have gone."

Stephen and I exchanged a look.

"The others yet live, do they not?" I said. "The priest and the sorcerer."

"They are yet held at the gaol in the castle. If we go there and are reported, we are likely to be seized by the Bishop's soldiers."

"Then we must move swiftly and if they do attempt to take us, we will cut our way free. Are we agreed?" Walt and Rob were quick to do so and Stephen hesitated only for a moment. "How much silver do you have on you, Stephen?"

We made our way to the prison as quickly and quietly as we could. With the help of fistfuls of coins, Stephen quickly talked the gaolers into granting us access to the guilty servants who had somehow avoided the sentence of death.

While my men watched the exits, the gaolers escorted Stephen and I through to the cell of Dominus Eustache Blanchet, who was horrified to see me step into his cell.

"Where is he?" I said, unable to keep the snarl from my face. "Where?"

"Who, my lord?"

I stepped over him and resisted the urge to thrash him senseless. "Gilles de Rais has fled. Following his execution, he has fled. And you know, by God, you know where he has gone, and you will tell me."

"Surely, sir, he cannot have survived the noose and fire," Blanchet cried. "Do you think he is coming for me, my lord? Because I turned on him and confessed and so condemned him?"

I slapped him and shoved him over and slapped him again. "Can you truly be so stupid? Is it a part that you play so well or are you a simpleton? You may have convinced the court but you do not fool me. You know what your master is. You know what the others were. And you must have known his plan to survive his execution. Tell me where he went!"

He sobbed and fouled himself and trembled, begging

forgiveness for not knowing anything, tears running down his face. He swore that he would say whatever I wanted him to say, if only I would tell him what it was.

Stephen pulled me back. "I believe him, Richard. He is ignorant, of this at least."

"I am going to kill him," I said.

Blanchet whimpered and closed his eyes, his lips moving silently.

"He is not an immortal," Stephen said. "For the sake of your own soul, Richard, do not murder him."

"Damn you, Stephen," I said and pushed by him to where the gaoler stood waiting. "Where is Prelati?" I cried.

We were shown to his cell where, having heard my brutal interrogation through the walls, he already crouched in the corner.

"Sorcerer," I said from the doorway.

"I know nothing!" he shouted as I advanced on him and dragged him from the corner by the hair.

"Blanchet is a simpleton," I snarled in his face. "But nothing gets by you, does it, Francis." I wrapped my hand tight about his throat and squeezed. "You know what Gilles was. You know that he has avoided death for decades and you know that he has cheated it once again with this trickery. If you wish to avoid your own demise in the next few moments, you will tell me where he has gone."

He did his best to nod and I loosened my grip enough for him to speak. "I believed when he gave himself up that he had some way to escape. When the murders could no longer be denied, he sacrificed himself and us also, so that he could get away and carry on elsewhere, with the man Gilles de Rais considered to be dead. That was why he contrived to give himself up, it was obvious and he even admitted as much, in his way. But he would tell me nothing more and whenever I pushed him he would strike me and rage at me. I was certain he would kill me in one of his black moods even before we were finally arrested and so—"

I slapped his face to shut him up.

"There were men supplying him with blood," I said. "After his arrest, here in this castle. Who was helping him? What are their names?"

He gasped for breath. "I never knew any of that. He would never have told me. I was not one of them and he would not make me so. He used me and discarded me."

I let go of his throat but stood over him, ready to throttle the life from him at a moment's notice.

"And so get your revenge on him and tell me where he went."

"If I knew, I would tell it gladly."

I almost killed him from the frustration. It was maddening. But I pulled myself back from the brink and instead asked him a question.

"Where do you think your lord would go? Which one of his own castles? And if not one of his own, who were his allies? Surely, there were other lords or knights nearby who would shelter him in their home and you, who spent so much time at his side, you would know of them. So, who would put him up in his hour of need?"

He frowned, casting his red-rimmed eyes up and down me

momentarily before answering. "Do you have any conception of his riches? Of how many men served him and serve him still? He owns a score of fortresses, a hundred villages, thousands of people. When we served him in his crimes and in his other deeds we used half a hundred peasant homes, spread across his lands. So many places, bought and paid for, or taken from men that we killed for him. It is conceivable he is at any one of them. But for how long? And I doubt he has gone to any place associated with the names Gilles de Rais, sir. Even in his arrogance, he would not be so witless as that. But in truth, my lord may end up hidden a dozen miles from here in some foul, dilapidated peasant house or in a grand palace in the East, feted by the Turks."

"You are a talker," I said, squeezed his throat once more. "A man with weasel words who thinks himself so very clever. Well, let me see you talk your way out of strangulation." His eyes grew wild and round and he thrashed and clawed at my throat and I revelled in his fear and suffering, which he had himself certainly inflicted on children before they were murdered.

"You can't do that!" the gaoler said, grabbing me to no effect before appealing to Stephen. "He can't do that, sir, or I'll get strung up myself for allowing it."

I did not care and would have committed another murder but Rob banged into the open door, breathing heavily. "Some bastard," he said, "tipped off the Bishop's men. They're on their way."

Growling, I pushed Prelati down and stalked out of his cell, hearing him gasping for breath as I did so. Following Rob, I hurried toward the way out of the gaol.

"When they come, we will subdue the Bishop's men and then question them," I said to Stephen. "One by one, to find who has helped him escape."

"You assaulted the Bishop of Nantes," Stephen said, lowering his voice. "Once we are cornered they will send more and more until you can kill no more. If we do not leave Nantes almost immediately, they will throw us in here with Prelati and Blanchet."

"He ain't wrong, sir," Rob said.

"We got to leg it now," Walt cried as we reached him.

"God save me from my temper," I muttered, recalling what I had said and done to the Bishop of Nantes in his own palace. "Come, then. Let us be gone from here. All we can do is go south and search those places that we can find. Someone will have seen something."

We made our escape from Nantes, with all of our horses, our belongings, and our valets. The enormous crowds were well on their way to drunkenness and the soldiers had their hands full keeping order so we slipped out without any trouble. Still, I looked behind me repeatedly as we rode to our inn at Mortagne which we reached as night fell.

∞

"Can it be true?" the innkeeper Bouchard-Menard asked when we arrived. "Is the demon finally dead?" He stood in the middle of the communal room downstairs with a big, dumb smile on his face and two cups of wine in his hands.

"Yes," I said, lying. "Gilles de Rais is dead."

"Praise God," he said, weeping. "God bless you, good fellows, for all what you have done."

"We shall need food and wine for travelling. Five days' worth for seven men, if you have it and we are leaving well before sunrise," I said to him. "Now, what do we owe you?"

While the valets packed the remainder of our belongings, we sat inside by an open window facing the courtyard, eating in silence. I chafed to be gone, to be chasing after our quarry before he got too far, but also knew we had to wait until morning. It was obvious that the men needed sleep and I found my own eyes closing and my head nodding close to my stew. The poultry was soft and nourishing, and the broth was savoury indeed, laden with salt and fresh herbs and I knew it would likely be the last hot meal I would have for some time.

"Bleed the valets," I said to Rob. "You three all must have blood. We will ride hard in the morning and for every day after until we find him. Wherever he has gone."

"Going to be hard on the lads," Rob observed. "Keeping up with us."

"We will run them ragged and send them back to Normandy and London, if they cannot keep pace. There is plenty more mortal blood for the taking in France."

My men did not like it. Not treating loyal men so poorly, nor risking their regular blood supply. But what were such things compared to Gilles de Rais escaping justice?

"Horses, too," Walt said. "Already looking ropey. Noticed that mare favouring a leg on the way here and the grey's breathing ain't improving, none."

I nodded. "How are our finances?" I asked Stephen.

"Well enough to keep us in food and horses for a month or two," he replied. "After that, we shall have to travel to Rouen to collect additional coin."

The thought of chasing around blindly through the country for more than a month turned my stomach and I put down my spoon.

"Can't we just take what we need?" Walt asked. "We done it before."

"That was war," I said.

"What," Walt replied. "Ain't we at war still now? Ain't we Englishmen and ain't this France?"

"Keep your voice down," Stephen hissed, looking around to see if anyone had heard while Rob laughed.

Outside, the hooves of a single horse sounded on the cobbles of the courtyard. I thought nothing of it because so many came and went at such times but then a voice, filled with anguish, cried out.

"Richard! Where be Richard?"

Looking out of the window, I saw a man attempt to dismount a skittish horse before falling to the ground. His horse danced away from him and I saw in the lamplight that the man's belly and loins were shining with fresh blood.

"Dear God," I said, rushing to the doorway. "Is that Paillart? Stephen, that is Ameline Moussillon's servant."

With Bouchard-Menard clearing the way, we carried him into

the ale room and laid him on a cleared table. Stephen opened his clothes while the innkeeper generously poured wine into Paillart's mouth and over the wounds on his belly.

The wounds stank of shit and bile, and I knew his guts had been hewn by a blade. Such a wound would certainly go bad and rot a man inside out, sooner or later.

"I am killed," Paillart said as he smelled it also, his voice rasping and his face pale. "She has killed me."

For a moment, I thought he meant Ameline had been the one who stabbed him but then I shook myself, for that could not possibly be true. "Who has killed you?"

"The damned girl. The girl."

"Tell me what has happened, quickly. Who is the girl who did this to you?"

"No true girl. A demon," he said, gasping. "A demon in human flesh. She broke through my master's door with her bare hands. My master attempted to seize her but she threw him. Across the room, into the wall. I stabbed her in the back, ran her through right and proper." He laughed in disbelief as he recalled it, eyes wild. "She withdrew my blade from her body and used it on me. As you may see, sirs. She held my master down and sucked blood from his throat until he struggled no more. Dear Ameline attempted to save her father but the girl dragged Ameline away. The demon girl looked at me, with her demon eyes. Tell Richard of Ashbury what has befallen his beloved, she said. Tell it to Richard. That's you sir, is it not? It must be. And then they was gone. She took Ameline, out the door to where others waited, men with horses, and they trussed her up and..." He gasped. "You

312

must save her, sir. Save her from the demon."

"Who was the demon?" I asked. "A child?"

"La Meffraye's girl. Her familiar. Evil creature. Pure evil."

I staggered away, clutching my head at the implications.

"The girl," Stephen said, coming up behind me. "The young woman that we heard about who accompanied the Terror in her business taking the children. She was a revenant all along."

"Perhaps he made more revenants before his end," I said. "In order to carry out this task."

"Strong, eh?" Walt said, holding up Paillart's head so that Rob could pour some brandy wine into his mouth. "Could you break through a door with your bare hands, Rob?"

He had been in possession of an archer's strength in his mortal life and his immortality had increased it beyond measure. "The physician's house, in Tilleuls? Solid oak door with iron fixings, weren't it? Not bloody likely."

Stephen scoffed. "He exaggerates," he said, indicating Paillart, whose eyes were rolling. "There were others there who no doubt threw down the door prior to the girl's assault."

"Maybe," Walt allowed, and lowered Paillart's head back to the table where the man closed his eyes. He was not far from his death.

"Why would he make some young woman into one at all?" I asked, speaking half to myself. "But not Prelati or the priest or Roger de Briqueville or even La Meffraye herself?"

Walt scratched his nose. "Wouldn't want to stare at some dried-up old bird for a hundred years, would you? Get yourself a nice, round young woman instead, right? Lovely."

"But he does not like young women, does he," I said.

"Well," Rob said, a small smile on his face. "Only one."

I looked at him, not getting the joke.

"Joan of Lorraine," he said, sheepishly.

We looked at each other, arriving at the same enormous thought like a thunderclap.

"But it cannot be," Stephen said. "She burned."

I nodded. "People think that Gilles de Rais burned. We know differently."

"But Joan was burned to ashes." Walt said.

"Someone was burned," I replied. "Some poor girl. Who's to say that burned girl was the same Joan?"

"Well," Stephen said, "it should be easy enough to resolve. Did La Meffraye's granddaughter look like Joan?"

"I never saw her. She was not present when the old woman was arrested. Did you see the girl, Walt? Rob?" They all shook their heads. "Surely, though it cannot be that Joan not only avoided her execution, and that she truly was an immortal, as we expected, but that she has been under our noses for months."

"And abducting children," Walt said.

"And feeding on them, perhaps every day," Rob said. "And so growing strong enough to break down a solid oak door with her bare hands."

"Do you really think it can be true?" Stephen said.

I walked to the door and looked out at the night, recalling the fierceness of the young woman at her trial. Her impossible leap from that tower in an effort to escape captivity. A leap that only an immortal could hope to survive. My heart raced, filled with fear and guilt for Ameline, and the death of her poor father. I pushed the feelings away, for I needed my wits about me.

"He's gone," Walt said, his hand on Paillart's chest. "Poor old bastard's had it."

"Remember this man in your prayers," I said. "For with the last of his strength, he did his duty."

The innkeeper's servants carried his body into a storeroom and began scrubbing at the blood and so we filed into the courtyard to continue our discussion.

"The demon girl must be Joan, the Maiden of Orléans," I said. "But even if she is not, she told Paillart that she wants me to follow her. Which means that such a thing is possible. But to follow her, we need a destination. A place that we know. So, tell me, where has she gone?"

"Tiffauges?" Walt asked. "Machecoul?"

"Any truly likely suggestions?" I asked the others.

"Where was Joan from?" Rob said. "Lorraine, no? People go home when they get afraid."

Rob was a family man at heart and wanted nothing more than to go home, so that was where his mind would run.

My own mind returned to thoughts of Ameline. The poor girl had simply been at home with her father, living her life, and she was taken in such a manner only because of me. Because of my actions.

"If the girl ever was from Lorraine in the first place," I said. "If she was a revenant at the time, and surely she was, then why believe anything else about her? She was a myth, originally, that notion of a maiden from Lorraine who would be the saviour of

315

France and so surely it was a prophecy that Gilles fulfilled when he created her. He moulded this girl into the shape of that myth and then set her off to charm the lords, and the people, and even the Dauphin. Her true home, where the human girl was born before she was made, could be anywhere in France."

Stephen massaged his temples. "Reason would dictate that you know where she went."

"Stephen, you ever assume that others are as reasonable and logical as you are. Most men are fools, monsters, or madmen, and women are even worse. The girl may have lost her mind long ago. In fact, if she is Joan the Maiden then surely we know she is madder than a box of frogs and nothing she says or does can be assumed to be due to reason."

"That is noted," Stephen said. "So, to where would a madwoman go?"

"Paris?" Rob said.

"She failed to take Paris, she would not return there," I said.

Stephen turned. "What makes you speak with such certainty?"

I could not say but something I had said to Ameline came back to me.

People stay away from pain, like an animal fleeing attack, or a child flinching from a hot candle. But we are also drawn to places where we once felt strength and love. And no doubt that is why he returns home.

"Where was Joan's greatest victory?" I said.

"Patay," Rob said, his face darkening. Of course that was where his mind would turn, the place where thousands of archers were cut down.

"That was Gilles de Rais' victory more than hers," I said. "Besides, what is there at Patay? A few houses? Fields, a woodland? It is nothing."

"Bloody Orléans, weren't it," Walt said. "They smashed us, over and over, when they had no right to and they did it because she riled them up into believing it."

"What is in Orléans?" Stephen asked. "Why would she go there?"

"She must be with the Marshal," Rob said. "Is that not what we think, sirs? Joan may have taken Mistress Moussillon but where she has gone, she has gone with Gilles de Rais at her side. The pair of them together won Orléans. And he was rich beyond mortal imagination. He could have bought anything, on the sly, through middlemen and agents. Like you do, Stephen."

"Dom Eustache Blanchet," I said. "He said something about Orléans during his confession, did he not, Stephen? What was it?"

Stephen frowned. "He went there with Prelati on the way back from Florence."

"By God, yes. Blanchet said he went to Gilles de Rais' house in Orléans. Prepare the horses. We will not wait for sunrise. We ride for Orléans."

21

Desperate Pursuit

Oct 1440

IT WAS A HUNDRED AND EIGHTY MILES up the Loire to Orléans. Pushing the horses, it took us four days of riding ten hours a day, through bitter rain and the howling winds of the fall. Every mile of it, I swore vengeance and murder and pictured myself tearing my enemies to pieces when I caught up with them.

But also I recalled my conversations with Gilles and his servants. I remembered all over again the battles I had fought where Joan had been their talisman and Gilles had been their commander. Searching my memories for the times when I should have said or done this or that thing differently. If I had acted with great virtue and clarity of purpose. If I had just killed them both myself years ago instead of acting like a lawful commoner instead of a righteous lord of war.

"I have been going over my words with Gilles," I said on the first night when we stopped, exhausted, at nightfall, at a small inn beside the road. "He confessed when he realised he would have to speak about Joan during his torture. Like a fool, I believed he wished to protect her good name. But in truth, he wished to hide the fact that she was still alive."

"You could not have known," Stephen said.

"More like he was hiding his plan," Rob said. "Didn't want to admit he was going to get taken away."

"Yes," Stephen said, as if struck by inspiration. "Surely, Richard, it was his intent to confess all along. Think on it. It was only due to his confession and his vile apologies that he was able to strike his deal to avoid being burned to ashes."

"Why delay such a confession, then?" I asked.

"Can't admit you done wrong right off," Walt said. "People don't believe it if you do that."

Stephen nodded. "The Inquisition would have put him to the Question if he had confessed at the outset. As it was, he seemed contrite and so avoided giving up his plan."

"Might be they took time to plan it," Rob said. "Who was them women who took his body away? Do you reckon Joan was one of them?"

I slammed my fist down on the table. "I should have taken my revenge from the first day. Damn the peasants and their need for justice. Damn the law. Damn the Bishop and the Duke. Next time, I will wait for none of it and I shall kill the bastards wherever I find them."

My men would not meet my eye. We retired early and got up and on the road before dawn, pushing the horses through the freezing dark until we were warmed by our exertions and then exhausted by them.

It seemed I was not the only one wrapped in my thoughts during the long days in the saddle.

"I think I saw her," Walt said suddenly, at the close of the second day while we shoved bread and cheese down our throats in a busy inn. He stared at his wine cup, a deep frown on his head.

"What are you talking about?" I asked. "When? At the execution?"

"No, no," he said. "At the church in Tilleuls. When you got them peasants to promise to make statements. When I come in, there was this woman at the back. Young, short, little thing she was, with a hood over her head even though she was inside the church."

"What makes you think it was her?" Stephen said.

"She was alone, keeping in the shadow. I thought at first maybe she was that old lady, the Terror, but then I see she was right young. Something off about her. The peasants kept away from her. Seemed like a spy. I thought maybe she was one of the Duke's or the Bishop's or maybe even the Marshal's but then when I went back to nab her after I spoke to you, Richard, she was gone. Weren't outside, neither. Forgot about it until just now. Sorry, Richard."

"You could not have known," I said, though internally I cursed his witlessness. "Do not give it another thought."

"She was under our very noses," Stephen said. "I wonder

where else she came so close to us?"

"He was nervous," Rob blurted out. "When we went to arrest him and you read out the charges, Stephen. Do you recall when he asked if the charges were for him alone?"

"My God," Stephen muttered. "How relieved he seemed when I named his servants also. I, too, thought it strange and now I realise it was that he dreaded the name of Joan of Orléans in the warrant."

"If we had made more effort to seize La Meffraye," Rob said, "you know, lain in wait for her more, we could have nabbed her and the girl at the same time."

"Only, you'd have thought her a girl, hiding under her hood, and gone to grab her and the little monster would have cut your head off," Walt said. "Be glad we never tried it."

"That is why she was always hooded," Stephen muttered. "And none knew her for a young woman of small stature. It was because she is a revenant and had to cover her skin even more than we do."

"And she needed to hide in case anyone did recognise her," Rob said. "Might be many thousands what saw her in Orléans and elsewhere."

"That old woman kept up the lies," Stephen said. "She claimed even to your face that the girl was her granddaughter, did she not?"

I rubbed my eyes and pinched the bridge of my nose. "It might be that I let my expectations get the better of me. Now I recall it, she said that the life of her family would be in danger if I found the girl. Something of that nature. They had threatened her family, I assume, should the secret be revealed."

"I thought I misheard," Rob muttered, before looking up. "So many times, the villagers spoke of the Terror, La Meffraye, and it seemed that they were speaking of the girl, not the old woman. The little demon, they called her. The demon spawn. Words such as that. And I thought they misspoke, or I misheard. But the Terror was the girl all along. La Meffraye was Joan of Orléans."

"It is all in the past," I said, still so angry at myself that I could barely speak of it. "All that matters is that we find her, in Orléans. Find her and kill her and tear Gilles limb from limb."

When we arrived at the city, our horses were in bad shape and our valets were miles and perhaps even days behind us.

But we did not need them. Walt, Rob, and Stephen had drunk their blood and I commanded them to reach Orléans when they could. If they found us dead, they were free to share our wealth between them. They were good lads and they wished us well as they begged our pardon for their weakness.

Orléans was almost unrecognisable without the English forts and camps outside the walls and the thousands of soldiers inside and out. We came into the city through the western gate just before it closed for the night and though the rain had stopped it was still bitterly cold and we were all sore when we dismounted to stable our horses. The stable hands claimed to be ignorant of the location of the house we sought, though they crossed themselves as they did so.

"I will pay you for the location," I said but none would so much as look at the silver coins I held.

"Where's the market?" Rob asked them, and they told him

readily enough.

We hid our weapons as best as we could, keeping them out of sight beneath our coats. Rob used his bowstave as a walking staff and kept his arrow bag close behind his back and covered himself with his cloak. Praying that we would be unchallenged, we pushed deeper into the city through the stream of people heading home, their business done for the day.

"Pardon me, sir," I said to a man closing up his leatherwork shop. "Can you direct me to the home of Marshal Gilles de Rais?"

He looked me up and down from beside the table that displayed his wares. I was filthy from the road and moving as stiffly as an old man from the hard riding. His son or apprentice began to answer but the leatherworker clipped the boy about the ear, spat on the floor and turned his back on me to finish closing his workshop.

"Don't be wanting to go there," a woman said from the shop next door. "It's cursed."

I walked up the street to her shop, which displayed an array of ready-made shoes. Her husband the cordwainer sat within the workshop behind her. "Where is it, good woman?"

"What business you got there?"

"We are not friends of the Marshal," I said. "Far from it, in fact."

She screwed up her face. "On the river. Past the bridge." Crossing herself, she closed her eyes. "Got red painted doors on the front, don't it. Red as blood."

We hurried on through the streets, looking for the house as darkness fell.

"There," Rob said. "Is that door red?"

If the doors were red, it was the russet colour of old blood. The house was enormous, a high wall built all around the perimeter, with two and three storeys and a tower on the riverside reaching even higher and the gateway with the red doors was high and wide enough to allow a mounted man or a small cart into the courtyard beyond.

We ducked into the shelter of a dark doorway across the street and a few yards up. The fine porch had an awning and hid us remarkably well from casual glances, though if the residents came or went then we would be swiftly ejected.

"Can't see no lamps lit within, can you?" Rob said.

"Perhaps we have it wrong," I said. "I have brought us to the wrong town, or to the wrong house within it."

Walt nodded. "There's light behind them shutters," he said, nodding. "Faint enough but it's there, sir."

"I will take your word for it," I said. Their eyes were better than mine.

"Is that smoke coming from the tower yonder?" Stephen muttered. "Or from a neighbouring house?"

Smoke rose from chimneys all over the city, of course, and so it was difficult to make out for certain. But it seemed as though the Marshal's residence was in use by someone, at least.

"Break it in, you reckon?" Walt said, nodding at the door.

"I'll use my axe," Rob said, patting the weapon where it was hidden beneath his cloak.

I was afraid to go in because I knew, in my heart, that Ameline would not be inside. Not alive, at least. It had been a ruse to bring me to a place of strength so that they could kill me, but they had no need to keep her alive and so she would be dead. Drunk dry and discarded, like so many others. Still, I had a faint glimmer of hope that I expected to soon be snuffed out.

"They are expecting us to come," I said. "They wanted this, precisely this, and we have done as they designed and so they will be well prepared for us to rush in. They know we are three, at least. How can the Marshal and one girl, revenant or not, expect to stop the three of us? The three soldiers that is, Stephen."

"Perhaps they are not within after all," Rob suggested, his eyes flicking up and around us. "Might be it is only mortal servants within, but the immortal lords sit watching this place, awaiting our arrival. Might they not trap us within and burn us alive?"

I shuddered at the thought. I had been in raging fires before and knew that there was no more agonising way to die. "It would have to be a quick fire to be sure of killing us before we escaped."

Walt cleared his throat and mumbled. "Hold up, my dear fellows. They have men within. Soldiers. Bound to be revenants."

"Perhaps," I said, nodding. "Perhaps he does have more men and so when I go rushing in, they will take me by force of numbers."

"Begging your pardon, Richard," Walt said. "It was no suggestion I was making but an observation." He pointed up and across the street at the Marshal's grand residence. "A man walks upon that wall, do you see the top of his helm bobbing along? He has a spear or polearm, which you can see bobbing beside him. And in the alcove there by the window, another man, unmoving."

"I thought it was a statue."

"On the tower," Rob said, nodding. "A man turned from the top with a crossbow in his hand. Gone now to the river side of the tower."

"Damn me but your eyes are good, lads," I said. "How many more does he have within? A dozen? A score?"

"Plate armour and mail, a steel helm," said Rob, nodding at the unmoving man in the shadowed alcove. "They are his famed army, are they not? Some of them, at least."

"How can we kill so many veterans, clad in such fine harness?" Stephen whispered, his eyes wide. "Four against a score? What if it is more? What if he has fifty revenants in there with him?"

I placed a hand on his shoulder. "Stephen, it is three against however many are within. I do not expect you, a monk, a merchant, and a lawyer, to fight soldiers. Revenants nor mortals, neither a score nor one alone."

"I am immortal," he said, shrugging my hand off his shoulder. "I have strength, I have speed. I can fight."

"You will help us, that is certain," I said. "But not by killing. That is our trade. Look at our brother Walter, here. His is a face made to do violence and one that declares to the world that he can do nothing else but that. Look at Rob, feel the breadth of his shoulders and the steel of his eyes and know that his trade has ever been the piercing and hewing of the King's enemies. Yours trade is and has always been your wits."

Stephen sighed. "Should I ready the horses?"

"I'm afraid that you may have the most dangerous task of all," I said, surprising him. "For you must spring the trap."

22

The Master

Oct 1440

CLINGING TO THE WALL, I inched my way out along the outer edge of the city wall with the dark river flowing below me. I could barely see my hands in the gloom and found my way more by feel than anything else.

We would attack the building from multiple sides at once and so take the enemy by surprise, cutting through whatever guards there were and forcing our way in to meet in the interior, tapping Gilles de Rais and the Maiden of Orléans before they could escape.

Against my men's wishes, I had taken the riskiest point of entry upon myself. With every sidling step, I regretted my decision.

My task was to climb the outer wall of the house's tower that thrust up in the corner of one wing, which meant first finding access to the river bank fifty yards away at a landing stage before picking my way along the walls that guarded the city from incursion by the river. It had not looked such a long way before I had committed to it and I had confidently declared it to be in a poor state of repair, with ivy clinging in patches and great chunks still missing from the damage caused by English cannonballs.

And yet, I found it was taking me far longer than I expected and already I was tired. The stone under my fingers was freezing and damp and I had lost most of the feeling in my fingertips immediately. The hard riding and lack of rest were taking their toll and I fretted that I would fail even before the assault began. Though night had fallen, I was exposed to view from anyone watching from across the river or from the bridge downstream. I also had the furthest to climb, all the way up the wall and then up the tower built alongside it. One slip and I would fall into the river.

I wore no armour and carried no weapon but my dagger, having learned from experience what an impediment they are and yet it meant placing myself at a disadvantage if I did make it to the top.

Walt and Rob were on the other side of the house and their task was to scale the perimeter wall from the street side without being observed or stopped by the citizenry. It was at least a far shorter climb that would allow them to carry their swords. Rob wanted to bring his damned war bow with him, but I ordered him to stop being so foolish.

Our assault was to be coordinated, as far as we could, and I was supposed to be in position near the top of the tower when the signal was given.

I climbed, as quickly as I dared. Breathing heavily, I chanced a look up at the wall and tower above me. It seemed almost impossibly far.

If I survive this night, I swore to myself, and even if I should live a thousand years, I shall never climb a wall again.

From the other side of the building, Stephen banged on the front door and cried out for them, in the best imitation of my voice he could muster, to answer the damned door and to let him in.

That was the signal.

I was far from the top of the tower.

Stephen was supposed to flee from the door after he cried out, and Walt and Rob would then throw themselves over the wall from the street below and begin their attack.

Gritting my teeth, I climbed faster up the crumbling, aged stonework, aiming now to climb up not to the top of the tower but the top of the perimeter wall directly above me. The top was almost within reach.

A man coughed, so close that I looked up, imagining that he would be looking down at me over the side.

There was no face there and a foot scraped on the boards of the wall walk as he moved on away from me.

I let out the breath I had been holding and launched myself up the final stretch, throwing myself over the top. The soldier stood twenty feet away at the end of the section of wall, about to turn to return along the wall toward me.

I yanked my dagger out and sprinted toward him.

He flinched in surprise but recovered quickly and drew his sword, stepping forward to break off my timing. He thrust the blade smartly, which suggested that he knew his business, but I twisted around it and slipped my knife hand up inside his arm and pushed my dagger into his throat as I checked him with my shoulder and brought him to the ground. I ripped my blade back, tearing his throat out and bathing the wall walk with his blood before he could let out a cry.

Nevertheless, I found myself exposed.

Looking down into the shadows of the inner courtyard below, there was a soldier looking up at me. He stared, as if unsurprised and unafraid.

I turned and looked up as a voice cried a warning from the top of the tower, echoing between the wings of the house.

"He is here! The river wall!"

Snatching up the dead man's sword, I pulled open the door at the end of the wall walk to find two soldiers rushing toward me from within, both dressed in armour and helm. One had a mace and the other a short-hafted war hammer, both men began roaring like madmen as they came on.

Retreating outside, I stepped over the dead man lying in the shadows and the first armoured man, his vision limited by his helm, tripped over the body and fell flat on his face. The man behind did not hesitate but jumped over his comrade and swung his war hammer overhead, trying to crush my skull. I rushed in, grasped his hand and ducked low into his body. Lifting him up, I heaved him over the side of the wall and a moment later I heard him splash into the black Loire below.

The first man was getting to his feet when I pulled up his helm and sawed through his throat with the sword.

A cry behind me forced me to spin about and back away. Good thing, too, because a crossbow bolt cracked into the stone where I had been standing. The man on the tower had shot down and then his shouts, too, joined the others echoing in the courtyard. More soldiers rushed from the wings of the house into the courtyard, a couple carrying lanterns that they held high, illuminating the lot of them.

I realised then that the trap Gilles de Rais had set was greater than I had imagined.

He had filled his house in Orléans with his veteran soldiers. The few on the outside were but a hint of what lay within. I wondered how many of the armoured veterans he had made into powerful revenants by the power of his blood. And I had climbed into the trap without armour, armed only with a dagger and now with a dead man's sword.

How many more were within? A dozen? A hundred?

I considered bellowing a warning for Walt and Rob to fall back, thinking that perhaps we could retreat from the building to try a better approach another time.

Yet, how could I flee? Even the slim chance that Ameline was still alive within somewhere meant that I could never have left her to her fate. No doubt, Gilles de Rais had known that about me and used my sense of honour, faded and fragile though it may have been at times, as a weapon against me.

And anyway, there could be no safe retreat. More soldiers were coming up behind me to close off the way out and so I plunged deeper into the east wing, where three soldiers met me in the first chamber.

They each brandished polearms with deadly hammers, axes and spear points arranged on the ends, but the ceilings and close walls meant they could hardly swing the things. Each man thrust his weapon at me and I darted forward past the iron heads and thrust my weight against the wooden shafts, sending the men reeling against each other. Quickly, I slashed at them with my sword and cut each of them down.

Shouting echoed through the wing and footsteps pounded on the stairs. When they came rushing from the stairwell, I came at them from the side and bundled them to the ground, my two blades, the sword and the dagger, flashing and stabbing them to brutal, bloody deaths.

Jumping over them, I hurried down the stairs only to find a dozen men below waiting for me in a small hall. Without hesitation, I rushed into them trusting my speed and skill and aggression to carry me through.

Killing three immediately, the others cornered me and I found a wound in my shoulder streaming blood. I had not noted receiving it and the sudden anger and fear pushed me to rush them again. They were fearful of my speed. They could not have witnessed anything like it in their entire lives and after throwing down a pair of them, the rest fled. Or rather, they tried to. I caught up with each man and speared and slashed and hammered them to death with their own weapons.

A gash had appeared over my temple and I recalled the desperate swing that caused it, fast and strong enough to cleave my head into two pieces had I not slipped the blow.

As I pushed open the door that led out into the courtyard, eight more men rushed me and pushed me back into the hall with a fury that for a time I could not match. These men were certainly revenants, and their speed was greater by far than any I had fought so far that night. In desperation, I retreated further and found myself with gashes opening on my arms and hands and on my jaw.

Still, as they cut me, I cut them, and my strokes had precision and timing that theirs lacked and soon the eight attackers became six and then I was chasing down the three that fled toward the front door of the house.

The wounds all over my body were terrible but I had cleared the entire wing of the house and no more came for me. I rushed back to the hall and out into the central courtyard, where I found an armed man creeping along in the shadow. I swung my gore-spattered blade at his face but he spoke and I checked my blow.

"Richard!"

"Walt? What are you doing? Come in here, out of sight.

When we stepped back into the doorway to the hall, I saw that he was breathing heavily and had blood all over his face and mouth.

"Thank Christ it's you, sir. Me and Rob cleared the other wing, murdered the lot of the bastards." He looked at the bodies in the hall. "As you did, it seems."

"And where is Rob now?"

"Got separated," Walt shook his head. "Heard him fighting

for a bit but then I couldn't find him and when I called, he didn't call back. Hiding maybe, or he's dead."

"Damn. What about Gilles? Joan?"

"Killed about a dozen of the bastards when I cleaned that wing." He jerked his thumb behind him. "No Gilles there. No demon maidens, neither."

"I also killed many soldiers and yet found no sign of our true enemies."

"Maybe they ain't here at all."

"The tower," I said, easing open the door to look up at it across the courtyard. "I was supposed to clear the tower but I never reached it. Come, through the courtyard, we shall finish this one way or another."

We crossed the dark courtyard quickly and Walt heaved open the door at the bottom which led into the base of the stairwell beyond.

"Thought it'd be locked," Walt said, a grin on his face as he half turned to me.

A crossbow clanged from the darkness within and I shouted a warning but the bolt hit Walt somewhere between his chest and his face with a wet thud. He fell back, his cry of pain cut off almost before he could utter it.

I charged through the doorway just as another bolt clanged from within, throwing myself down onto my face just in time so that the bolt missed me and shot over my hunched back.

Knowing I was close to death once more and at the mercy of anyone close by, I rolled over in order to get up.

A hand grasped my hair and a knife slashed over into my belly, cutting me deep once, twice, and almost a third time until I caught the attacker's wrist in both of mine. The wounds were agony and I was sickened greatly by the damage done. By God, he is strong, I thought, as strong as I, at least, and perhaps stronger. As I held his wrists and twisted, trying to pull him down off his feet while avoiding his blade, another man fell upon me, wrapping his arms about my legs.

I kicked out, not thrashing but with a swift blow from my heel. Through luck rather than judgement I caught him clean enough to crack his jaw or perhaps his nose.

The other man yanked his knife away from my grasp and swiftly drove that blade into my chest.

I had twisted before it plunged into my heart but still it pierced me between the ribs and I knew I would instead soon drown in blood if they did not slay me first.

Still kneeling behind my head, he drew his knife out and tried to cut my throat. Somehow, I got my hands up to my neck just in time and so instead of sawing through my neck he frantically worked the blade back and forth, cutting deep lacerations into my palms and fingers.

Grasping the sharp blade and twisting, I pulled it from him and rolled over. He lost his grip on his knife and I got my knees under me and drove myself into him so that he fell back against the lower steps of the stairwell, pulling the knife from his hands and stabbing it into his body once, then twice, and I was about to finish him off when the other man rushed me from behind.

I twisted and slashed out, catching him across the face. The blade cut across his eyes and through the bridge of his nose.

Screaming, he fell to the side and I turned to finish off the wounded man under me at the base of the stairs.

"Please," the man said, almost wailing. "No, no."

There was no reason to hesitate and yet I recognised the voice and it stilled my hand.

"It is you," I said, in the dim lamplight seeing that it was in fact Gilles de Rais cringing beneath my knife. He was the man who had almost killed me. Blood welled out of the wounds on my chest and I knew that he had done me mortal damage. Without human blood I would myself swiftly die and so I wanted nothing more than to cut off his head. He deserved to die, for all the murders he had committed, least of all my own.

"Where is she?" I asked, coughing up blood along with my words.

His eyes flicked up the stairs above us.

"Thank you," I said and placed the knife against his neck, though blood streamed from my lacerated hands and I struggled to keep hold of it.

"Wait, wait," he said, lifting his chin and inching up the steps as he strained to pull away. "Your woman will be killed."

"Ameline?" I stopped. "She is above us?"

"With my lady," he said, gasping and wincing.

I gritted my teeth. "With your..? Joan the Maiden is up there?"

His mouth twitched at the corners. "And she will kill your woman before you can stop her."

The flicker of hope kindled in me but then faded as I realised he would say anything to prologue his life a moment longer.

"If the Maiden harms Ameline then I will kill her

immediately. Nothing will stop me."

"I can save her," he replied, coughing up blood. "Save your woman. If you let me."

"A trick," I said, shaking my head as blood dripped from my mouth.

"I swear it."

"Meaningless words," I growled and pushed the knife against his neck.

"Kill me then," he said, closing his eyes and lifting his chin. "I beg you. End it, please. Please. End me now as I pray."

I rolled him over and pushed him. "Up, then. Up, up."

Staggering up the stairs with one hand over my chest and belly, I crept up behind him with my knife at the ready. The soldier I had blinded below continued to wail about his blindness, banging around at the base of the stair. I wondered if Walt was dead yet or if he was still lying in the dark courtyard, dying alone and in agony. He would have wanted me to try to save Ameline, for he was a knight at heart. It galled me to leave him behind but I was dying myself and I had only so long before I would bleed to death.

Shoving Gilles faster and faster, I crawled up, step after step. My head swam, and my vision clouded. One of my bloody shoes slipped on a step and I fell to a knee. Whipping my knife up, I saw Gilles peering down at me. He made no move to attack and instead turned and continued up.

We rounded the final bend and came immediately into the chamber at the top of the tower. A fire burned in a hearth on one side. A ladder led to a closed hatch in the ceiling.

Ameline stood upright in the centre of the room, her hands

bound and her face a mask of terror and exhaustion. Behind her, a low iron cage. Inside that cage, three young children huddled together in the far corner.

And there stood Joan. La Pucelle. The Maiden of Orléans. I recognised her pug nose, small mouth, and her wild, shrewd eyes.

Joan held a knife to Ameline's throat. Though the Maiden was far smaller, she was possessed with an immortal's strength and so kept her prisoner from freeing herself with a hand wrapped like a vice around Ameline's upper arm.

"Halt there, Richard," Joan said, sneering at me and pushing her knife against Ameline's skin, threatening to break it. "Unless you want to see this girl's blood spilt."

"How is it that you live?" I asked her, inching forward.

"My Gilles saved me," she said, smiling at me and then at him. "You did something right, once."

I inched forward again. "Who was it that you burned?"

She scoffed. "It is a simple thing to find a girl that the world has discarded. They are so many, and they can be bought, threatened, and owned, really rather easily. If you take one more step I shall cut this bitch's throat."

I froze.

Gilles cried out, clutching the wounds I had given him. "Joan, please, no."

"I knew you would fail," Joan said to Gilles, bitterly. "You useless dog. Look what you have brought us to. He has killed you."

"He dies also," Gilles said, gesturing to me as he fell sideways against a table near to the fireplace. "And his men are dead."

Joan looked me up and down. "Yes, yes, I see it. So, Richard, my useless Gilles has killed you after all. Finally."

"Not yet," I said, coughing up blood and spitting it to the floor after I spoke.

Joan scoffed. "Drink one of the children," she said to Gilles, jerking her head at the cage behind her.

"No," he said, slumping against the wall. "No, I will not."

"Do it," she hissed. "Quickly, while you still can."

"No more," he said, weeping and leaning his head back against the wall. "No more killing. No more. Not the children."

"You are weak," Joan said. "You were always weak at heart. Die, then. You may as well die, for your will is long broken. When my lord returns, you will be no help like this."

"Your lord?" I said, a chill about my heart because I thought I knew who she meant. And I dreaded it.

"My lord," Joan said, her eyes shining in the lamplight. "My lord, the Archangel Gabriel."

"She means Milord William de Ferrers," Gilles said, glancing at me as he pulled himself to his feet once more. "Your brother, sir."

"Brother," Joan said, scoffing at him before turning to me. "You are Judas. My angel said that he would deal with you when he returns to these lands."

I laughed but the pain of it racked my body. "Yes he said that," I said, wincing. "Said it a long time ago."

She lifted her chin and glared triumphantly. "He sent word. He comes. Even now as we speak, he comes with a great army that will save France and all Christendom from the heretics."

"You are the heretic," I said, not believing a word. "And a

lunatic."

She ground her teeth then snapped at Gilles. "Take a child before it is too late."

Gilles slid along the wall toward the fireplace where an ornate short sword leaned. I forced myself to straighten up, feeling my wounds open and more blood seep from me, and prepared to defend myself with my knife. Gilles grasped the sword, turned and brandished it.

Brandished it not at me, but at her.

"No more killing, Joan," he said, almost wailing. "I cannot bear it. I want only peace. All I did, for nothing. William comes not to save Christendom but to destroy it. Everything he said, everything he promised. It was all lies."

Joan snarled like an animal. "Unfaithful. Heretic!"

Beside her, Ameline attempted to pull away but Joan held her fast.

I was fading quickly, my sight darkening. My wounds were not healing swiftly enough and I lost more blood by the minute. I meant to save Ameline before I fell but could think of no way to achieve that. So I sought to draw things out further.

"Destroy Christendom?" I asked Gilles. "What does William mean to do?"

Gilles scoffed, disgusted. "He comes from the East with an army of Turks to overrun us. An army of a hundred thousand Turks who come to conquer Christendom forever, to conquer us and subjugate us under his rule for a thousand years. So his messenger said. I do not believe it, but the man swore it was true. He has betrayed Christ."

A messenger, I thought. A man. A man who could lead me to my brother. "I can believe it," I said. "He attempted it before, centuries ago, with Mongols instead of Turks. Where is this messenger?"

He shrugged. "Long gone. Two years past."

"Tell him nothing," Joan snapped. "Traitor."

"He dies," Gilles said. "What can he do?"

Joan looked me up and down, noting the blood pooling at my feet.

"So William made you both," I said. I wiped the blood from my mouth. I knew I would have to rush Joan and somehow reach her before her knife could mortally injure Ameline. "How many more of you are there?" I asked. "Who else have I missed all these years, other than you?"

"We are the last," Gilles said, his head dropping.

"We are the faithful," Joan said, raising her voice. "The only ones who had faith all these long years. We worked, we toiled. We were nothing, nothing at all, until he lifted us up and gave us eternal life and the true purpose. Oh, the glory. My angel, my sweet angel. How we toiled for thee."

"How did you so toil?" I asked, shifting forward.

She tossed her head back, smiling. "We began a rumour, a prophecy, that a maiden would come and save France. An armoured maiden from Lorraine. And then we worked to better ourselves. To learn the art of war and the war of art. Theology, poetry, philosophy. How we toiled. What riches we made. Always, we spread the word that the maiden would come. And then, when the time was right, I fulfilled the prophecy that I had written for myself two centuries prior." She laughed, a mad, peeling laugh and her knife pressed at Ameline's throat.

"Let her go or I shall kill you," I said, taking half a step forward.

"If you come closer, I will kill her," Joan said. "Then kill you all the same."

We both knew that if I did nothing, I would bleed to death on the floor and nothing would stop her killing Ameline and the children.

"No!" Gilles shouted.

His voice was filled with sudden and powerful anguish that I did not understand.

And then I did.

For I turned in time to see Rob come through the doorway with his bow in hand, an arrow nocked and pulled to his cheek. Blood streamed down from a gash on his head but his eyes were focused and his arrow point did not waver.

Joan was frozen in shock but Ameline was so close beside her.

I started to cry out to wait but Rob did not hesitate.

He loosed his arrow, the cord whipping through the air.

Rob's arrow hit Joan square in the chest and she fell back, dragging Ameline down with her.

As I lurched toward the two women, Gilles hefted his sword with a cry and ran forward, his wounds forgotten in his despair and his rage. I twisted, raising my knife and preparing to meet his attack once more.

But he was not coming for me.

His eyes shining with mad grief, he swung a wild cut overhead and brought it down, meaning to split Rob's skull in two. Surprised by the sudden flank attack, and the speed and ferocity of it, it was all Rob could do to raise his left forearm to protect his head and rush in to grasp his attacker.

The sword blade sliced through Rob's arm above the wrist and his hand tumbled to the floor as Gilles and Rob clashed together, both growling like beasts.

Ameline screamed as she struggled to get away from Joan who grasped her long hair in a hand.

I rushed in and fell on Joan, breaking her grasp and pulling Ameline away to safety before pushing her aside. Blood poured from my wounds as I looked down at Joan. The great arrow, a yard long and as thick as a thumb, had run her through the chest, wedging itself fast between her ribs or perhaps in her spine.

Turning, I watched Rob, one-handed now, stabbing Gilles in the guts with his own sword as he stood over him. It was done.

Beneath me, Joan gasped, her arms flailing. It seemed that she had lost the ability to speak and perhaps to stand.

"You killed all those children," I said. "It was you and him together."

She coughed up a mouthful of blood and spat it out. "My lord comes. My lord comes to begin a new age. And... to kill you."

I scoffed. "I have stopped him before. I shall do so again." I looked up at the children in the cage and at Ameline, who hunched against the wall. "Look away, children."

"Do not kill her," Gilles cried from the centre of the room, pleading. He crawled away from Rob, who tracked him slowly with his sword at the ready.

I pulled her up by the hair, cut into her neck and threw her across the room into the fireplace.

"Joan," Gilles wailed, slithering forward. Rob moved to finish him off.

"Leave him be," I commanded.

Rob stopped, confused.

Gilles fell to his knees deep in the fireplace and reached into the hearth to drag Joan out. Before he could do so, I grabbed the nearest lamp and threw it at them. It smashed and the oil burst over Gilles and Joan, immediately bursting into flame.

They screamed as they burned and as they died, clutching each other to the last, the flames burning hot until they screamed no more.

"Rob?"

"I'm alive," he said, clutching his arm while he stared at his severed hand where it lay on the floor. His face was white.

"Ameline," I said.

She stared at me, her eyes white in her dirty face. "Get away."

"I will not harm you."

"You are like them?" she asked, eyes flicking to the burning corpses. "A drinker of blood? Ageless. Monstrous."

I knew I was dying and could not bear that she would think so badly of me after I was gone. "Ageless, yes. But not like them. Never an innocent." Slumping against the wall, I eased myself to the floor and closed my eyes. "Be sure to free those children, won't you, Rob?"

He moved toward the cage. "Might need two hands, Richard."

"I will do it," Ameline said.

"God bless you," I muttered, feeling myself going.

"Blood heals you?" she asked.

I nodded, not daring to ask. She had suffered so much and suffered it because of me. I could not ask her. Better to die.

"Drink mine," she said, taking up my knife.

At heart, she was ever the healer.

Rushing down the tower, I cut off the head of the blind crossbowman who lurked still, hoping to catch us as we escaped.

We reached Walt, mere moments before he died, and I withdrew the bolt from his neck, spilling even more blood from his terrible wound. He clung on to the last vestiges of life for long enough to drink of Ameline's blood and was healed. Rob also drank, and soon his stump stopped bleeding and began to mend itself. Together with the children, we made our way out the building. The townsfolk of Orléans had heard the commotion and greeted us warily at first until we explained that we were agents for the Bishop of Nantes and had freed the children from the Marshal's soldiers. Then, they gave us wine and food and bandaged our wounds and found us rooms at an inn.

Two days later, we escorted the children and Ameline back home, to Brittany.

2 3

Invasion

Oct 1440

POOR ROB. THE LOSS OF HIS HAND meant he could no longer draw his bow and that more than anything else broke his heart. We had all known men who had suffered such injuries in battle and so knew also that it takes a man time to come to terms with becoming an invalid. He had to learn new ways to dress and care for himself, and to eat and fight. But one thing that we had plenty of was time. And life is easier when one has servants to help fasten your clothing.

Walt had taken a bolt to the neck and had bled so profusely and come so close to death that even with days' worth of blood in him, the skin where the wound had been remained scarred and he spoke with a hoarseness that he had not had before.

"You might never shoot a bow again," Walt rasped at Rob on

the road back to Nantes. Ameline and the children slept in the chamber upstairs at the inn while we toasted our survival below. "But what a final shot that must have been, eh? Wish I had seen that, by God. As far as final shots go, to kill the Maiden of Orléans and to save Richard, that gaggle of children, and a beautiful maiden all with a single arrow." He slapped his knee and laughed until he winced and held his neck.

"I suppose that is true," Rob said, attempting to smile.

"It was the finest shot in all the world," I said. "And I take back every jest and gibe I ever spoke against that bow, for you were right to carry it as you did. With that arrow, you ended the last of William's servants. The last in Christendom, at least."

"Yes," Rob agreed. "A hand is no price at all to pay for such a victory."

"A fine thing to say," Stephen said.

It was too soon for Rob to mean the words that he spoke, but he would, in time.

We were wanted men, in Nantes, for the assault I had committed on the Bishop, and for my assault of prisoners and bribery of the gaolers and all the other mischief we had caused. The lords of Brittany wished to put the entire matter quietly to bed and so we had to be careful. At the final stretch, we sent Ameline driving the wagon into Nantes with the children in the back. They were yet terrified beyond words and whether their spirits and their wits ever recovered from their abduction, I did not know. At least they had their lives.

"I am sorry," I said to Ameline. "They did this to you because of me."

She had healed me with her blood and did not believe I was evil, yet she could not stand to lay eyes on me.

"I know," she replied. "Because they believed you cared for me."

"They were right about that, at least. But still, I wish that I had not put you in such danger."

She nodded, absently. "I must see to burying my father. And Paillart."

"I am sorry."

Her eyes roamed the landscape before fixing on mine again. "I will never be able to speak of this. To anyone. Not without them thinking me mad."

"The truth is that it is over," I said.

"Is it?" she asked, her eyes looking through me.

The wagon rumbled on toward Nantes and I sat in the saddle with my men watching her and the children go.

∞

Astonishing as it may seem, a number of the accomplices avoided justice. After my abduction of him from that tower, Roger de Briqueville had provided the evidence necessary to produce the arrest warrant for Gilles. He was certainly guilty of being present at a number of murders and as far as I am concerned that was enough for him to be hanged. But Roger was a knight from a good family and had a rich and noble father. Ultimately, the man was freed and entered the service of Pregent de Coetivy, an Admiral who proceeded to request a pardon for his new servant. The letters of pardon pass Roger off as an unwitting and unknowing participant in the crimes and who, upon discovering them, immediately left the company and service of his lord. Those letters paint the knight as a good and decent man but there is no doubt this Admiral Pregent de Coetivy wanted Roger to provide some vile, base service suited to his depraved mind. So, he got away with murder, and more than one, but he was not the first mortal to do so and was not the last.

Francisco Prelati, the vile cleric, alchemist, sorcerer, and mountebank, managed to avoid the noose but was condemned by the court to life in prison. Practised charlatan and rogue that he was, with his gift of the gab and sleight of hand, he somehow managed to escape from gaol. From there, he found his way into the service of another enormously wealthy nobleman, Rene de Anjou, who he convinced he could make richer by the alchemical creation of gold. The gullible Rene even made Prelati into the captain of La-Roche-sur-Yon, to where flocked other former servants of the Baron de Rais, including the pathetic priest Dominus Eustache Blanchet.

The damned prideful idiot that he was, Prelati could not contain his delusions of power and he had a minor lord named Geoffroy Le Ferron arrested as he passed through La-Roche. Le Ferron was the brother of the priest that Gilles de Rais had abducted years before and Prelati meant to exact some sort of revenge for all that had befallen him and his old master since that abduction. But Prelati had bitten off more than he could chew, and the affair brought to light his escape and his new crime resulted in Prelati being hanged. Finally, justice had been done.

Dominus Blanchet had been protected by the Church and received a sentence of banishment from Brittany, which was appallingly lenient. Especially as he left for a short time but then returned until Prelati was killed and his last allies were gone. For all I know, the weasel monk and priest lived a long life.

And then there was Perrine Martin, La Meffraye, the Terror of Tiffauges and Machecoul, who had personally taken away so many boys over the years with her tricks and honeyed words and heartlessness. She had claimed to be acting only as commanded by her lord. She said also that if she had not done as they asked, Joan the Maiden would have murdered all of Perrine's family. But still, there had to be some punishment for someone who could knowingly supply innocent boys for slaughter.

But they let her go.

If she had been a man, she would have been hung and burned also but convinced that an old woman could never have a will of her own in such crimes, they simply opened the door to her prison and set her free. Ever a cunning one, she immediately disappeared, along with her family.

There was an entire network of servants and associates who had been involved to a greater or lesser extent. Men like the porter at Tiffauges, Miton, and all the other porters who certainly had known about what was going on. Servants who scrubbed away the blood and washed clothes or burned mounds of linen. Others who heard the screams of the tortured and the dying.

If I had been able to remain in Brittany, I am not sure I would have been able to resist executing the worst of them. Prelati certainly deserved death, as did Briqueville.

But I had business in the East.

The war between England and France limped on a few more years, with treaty and truce bringing the conflict to an end. Altogether it had been a hundred and sixteen years and I had been there since the start and for almost all of it, on and off.

In the end, what had it all been for?

Henry VI was the weakest king England had ever known. He gave away all we had won for his kingdom in return for peace. It was the most pathetic capitulation imaginable but then he was a weak and useless man, so what else could one expect? If only his mighty father had not died so young. His weakness of character and the madness that came to take his mind led to his loss of the throne to Edward IV. From what I hear, he was a good man, an excellent knight, but another lacklustre king. He ruled until 1483 but the nobility of England warred over control of the crown for decades in a conflict that became known as the Wars of the Roses.

I did not take part in those wars, though I wish I had been able to knock some sense into the damned lot of them. In time, I would return to England when a new dynasty ruled. That of the Tudors.

After so long looking inward, England would emerge onto the world stage once more and I would be there with them as we reached out to counter the rampaging Spanish and began to settle in the New World. Most of the Tudors were a miserable bunch but Elizabeth was quite something else entirely.

As far as the world was concerned, La Pucelle died a heretic. But the French knew she had been wronged. A posthumous retrial for Joan was opened after the war ended. The Pope authorised the proceeding, known as the nullification trial, and its purpose was to investigate whether the original trial of condemnation and its verdict had been handled justly and according to canon law. Investigations started with an inquest by Guillaume Bouillé, a theologian and former rector of the Sorbonne. A good man, so Stephen said.

They found a huge number of strange and contradictory accounts with regards to her supposed upbringing, but they brushed all that aside lest it affect the outcome of the new trial. It was to be fair and legal in all ways, so they said, which meant that they intended to find her innocent and clear her name.

Before even reaching a new verdict, the Church declared that a religious play in her honour at Orléans would allow attendees to gain an indulgence by making a pilgrimage to the event. Which tells you all you need to know about the fairness of the process.

In 1456, they declared Joan innocent, of course, and also that she died a martyr. What is more, they formally accused the now-dead bishop who had conducted the first trial with heresy for having convicted an innocent woman in pursuit of secular, political outcomes at the behest of a foreign kingdom. Of course, they were not wrong about that, at least.

Over time, her legend grew until she became something like a talisman for the French people, and for the lords of the Church in that nation. At some point, they began calling her Joan of Arc, as they believed that was her father's name. In truth, he was likely just some poor fool who had been paid to say the girl was his and had become trapped in the lie.

During the Wars of the Reformation, Joan became a symbol of the Catholic League, who were an order dedicated to eradicating the Huguenots and Calvinists from France. In the 19th century, the bishop of Orléans led the efforts which culminated in Joan of Arc's beatification in 1909. This meant that Joan had not only officially entered Heaven but could now intercede on behalf of those who prayed in her name.

What she really did, along with Gilles, was rile up the French so much that they threw us out of France. The commoners had for a century been subjugated in misery while we rampaged through their land but then Joan had come and through her madness, on behalf of William, had bestirred the passions of those same people to such an extent that neither Gilles nor Joan could control them. No one knew the truth about her and so they made her into whatever they needed her to be, whether they wanted her to be a heroine or villainess. Who was the real Joan? Whatever she was in life, in death she became a symbol of something great. There was a real Joan and there is the myth of Joan. It is the myth that has the power and always did.

But there need be no wonder for anyone, for she always insisted, no matter how they threatened and mistreated her, that she was guided by the voice of an angel. It is only I who knew that the voice she imagined all those centuries was William's.

He had abandoned her, and Gilles, and all the other monsters he created, to their fates. And when he sent word of his return, it was too late. The centuries of death and murder had taken their toll on their souls and Joan and Gilles had been driven mad. Driven to consume ever greater numbers of children in order to increase their power, they had succumbed to the relentless damage it had done to their souls.

Gilles would be remembered down the centuries as the beloved captain and companion of Joan but mainly of course for his enormous crimes. He has taken all of the blame when it was equally Joan's, or perhaps much more so, and so he has entered history as one of the first and greatest serial killers. Some of the other men who share that appellation were the sons of Priskos. Those murderers also I tracked down and killed in the years to come, one near Cologne and the other in Bavaria. But none had the power and the wealth and authority that had allowed Gilles de Rais and his servants to commit the crimes they did, for as long as they did.

In all my long years, I swear I witnessed no crimes so depraved and so evil.

∞

Watching her drive that wagon toward Nantes, I knew Ameline's heart was broken. The loss of her father was too great to be overcome quickly, if at all, and she was alone in the world. I wanted to stay and take care of her but I could not.

"Perhaps I could see her right," I muttered. "Keep an eye on her for a while. From afar."

"We must be gone," Stephen said. "There are too many questions. The Bishop's warrant for our arrest is still in effect. The Duke's soldiers are looking for us."

"Who will look after her if I do not?" I asked him.

"You cannot save everyone, Richard."

I turned on him. "I do not wish to save everyone. Only her."

It was my actions that caused her such loss, such pain but I could not undo it. Some deeds simply cannot be undone.

"You have saved her," he insisted. "We saved everyone in this land from Gilles. From Joan. There will be no more murders and missing children. The weight of the curse has been lifted and the fear will be thrown off. The people will heal, in time. The land can be lived on again, fully lived. Marriages will be celebrated joyfully, and their children will be able to play and grow to adulthood without threat."

"In time, yes," I said. "But she needs someone now."

"She has property," Stephen said. "Some wealth, an education. She is a beauty. There will be suitors nonstop, now, and one of them will make her a good husband."

He was right enough but I wished so very much for that husband to be me.

I knew I was not evil and prayed that I would never become so. Perhaps it was in me to turn to depravity, like Gilles and Joan had done, and if I gave in to it then I could become just as deranged and Satanic as they had. Whether it was the nature of William's blood rather than mine, or if there was something especially rotten in the both of them to begin with, they had over the decades and centuries, turned into demons themselves.

There was only one way that I knew to stop myself from taking the same path. Whether he is a commoner or a lord, a man must strive to live a virtuous life. When confronted with the choice of virtue or sin, one simply must choose virtue. One will not succeed, not always. But as long as one lives, the choice between virtue and sin remains in every act, in every day, and one must wrestle oneself onto the right course. It is simpler for a sinful man to chose sin than virtue but when one is virtuous in his heart, acting virtuously becomes easier every day.

"Come, then," I said, turning my horse. "Let us be gone."

"Too right," Walt said. "If I never see Brittany again, it'll be too bloody soon."

Of course I could not stay. For I knew that William had finally returned, just as he had promised he would. It had been almost two hundred years, as hard as it was for me to believe, but he was finally coming. Just as I had both dreaded and longed for all that time.

And he was returning to conquer Christendom at the head of an army of a hundred thousand Turks.

I did not know it then but the only man standing in his way was from a small, mountainous principality called Wallachia. A man who would become a hero of his country. A hero, in fact, for all Christendom, although he is not remembered that way.

He is remembered as Vlad the Impaler.

A man known to his own people as the Son of the Dragon.

They called him Dracula.

AUTHOR'S NOTE

Richard's story continues in *Vampire Impaler the Immortal Knight Chronicles Book 6*

If you enjoyed *Vampire Heretic* please leave a review online! Even a couple of lines saying what you liked about the story would be an enormous help and would make the series more visible to new readers.

You can find out more and get in touch with me at dandavisauthor.com

BOOKS BY DAN DAVIS

The GALACTIC ARENA Series
Science fiction

Inhuman Contact
Onca's Duty
Orb Station Zero
Earth Colony Sentinel

The IMMORTAL KNIGHT Chronicles
Historical Fiction - with Vampires

Vampire Crusader
Vampire Outlaw
Vampire Khan
Vampire Knight
Vampire Heretic

For a complete and up-to-date list of Dan's available books, visit: **http://dandavisauthor.com/books/**

365

Printed in Poland
by Amazon Fulfillment
Poland Sp. z o.o., Wrocław